BOUND BY BLOOD

CRESCENT CITY WOLF PACK BOOK THREE

CARRIE PULKINEN

This is a work of fiction. Names, characters, places, and incidents are either the product of the author's imagination or are used fictitiously, and any resemblance to actual persons living or dead, business establishments, events, or locales, is entirely coincidental.

Bound by Blood

Contact Information: www.CarriePulkinen.com

First Edition, 2018
ISBN: 978-0-9998436-4-2

CHAPTER ONE

Alexis Gentry tugged at the top of her strapless bridesmaid gown as she paced across the dance floor toward her sister. She could count on one hand the number of times she'd needed a formal dress in her life, and Macey's wedding made number three. After barely scrounging up enough money to pay for the two-hundred-dollar dress, the thought of only getting to wear it once had made her cringe.

Macey had chosen a beautiful burgundy satin number, though, and if Alexis found herself needing to attend another formal pack gathering in the future, thankfully, this dress would do the trick. Not that she *ever* planned to attend another pack meeting. With her sister mated to the alpha, she was already closer to this pack than she'd intended to get.

A pair of crystal chandeliers illuminated the hotel ballroom, and hundreds of people milled about the massive space, dancing and drinking to celebrate the alpha's wedding. Had she ever been in the presence of this many werewolves at once? She shook her head. Macey's human friends didn't have a clue.

Plush carpet squished beneath her shoes as she stepped off the wooden floor and approached her sister. Delicate beadwork accented the top and bottom edges of Macey's simple, white gown, and a pair of satin stilettos added four inches to her petite height.

"You're the most beautiful bride I've ever seen." Alexis hugged her, and a strange pressure formed in the back of her eyes as her throat thickened. She released her hold and straightened the top of her dress again.

Macey smiled as she brushed a strand of hair from her forehead. She'd piled her long, blonde locks on top of her head in elegant curls, and a few shiny spirals cascaded around her face, accenting her eyes. "Thank you. That gown looks gorgeous on you."

Gorgeous, but completely impractical. If she wasn't careful, the damn thing might end up around her waist before the night ended.

"I've got you to thank for that." She returned the smile and scanned the room, hoping to catch another glimpse of Macey's sexy detective partner, Bryce Samuels. She'd met him several months ago, when she and Macey had first reunited after a twenty-year separation, and her wolf had insisted she at least say hello to him every time she'd swung through town since.

Her duties as maid of honor had kept her too busy to speak to him so far, but now that the formalities had ended, she could placate her wolf with a short conversation with the man. When she couldn't find him, an odd mix of disappointment and relief spiraled through her chest and came out as a sigh.

Macey touched her elbow. "Are you going to be in town when I get back from my honeymoon?"

"Oh." She bit her bottom lip. "No, I found a job a few towns over that will take me a while to complete. Room and board are included." That last part was a lie. She wouldn't room with the person offering if he tripled the payment. She'd learned her lesson with Eric two years ago, and she would never go back to that abusive bastard again. But she couldn't resist the money he'd offered, and small-town motels were cheap enough. Or she'd sleep in her car; she was accustomed to both. Either way, she'd do the job, get the money, and get the hell out.

Her sister's brow pinched. "You could stay at my place while I'm gone, and then work for Luke when we get back. If you need money, I can—"

"I don't need a handout." The last thing she wanted was for her little sister to think she couldn't take care of herself. "Anyway, I've already agreed to do this job. It's not that far away; I'll stop by and see you when I can."

"You know you're always welcome—"

"So…" She couldn't bear another second of their current conversation. Macey only *thought* she wanted her to stick around. "What's it like working with Bryce? He seems a little cocky." And too hot for his own good. Why did she always find herself attracted to men like that? "Does he get on your nerves?"

Macey sighed. "He is a little sure of himself, but he's got a big heart. I love him like a brother."

"He doesn't wear a wedding ring. Does he have a girlfriend?" She clamped her mouth shut. Her voice had sounded way more hopeful than she'd intended.

Her sister cut her a sideways glance. "Bryce hasn't had

a relationship that's lasted past the third date as far as I know. We don't share a lot about our personal lives."

"I remember." Bryce didn't even know Macey had a sister until a few months ago. Alexis gritted her teeth to quell her irritation, reminding herself *she* had been the one to run away. She couldn't expect Macey to tell her partner about a sister she hadn't seen since she was ten. "You spend all day with the guy. What *do* you talk about?"

"Work. Shallow stuff. We joke around a lot." She shrugged. "Bryce has lost most of his family. He's not the most emotionally open person, but I can't imagine working with anyone else."

A man with baggage, emotional scars, who didn't like to share himself. He sounded exactly like her type, but she was done with men. Especially men who needed saving. She'd spent her entire adult life trying to heal people's wounded souls, thinking that maybe if she fixed someone else, she could fix herself in the process.

Her enhanced healing powers only worked on physical wounds, though, not emotional ones, and she should have learned that lesson by now. She was attracted to damaged men because she was damaged beyond repair herself.

But she couldn't ignore the flutter in her stomach as she caught Bryce's eye through the balcony window. Her lips curved into an involuntary smile, so she pressed them together and lowered her gaze to the floor. "Good thing he's your partner, then. You don't have to work with anyone else."

"He won't be for long."

She glanced at Macey. "Is he moving?"

"He's up for a promotion to sergeant, and he's applied for a position as a negotiator. He's been studying for it, so

I know he'll get it." Her shoulders drooped. "I'm going to miss him. Everything in my life seems to be changing."

"Change is the only constant in my life." The one thing she could depend on.

"It doesn't have to be that way."

"Hell of a party, ladies." James sidled next to them and tossed back the contents of his glass. "Can I buy you a drink?" He winked before raising his dark brows.

Alexis laughed. "At the *open* bar? Sure. Why not?" She smiled at Macey. "I'll talk to you later."

Taking a deep breath of relief, she followed James toward the bar. "Thanks for that."

He paused and turned to her. "You looked like you needed a little help. Family squabble?"

She cast her gaze to her sister as Luke swept her into a spin on the dance floor. The band belted out a slow version of Frank Sinatra's "My Way," and she chuckled at the appropriateness of the song. "Not a squabble. She expects me to drop everything in my life and settle down in New Orleans to be with her. I can't do that."

James shuffled toward the line at the bar. "I hear ya. You've got a life to live too."

"Exactly. I'm a rogue. Always have been. She can't expect that to change. People don't change."

He rubbed at the scruff on his chin. "That's where you're wrong. People *can* change if they want to."

"Situations change. People don't." She'd learned that the hard way. Several times.

He arched an eyebrow as he stepped toward the bar. "If you say so. What are you drinking?"

"Whiskey, neat."

James turned to the bartender, and Alexis gazed

toward the window where she'd seen Bryce, but he was gone.

"Excuse me, ma'am, would you care to dance?" Bryce's deep, rumbly voice came from right behind her, and she jumped.

Her heart fluttered, and she pressed a hand to her chest as she spun to face him, discreetly running a finger over the top of her dress to be sure nothing had popped out when she'd startled. A quick glance down assured everything was in place. "Do you always sneak up on women like that? Trying to shock me into saying yes?"

Shrugging one shoulder, he grinned and held out a hand. "Whatever works."

His dark suit accentuated his broad shoulders, and he wore a gray shirt with a charcoal tie. Alexis pressed her lips together and glanced at his outstretched arm before looking into his eyes. That was her first mistake. The little brown flecks in his hazel irises seemed to sparkle with his smile, drawing her in and holding her. Mistake number two happened when she placed her hand in his and let him lead her to the dance floor.

She hadn't thought about it. Her arm acted of its own free will, extending toward his until their palms touched and his fingers closed around hers. By the time she realized what she'd done, Bryce's right hand rested on her hip, and his left hand held a firm grip on hers.

James caught her gaze as he sauntered toward the dance floor with two glasses of whiskey in his hands. He grinned and tossed back one of the shots before taking a sip of the other and winking. What had she gotten herself into?

"It was a nice wedding."

Bryce's voice drew her attention, and she glanced at his

lips before looking into his eyes. Mistake number three. No lips should look that inviting. She swallowed the dryness from her mouth. "Yeah. It was."

He chuckled. "I never thought I'd see the day Macey got married."

"Why do you say that?"

"She never was one to share much about her emotions. I'm glad to see she finally let someone in." He tugged her closer as he eased into a spin.

With her face this close to his neck, she couldn't help but take a sniff. He had a masculine, woodsy scent with a hint of citrus that made her mouth water. Damn it, why did he have to smell so good? She cleared her throat. "Funny. She said the same thing about you."

"She knows me better than anyone." As the spin slowed, he loosened his grip, putting some much-needed space between them. "It's been a while since I've seen you."

"You've seen me every time I've been in town."

"You should be in town more often then." He looked into her eyes, and a familiar sensation stirred in her soul.

A sense of longing tightened her chest—a feeling that seemed to grow stronger every time she was near this man. The same words coming from her sister would have irritated her, but for some reason, when Bryce suggested she should be around more often, something deep inside her wanted to agree.

Snap out of it. She needed to put an end to these stirrings right now. She was done with emotionally unavailable men. Why did she keep having to remind herself of that? "I'm a busy woman. I stop by when I have time."

He nodded. "I respect that."

Sure, he did.

"Do you want to have dinner with me tomorrow night?" So much for respecting her busy life.

No, she definitely did not need to have dinner with him. "I'm leaving town tomorrow. I don't know when I'll be back."

"How about tonight then?"

"We already ate."

He pursed his lips as if he were thinking. "How about this? After this shindig is over, we'll go to Café du Monde for a *café au lait* and maybe split an order of beignets. Will that work?"

The man was persistent; she'd give him that. "I prefer my coffee black."

He grinned. "Got it. *Café* without the *lait.* No problem; we can do that too."

Why was she having such a hard time telling him no? Half of her wanted to say to hell with the job she had lined up and stay in New Orleans so she could have that dinner date with Bryce. The other half—the logical half—wanted to turn tail and run out the door right now. She didn't need yet another man's emotional baggage weighing her down, trying to drown her. She'd been there, done that too many times already.

Maybe spending some alone time with Bryce would wake her up to the fact that he was no different than any other man she'd tried to save. He was damaged goods, like all the guys she'd fallen for, and that would never change, no matter how hard she tried to fix him. Then she could squelch that nagging message her wolf had been trying to wriggle into her brain since the moment she met him.

"I do love beignets, but it will be awfully late."

He shrugged. "I don't mind if you don't. I work nights, so I'm used to it."

"Not for long, I hear. Macey said you might be getting a promotion."

He eased her into another spin, and his masculine scent danced in her senses again. Having coffee with him would also satisfy the half of her that wanted to get to know him better. Well, that half wouldn't be completely satisfied until she'd gotten to know what was beneath his tailored suit, but that would never happen. Not if she could help it.

Sliding his arm around her waist, he tugged her closer so their hips touched, and against her better judgment, she didn't pull away.

He grinned triumphantly, as if he thought he'd broken down one of her walls, but he had no idea who he was dealing with. Her walls were fortified with titanium.

"Did Macey use the word *might?* Surely she thinks more highly of me than that."

She fought her eye roll. If he kept up the cocky attitude, she'd have no problem telling him goodbye after coffee tonight. "I didn't mean to bruise your ego. What were her exact words?" She gazed at the ceiling, feigning deep thought.

He let out an irritated *hmph.* "It takes a lot more than that to hurt my pride."

She narrowed her eyes at him. Something told her he wasn't as tough as he pretended to be. "She said you were up for a promotion and wouldn't be her partner much longer."

His grin returned. "That's more like it. I knew she had faith in me. I'm going to be promoted to sergeant." He straightened his spine, inclining his chin like he had no doubt the job was his. "A spot as negotiator opened up, so I applied for that too. I want to get into community policing—be present at the area schools, get to know the kids. Hopefully I can save a few lives so no one will have to investigate their deaths later."

"That's noble of you." And a little bit hot.

He shrugged. "Being a homicide detective is noble too, but this is what I've always wanted to do. My life's purpose."

The song ended, and as she stepped away, Bryce tightened his grip on her hand. The band played a cover of Billy Joel's "Just the Way You Are," and he tugged her to his body.

"One more dance? I love this song."

"Sure." And there she was telling him yes again, when she should have said no. His muscles were firm beneath his suit, and as he slid his arm tighter around her waist, she leaned into him, allowing herself…at least for the moment…to enjoy the feel of his strong arms wrapped around her.

She'd never dated a human before. Maybe Bryce would be different since he wasn't a werewolf. Maybe without an animal side, he… *No, no, no.* She'd made a promise to herself, and she intended to keep it. No more relationships.

The song ended, and she stepped away before he could pull her into another inviting embrace. "I need to use the restroom."

He walked with her to the edge of the dance floor. "No problem. I'll find you again before the party ends."

She flashed a weak smile, turned on her heel, and strode out of the ballroom. And hopefully out of Bryce's life forever.

Bryce shoved his hands in his pockets and watched as Alexis strutted away. Her maroon dress hugged her curves in all the right places, and her hips swayed in time with the music as she drifted through the door. *What a woman.*

He couldn't fight his smile. He'd jokingly asked her out a few times...well, every time he'd seen her since they first met, but she'd never taken him seriously, especially since Macey was always around when he did it. After a pep talk from Chase's wife, Rain, on the balcony, Bryce had gathered up the courage to ask her out for real this time, and his pulse was sprinting from her answer.

Wait...she hadn't exactly said yes, had she?

She hadn't said no either, though.

Alexis was mysterious, and he liked that about her. Most of the women he'd dated wanted to spill all their secrets and load him down with their problems before they'd gotten to second base. Not Alexis. She was a woman who knew how to handle herself.

He'd had to fight the urge to slide his fingers into her silky, blonde hair while they were dancing. She smelled like cinnamon and vanilla, and she'd fit in his arms perfectly. He could get used to holding a woman like that.

"You're smiling." Rain grinned as she and Chase moved closer to him from the dance floor. Her long, dark curls swished across her back as her husband spun her under his arm before pausing in front of Bryce. "I guess it went well?"

He tried to flatten his mouth into a neutral expression. "We're having coffee tonight."

"Good for you." Rain waved as Chase led her into another turn.

His own smile returned as soon as she looked away, so he sauntered to the bar and ordered a Jameson. Sipping his whiskey, he kept an eye on the door, watching for Alexis to return.

He couldn't explain the way he felt about the woman. There was something about her that made him want to dive into her mystery and swim through her soul. Independent and strong, she didn't give a damn what anyone else thought of her. She was who she was, and she made no apologies. He could learn a lot from a woman like Alexis.

The band played three more songs, and Bryce ordered another drink. After another three numbers, she still hadn't returned, and a sinking feeling formed in his stomach.

Grabbing his third drink from the bar, he found Macey sitting at a table near the wall. He strolled toward her and settled into a chair. "Congratulations, again."

She smiled. "Thanks. Thirty more minutes, and we can get the hell out of here. I've dealt with enough people for one day."

He chuckled. "I bet."

"I saw you dancing with Alexis." Her brow puckered, her eyes holding way too much concern.

His stomach sank a little further. "I'm supposed to take her out for coffee after this is over, but I haven't seen her in a while." He set his drink down and drummed his fingers on the cloth.

Macey reached across the table and stilled his hand. "She left."

He blinked. "She went to the restroom. She's coming back."

"She left fifteen minutes ago. Said she wanted to make the drive to her new job tonight so she'd be fresh in the morning."

"She..." He let out a heavy sigh. "She didn't tell me that."

Macey squeezed his hand before leaning back in her chair and crossing her arms. "Her excuse was a load of bull if that makes you feel any better. Between me trying to get her to stay at my house while I'm gone and you asking her out, we probably scared her away. What else did you talk about?"

"Nothing really. I was my usual charming self. Don't think I've ever scared a woman away before." He tossed back the whiskey and focused on the burn it caused on its way down to his stomach. At least that was a welcome burn.

"She's skittish. It may not feel like it now, but it's better this way."

He arched an eyebrow.

"She ran away when she was thirteen. I didn't see her for twenty years, and now she's been in and out of my life so many times in the past year that I've lost count. I love her, but...Alexis always leaves. It's the only dependable thing about her."

There had to be more to it than that, but if the woman didn't want to go out with him, he wouldn't push it anymore. Despite what he led people to believe, he was no stranger to rejection. It had been a while since it had happened, but he'd get over it. He always did.

Plastering on his most confident grin, he straightened his spine. "She's still pretty, though."

Macey rolled her eyes. "You're impossible."

CHAPTER TWO

(Three Months Later)

A feeling of dread twisted in Alexis's core as she stopped outside a one-story brick house in Pearl River, Louisiana. Three massive pine trees towered over the squat structure, creating an intricate pattern of needle-sharp shadows jutting across the front lawn, and a tricked-out black Ford Mustang took up most of the short driveway. She let out her breath in a hiss. Eric's ego was probably parked right alongside it.

Sinking in her seat, she gripped the steering wheel in her sweaty hands and stared at the front door. Bile crept up the back of her throat. This was a bad idea. She hadn't spoken to Eric in two months. Not since she'd finished the job. He'd declined to pay her for the work when she'd refused to stay and be his mate. What made her think he'd pay her now?

Prying her hands from the steering wheel, she rested her fingers on the door latch, but she couldn't make herself open it.

She squeezed her eyes shut and rubbed her forehead.

Coming here hadn't been an option two years ago; it had been survival. When a Biloxi pack member's drug deal with the area rogues went awry and three of them wound up dead, Alexis—the only other rogue in town—had been blamed for the murders. Mississippi wasn't known for having the most civilized packs in the nation, so when the second-in-command had offered her a way out, she'd jumped at the chance to move to Pearl River and keep an eye on his son in exchange for her life.

Though she'd been paid to watch Eric and report his actions to the pack, she'd also tried to save him. To heal the wounds that made him into an abusive, cocksure, wannabe alpha male. She couldn't help it; healing—fixing people—was in her nature. But she couldn't fix someone's personality, and he'd given her plenty of bruises to prove it.

Eric wasn't mate material. Hell, there was only one person her wolf would allow her to take as a mate, and she'd been steering clear of him since her sister's wedding.

A rogue couldn't be tied down, and no matter how much she wanted to belong somewhere, she never would.

"What am I doing?" She eased her foot onto the gas pedal and continued down the street. She'd traded in her Honda Civic for a small stack of cash and this beat-up Ford when she'd finished the job. Eric wouldn't recognize it, and something in her gut told her she should keep it that way.

She drove to a strip center a half mile from the neighborhood and parked in front of a doughnut shop. A pair of police officers sat inside the small store, chatting up the waitress behind the counter. *How cliché.* A diner anchored one end of the center, while a small grocery store occupied the other. People wandered in and out of the shops and restaurants all day. Leaving her car here wouldn't raise suspicion.

With her phone and wallet locked in the glove box, she slipped the car key into her pocket and trekked up the street to Eric's house. Winter wind bit at her cheeks, whistling through the trees and whipping her hair into a mess. She crossed her arms over her chest to ward off the cold and marched up the driveway.

Alexis hovered her finger over the doorbell. *Go in, convince him to give me the money, and leave. That's all I have to do.* Then she'd never have to see the abusive bastard again. He owed it to her anyway. Soundproofing a room wasn't easy. Or cheap. Twenty-seven years old, and he wanted to start a metal band. *Meathead.*

When he'd called her three months ago, asking her to do the job, instinct had told her to say *hell no*. But even werewolves couldn't survive on hunting alone. Her human side needed to eat too, and the last twenty dollars she had to her name sat locked in the glove box of her car.

She rang the doorbell and waited. Silence answered. Her knuckles wrapped on the wood as she knocked. Nothing. "Eric, I know you're home. Answer the door."

He was probably in his music room, fumbling with the new guitar his daddy bought him. She twisted the knob. Cold metal bit into her palm as the latch disengaged, and she pushed open the door. Small town folk trusted their neighbors way more than they should have.

Alexis peeked her head inside. "Eric?" She stepped into the foyer.

Stifling heat blasted through a vent in the ceiling, and she slipped out of her jacket and dropped it on a ratty, overstuffed sofa in the living room. A football game played on an eighty-inch television. Surround-sound speakers hung from each corner of the room, but thankfully they were muted. A pizza box lay open on the kitchen counter, grease congealing on the surface of the leftover slices, and dirty dishes filled the sink.

She covered her nose. With a sense of smell ten times better than a human's, how could any werewolf live like this?

Eerie silence filled the home, and a sinking feeling twisted her gut tighter. Something was off. Her instinct to run battled with her curiosity to figure out what was going on. Curiosity won.

"This is a bad idea," she whispered as she crept down the hall, the beige carpet masking her footsteps—not that anyone inside a soundproof room would have heard her approaching. Her arm hairs stood on end as she rested her hand on the knob and twisted it. Figured. Eric felt the need to lock this door, but not the front one. Detaching the bobby pin from her keyring, she jiggled it in the lock to disengage it and flung open the door.

Her breath caught in her throat.

Eric crouched, in wolf form, his gray fur standing in a ridge down the center of his back. Saliva dripped from his bared teeth as he snarled over a trembling woman. Blood soaked through the thigh of her khaki pants. Eric's head snapped toward Alexis, his gaze locking with hers for a split second before she reacted.

"Eric, no!" She called on her wolf, her body tingling with magic as her form shifted. Plowing into his side, she knocked Eric off his feet, and the woman scrambled into a corner. Eric lunged at Alexis, clamping his jaws on her front leg. His teeth tore into her flesh, cracking her bone, and she yelped and jerked from his grasp. She threw herself toward him, and they tumbled over each other, fighting for dominance. Alexis didn't stand a chance against a wolf as powerful as Eric, but she couldn't let him tear a defenseless human to shreds.

The woman screamed. Alexis glanced her way to find the victim sitting beside a mangled, bloody body. Eric barreled into Alexis's side, knocking the breath from her lungs as she crashed to the floor. The woman stumbled to her feet before falling onto her side.

Why wasn't she running? The door was wide open.

The woman clutched her leg and peered at the torn flesh, gritting her teeth as her complexion paled. Alexis glanced at Eric. What was this sick bastard doing?

She bared her teeth, growling a warning for Eric to stay away as she backed toward her. The woman's chest heaved as she tried to scramble away. Eric crouched low, preparing to lunge. She had seconds at most.

Alexis placed her front paw on the victim's leg. A high-pitched squeal escaped the woman's throat, a mixture of garbled fear and pain. Magic pulsed from Alexis's core, and she focused it into her paw. She felt the woman's torn muscles stitch back together as the wound closed.

She clutched her leg. "How?"

Alexis's head spun, but she nudged her with her nose. She wanted to scream, "*Get out*," but her wolf mouth couldn't form words. Another nudge, and the woman shot to her feet and raced to the door.

Eric lunged for his victim. Alexis caught his back leg between her teeth and yanked him to the floor. The sharp tang of were blood oozed into her mouth as she tightened her grip on his leg. The woman took one last look at the body before sprinting away.

With his victim gone, Eric relaxed beneath her grasp. He shifted to human form, the sensation of matted fur turning to skin and denim on her tongue. She growled a warning, refusing to release her hold.

"C'mon, Alex. Let me go."

Her nostrils flared as she blew out a hard breath and tightened her jaw. Nausea churned in her stomach, her power waning from the energy she'd expended to heal the human. She'd need rest to regain her strength, but she couldn't let Eric see her weakness.

He winced. "I wasn't trying to kill her."

Yeah, right. She flicked her gaze toward the crumpled corpse in the corner.

"That was an accident." He shrugged. "Let me go, and I'll explain." His eyes didn't hold a single hint of remorse, but that shouldn't have surprised her. He'd tried to convince her she deserved the beating he'd given her, right before she'd run away.

She released her grip on his leg and backed up. Ribbons of blood flowed down his skin, splattering on the tile floor. She hesitated to shift. Eric was stronger than her no matter what form he took. As a man, he stood six-four with two hundred pounds of pure muscle. In her weakened state, at least as a wolf, she'd have a fighting chance if he tried to pull something.

He rubbed at the gash in his leg, wiping the thickening blood from the wound. The flow was already subsiding. "I haven't seen you in two months, sweetheart. Show me your pretty face."

Asshole. Alexis blew out a hard breath and shifted to human form. The gash on her arm had already healed, and the bone had mended where it cracked.

Eric rose to his feet and dusted off his shirt, flexing his pecs so the garment strained across his chest and grinning like they'd had a friendly wrestling match rather than a full-blown fight. His charming smile added an innocent look to his sharp, handsome features. But a coldness hovered behind his eyes, turning the light blue irises to ice. "That's better. Now we can talk like civilized people."

"Civilized?" She looked at the heap of flesh in the corner and shuddered. "Nothing about this setup is civilized."

"No? I soundproofed the room so it wouldn't disturb the neighbors. Well, *you* soundproofed it actually. Great job, by the way. You've always been good with your hands." His gaze raked up and down her body as he took a step toward her.

Her heart rate kicked up, but she held her ground and stared him hard in the eyes. "What's going on here?"

He walked his fingers up her arm, and chills crept down her spine. "Why don't you come to the bedroom, and I'll tell you all about it?"

"Not a chance." She slapped his hand away, but he caught her by the wrist.

"I knew you'd come back to me."

"I came back for the money you owe me." She jerked from his grasp. "If you weren't trying to kill her, what were you doing to that woman?"

Sighing, he stepped toward the man in the corner. "I was really hoping he'd pull through." He nudged the body with his boot. "Of course, if I'd have known about your little gift of healing, I would have waited until you got here. How long have you known you could do that? I'm hurt that you kept it from me after everything else we've shared."

She clenched her jaw. "We never *shared* anything. I gave. You took. Now, you've got thirty seconds to tell me what the hell is going on or—"

"Or what? What will you do? Run to your sister's pack in New Orleans? They won't help you. This isn't their territory." A wicked grin turned up the corner of his mouth. "And you're just a rogue."

That sinking feeling she'd felt earlier slammed her stomach into her knees. *Just a rogue.* That was all she'd ever be. Even with her blood-ties to the pack, the law forbade them from interfering outside their territory.

She was on her own.

He rolled the corpse onto its back and rotated the head from side to side. "Damn. Definitely dead. I'll have to find another one."

"Another one?" She gaped.

"Well, you turned my next patient loose, didn't you? I'm not a murderer. I'm trying to help these people." He crossed his thick arms over his chest, purposely flexing his biceps.

She mirrored his posture, though she left the flexing to the meathead. "By tearing them to pieces?"

"I want a pack of my own. I deserve to be alpha, no matter what my old man thinks. I need at least twenty members before the national congress will even consider giving me pack status, but there aren't enough weres out here that are willing to follow. Right now, I have three: Trevor, Justin, and you."

She scoffed. "You don't have me. And what does that have to do with killing humans?"

"Like I said, I'm not trying to kill them. I'm trying to turn them. Make them into werewolves."

Her eyes widened. "That's illegal." And impossible. Even a rogue knew that.

He lifted one shoulder in a dismissive shrug. "Since when do you care about laws?"

Was he completely insane? "You can't turn someone into a werewolf by attacking him."

He gave the body another kick. "No? You've never been part of a pack, but the first and most important law weres learn is never to attack a human while in wolf form…unless it's a fight to the death."

She clenched her fists. "I'm aware of the laws." Alexis had been on her own since she started shifting at thirteen years old, and the first rogue werewolf she'd met had taught her the rules. She shuddered at the memory of the *other* things he'd taught her.

"So? Why do you think that law was created?"

"Because attacking humans is wrong." Werewolves were supposed to be peacekeepers, not monsters.

He chuckled and shook his head, giving her that condescending look he always used when he wanted to make her feel stupid. "Because if you leave them alive, they'll turn into werewolves themselves. My dad is second of the Biloxi pack; he has access to ancient records. I've read about humans being turned. That's why the congress outlawed attacking humans without killing them. To keep people from trying this." He opened his arms, gesturing to the dead man in the corner.

She swallowed the sour taste from the back of her throat. "This is barbaric."

"I won't argue with that. But once I master the process, it'll be much more efficient. Finding the right balance of blood loss and venom is proving impossible, but you can help. If I attack them, you can heal them right before they die. Then if the change doesn't take, we can try again and again. We'll be a team. What do you say?" His charming smile returned as if he'd asked her to go to an amusement park rather than become an accessory to murder.

"You're sick." *And deranged.* Werewolf venom? There was no way in hell she'd take part in this. She backed toward the door.

He wiped his hands on his pants and stepped toward her. "We could be more than a team, babe. If I'm going to be alpha, I'll need a mate. We already know we're compatible in the sack." He reached for her hand.

Her wolf revolted, the thought of going to bed with him making her skin crawl. She crossed her arms and took another step toward the door. "No way. I want the money you owe me, and I'm leaving."

He winked. "I'll give you the money if you stay."

"Keep dreaming." She stumbled through the threshold into the hallway. Sure, she was broke, but no amount of cash made any of this okay. She'd find another job somewhere. Sell what few belongings she had left. Hell, she'd cut out her own kidney and sell it on the black market before she'd take part in Eric's macabre plan. "Does your dad know you're doing this?"

"That dick wad doesn't know shit. I'm not the fuck-up he thinks I am." He prowled toward her. "C'mon, Alex. Don't make this difficult. You know I care about you, and you care about me too."

Her lip curled. "No, I don't."

"You used to."

She clutched the doorframe, every muscle in her body tensing to bolt. "That was before I got to know you." When she'd had her blinders on. Before she'd figured out she couldn't fix a broken soul. Eric *wasn't* the fuck-up his father thought he was…he was worse.

He sighed. "You know I can't let you leave. I've told

you too much. Stay with me. Be my mate, and I'll take care of you. You'll never have to worry about money again. My old man's cash flow will cover everything."

She backed down the hall toward the front door, never tearing her gaze away from the deranged man who pursued her. He didn't know it, but his dad's money had been the reason she went to Pearl River in the first place. He was the one who'd financed her undercover mission, and now it seemed she'd have to do some pro bono work for her old boss. "You can't make your own pack out of innocent humans. I won't let you do this."

"How are you going to stop me?" He lunged, wrapping his arms around her waist and dragging her to the floor. Her head hit the fireplace hearth with a crack, and splitting pain shot through her temple. Darkness tunneled her vision. She blinked away the stars that swam in her eyes as she struggled beneath him, but she may as well have been wedged beneath a concrete block. He had the strength of an alpha, but no pack would ever accept Eric as leader.

He pinned her shoulders to the ground. "Please don't make me kill you. I'd much rather make love to you."

As her vision cleared, she spotted a canister of fireplace tools to her left. If she could get her hands on the poker... Her breathing slowed in spite of her racing heart. She tried to relax. To play the part of the lesser wolf giving in to the alpha's advances. She curved her lips into a seductive smile and sighed. "You're right, Eric."

"I am?" He loosened his grip on her shoulders.

"Of course. It's a genius plan. Making your own pack from scratch, they'll do whatever you tell them to. You can train them." She licked her lips. "Think of the power."

He released her and rose to his feet. "Exactly, baby.

And with your healing powers, no one else has to die. Think of all the lives you'll be saving." He didn't offer her a hand up. Typical.

The room spun as she stood, but she held her seductive expression, running her fingers along the mantel and stepping toward him. "I'd be a fool not to stay with you, wouldn't I?"

"I knew you'd come around." He grinned and adjusted his crotch. "Let's go back to the bedroom and make things official."

She rested her hand on the handle of the poker. "There's one problem with that." She tightened her grip.

He crossed his arms and raised his eyebrows. "Oh, there is?"

"I wouldn't touch you with a ten-foot pole." Gripping the poker, she swung it at his head. The pointed end sliced through his cheek, the shock of impact knocking him to the ground.

"Three foot, maybe. But not ten." Her weapon clattered on the floor as she turned and sprinted out the door.

"Damn it, Alex! I didn't want to kill you." Eric barreled after her, gripping his bloody cheek in his hand.

Alexis tore through the front yard and darted across the country road into a field. She didn't dare look back. She could feel him getting closer as she ventured farther and farther into the grassy pasture. As she hurdled a barbed wire fence, her pant leg caught on a spike. The fabric ripped, and she crashed to the ground, taking in a mouthful of bitter grass and dirt. Spitting out the mess, she scrambled to her feet as Eric leapt the fence and caught her by the arm. He hauled her to his body, gripping her from behind.

His breath was hot against her ear. "Maybe I'll kill

your sister too. That's a fair trade, huh? Stay with me and Macey lives."

He lifted her from the ground, and she planted her boot square in his knee. His scream muffled the loud pop of the joint dislocating. She wiggled free and sprinted through the field. The gash on his face had already healed; his knee wouldn't take long. She'd bought herself seconds at most.

She could shift and fight him as a wolf. At least the fight would lean toward fair. But to shift in public, in daylight, and expose herself to humans, would earn her one of the harshest punishments the werewolf congress handed out. Rogue or not, some rules simply could not be broken. She could never beat him anyway. The guy was a machine. Her best option was to run, but to where?

She poured on the speed, but not enough. Even with the injured leg, he gained on her. He caught the hem of her shirt and yanked. She stumbled. His arms wrapped around her waist, and he tackled her to the ground. She scrambled away, kicking him in the face, and jumped to her feet again. An electrical transmission tower stood ten feet away, and she darted toward it.

Gripping the cold steel beams, she hauled herself up. Hand over hand she climbed the structure towering one hundred feet into the air. She didn't have a clue what she'd do once she reached the top, but it didn't matter. Eric wouldn't follow her ascent.

She climbed until her palms bled and her arms shook with exhaustion. Eric grabbed the tower and pulled himself onto the first crossbar. Alexis froze. Was he actually going to climb it? Cursing, he jumped to the ground and spat at the steel.

"Damn it, bitch, you know I'm afraid of heights." His

body shook with rage. "You can't stay up there forever. As soon as you come down, you're dead." He fought the urge to shift; his eyes strained with the pain and concentration it took to hold back his wolf. The intensity of the situation called on her own beast as well, but even Eric knew better than to shift in public.

The wind picked up, whipping through her hair and cutting through her clothes like knives. She gripped the cold steel tighter, wrapping an arm around the bar and hooking it with her elbow, using all her energy to hang on. Her muscles trembled, fatigue threatening to make her fall.

What the hell was she supposed to do now? Like most times in her life, she'd acted rashly, climbing the tower without considering the consequences. Now she was screwed—like a kitten stuck in a tree, but no fireman would come along and rescue her. Unless…

Eric stood on the ground below, smiling as she struggled. "You might as well come down. What else are you gonna do?"

"What's going on out here?" A heavy-set woman wearing a bathrobe and rubber boots stomped toward Eric. "What's all this racket about?"

This was her chance. She couldn't out run him. She couldn't beat him in a fight. But she could always outsmart him. "I'm going to jump," she called to the surly neighbor below. "It's all his fault."

The woman's head snapped up, her eyes widening as she realized Alexis hung at the top of the tower. "What did you do to her?" She smacked Eric on the shoulder, and he flinched, ducking his head. A wannabe alpha…scared of an old woman. Alexis chuckled.

"Me? I…I didn't do anything. I don't even know her. I

saw her out here climbing the tower, and I came to see what she was up to." He glared at Alexis, and a vein throbbed on the side of his forehead.

For her plan to work, she needed a bigger crowd. More witnesses. "I'll do it." She pretended to slip on a beam and let out an emphatic scream.

"You stay put, young lady. I'm calling for help right now." The old woman pulled a phone out of her bathrobe pocket and pressed it to her ear.

"Help me! I can't hold on!" She smirked at Eric, and his vein throbbed harder.

More neighbors appeared from their houses and rushed into the field. Eric held up his hands, swearing he had no idea who she was. The police were on their way. If she came down now, with all these witnesses, she'd be able to get away.

But she knew Eric too well. He wouldn't stop until she was by his side or dead, and she wouldn't give him the pleasure of achieving either.

He'd threatened her sister's life, though. There was only one thing she could do to keep Macey safe. He had to *think* she was dead.

She swallowed hard and leaned away from the tower. A square of concrete surrounded the structure—not a soft landing pad. If she jumped out far enough, she might be able to make it to the grass. Either way, the fall would be fatal for a human. Even a normal werewolf wouldn't survive, but she was banking on being *not* normal, hoping her enhanced healing powers would keep her alive.

If she didn't survive, at least Macey would be safe. Eric would have no reason to go after her if Alexis were dead. Her sister's life was worth more than a miserable rogue's.

Closing her eyes, she said a prayer to whatever gods

might be listening and let go. The collective gasp from the crowd rang in her ears as she plummeted to the ground. The impact shattered her bones. Searing pain rolled through her body like a wildfire, consuming her in its torrid hell. She wanted to scream, but she couldn't move. She couldn't breathe. She lay there an eternity before blissful darkness swallowed her whole.

"No! Oh, God no." Eric Anderson watched in horror as Alexis fell from the tower. She hit the ground with a jarring *thud*, and silence engulfed him. He rushed to her side and pressed his fingers to her neck. No pulse. A pool of blood spread on the concrete beneath her head, and her legs jutted out at unnatural angles.

Broken. Everything was broken.

Old Mrs. Livingston waddled over to him. "Ambulance is on its way, but it looks like we're too late for that."

His mind reeled. She couldn't really be dead. Any second now, she'd start breathing again. She was a werewolf; she had to survive. She was supposed to be his mate. She was the answer to all his problems. *Shit!* What had he done?

A siren sounded in the distance. He dropped to his knees to compress her chest. Maybe he could get her heart beating again. As soon as he pressed on her breastbone, a rib snapped. He jerked his hands away. "She can't be dead."

The paramedics arrived and ushered everyone away. Eric peered over their shoulders as they examined her. An EMT checked her pulse in her neck. Another one tried her wrist. He covered her mouth and nose with a mask and squeezed a plastic bubble, forcing air into her lungs, and a sickening, gurgling sound resonated from her throat. They started chest compressions, but they didn't try hard enough. Within a few minutes, they gave up.

"What are you doing? Get your ass back over there and use a defibrillator or something. She's not breathing!" He needed her powers, damn it. They couldn't let her die.

A dark haired EMT shook her head. "I'm afraid there's nothing else we can do. She's gone."

The words slammed into his head like a baseball bat shattering his skull. "No." She couldn't be.

A police officer tapped him on the shoulder. "I need to ask you a few questions, Mr.—?"

"Anderson." The police? What the hell was he supposed to do now? His father would shit a brick if he got into trouble with the fuzz again. He might even cut him off. Technically, Eric belonged to the Biloxi pack. He had to obey their laws.

"How did you know the victim?"

"Victim?" His hands trembled. Alexis wasn't a victim. He hadn't done anything wrong. "She killed herself."

"Right." The pig pushed his glasses up his greasy nose. "And how did you know her? Girlfriend? Relative?"

He shook his head. "I didn't know her at all. I looked out my window and saw her climbing, so I came out here."

"Why didn't you call for help?"

"I…Mrs. Livingston called. I was trying to talk her down." If he acted innocent, like he had nothing to do with it, they'd have to let him go. He'd lost his potential mate, but at least she wouldn't be able to screw up his plans.

The pig asked him a few more questions and seemed

satisfied with his answers. As soon as he left him alone, he stepped away from the crowd and pulled out his phone.

"Trevor, it's Eric. We've got a problem. That Jane Doe you picked up for me this morning?"

"She met your requirements." Panic raised Trevor's voice an octave. He was about as useless as a werewolf could be, but at least he followed orders. "I did exactly what you asked."

"I know, but she got away. I need you to go find her. Now."

He paused. "Umm…I would, boss. But I'm at work, and if I miss any more shifts, they'll fire me. Can I go find her this evening?"

"I don't give a damn if you're in the middle of open heart surgery, you'll go find that woman now or I will make your life a living hell. Do you understand me?" He had to get that Jane back before she went around spreading stories about werewolves. The last thing he needed was to have the congress on his back about exposing their kind. And if they ever found out he was trying to turn humans, he'd be a dead man.

Trevor cleared his voice. "Yes, sir. I'll get right on that."

"Good."

He shoved his phone into his pocket and strolled toward the scene. The paramedics loaded Alexis's body onto a stretcher and covered her head with a sheet. If she hadn't started breathing by now, there was no way she'd recover.

A pang of regret flashed through his chest, and he winced. He'd miss the blonde bombshell, that was for sure, but he'd miss her healing powers more. That shit would have come in handy. He'd master the art of making a werewolf soon enough, though.

He ran his hand along the small dent in the back of his skull where his dad had hit him with a baseball bat when he was a teen. He'd spent his entire life trying to make that man happy and avoiding the beatings that ensued when he failed. Then the dick wad had banished him to this God-forsaken town to "keep him out of trouble." He'd show the old man trouble. Once he ran a pack of his own, his dad would have to respect him.

CHAPTER THREE

BRYCE PARKED ON THE CURB IN THE CENTRAL Business District and popped a stick of gum into his mouth as he stepped out of his car. A brisk December breeze tumbled through the streets, stinging his cheeks like the cold slap of an ex-lover. He zipped up his jacket and squinted toward the top of the twelve-story brick building. The structure seemed squat compared to the towers of steel and glass soaring around it, but it was tall enough to be deadly. Shielding his eyes from the sinking sun, he could barely make out the jumper's silhouette. A heavy-set man balanced on the ledge, his back pressed against the brick.

Bryce strode toward the police tape cordoning off the area and nodded at the officer in charge of crowd control.

The officer returned the nod. "Sergeant."

"What have we got?"

"Seventeen-year-old male snuck into an empty office," the uniform replied. "Johnson's been up there thirty minutes. No luck talking him down."

Christ, he's just a kid. "Got a name?"

The officer mumbled into his radio and nodded as the reply came through. "Michael Benson."

Bryce choked on his gum, the mint burning its way down his throat to sour in his stomach. "Shit."

"One of yours?"

"My neighbor." He shoved his way through the crowd that had gathered and jogged into the building. Jabbing the button for the eleventh floor, he twisted his brother's college ring on his finger and prayed he'd make it up there before the kid did anything stupid.

The elevator doors opened, sending a blast of frigid air into the compartment. Cold sweat beaded on his forehead. The drab beige hall stood empty, save for a lone guard standing outside the office doorway. Bryce nodded to the man and stepped inside. Papers lay strewn across the floor, the winter wind having scattered them in its wake. Most modern buildings in the Central Business District didn't have windows that could open, but this structure was from a time before central AC rendered them obsolete.

"Why don't you come inside, and we can talk about it?" Lieutenant Able Johnson, lead negotiator, reached a hand toward the kid on the ledge, but Michael scooted farther away.

"I got this, boss." Bryce waited for Johnson to crawl down from the window before sliding into his place.

Johnson nodded. "Remember. Start gentle. The kid's scared shitless."

"Have a little faith." Bryce had only been in the unit two months, but this was Michael. If anyone could talk the kid down, it was him. He latched on a harness and eased his way out onto the ledge, careful to keep his legs inside the window.

His heart raced. Even with the safety cord snugly secured, he kept one foot hooked under the edge of a desk. Instinct forced him to look down, and his stomach rolled. He took a deep breath and closed his eyes for a long blink. Rule number one—don't look down. Why did he forget that?

"Hey, Michael."

The kid swallowed hard. "Sergeant Samuels? What are —" His foot slipped off the ledge, but he caught himself on the edge of the window. A strangled squeal emanated from his throat as he dug his fingernails into the brick.

"You're okay." Bryce scooted closer. The kid was a mess. Bright-red capillaries zigzagged across the whites of his eyes, and his dark umber skin held an ashen tinge. It couldn't have been more than forty degrees outside, but sweat poured down his face, soaking the neckline of his sweatshirt.

"No." He shook his head and bit his bottom lip. "I'm not. I'm a lard-ass who doesn't deserve to live."

Bryce inched closer. "Now, where on Earth would you get an idea like that?"

Shutting his eyes, he tipped his head back against the brick. "Social media."

Of course. "What happened?"

Michael sucked in a shaky breath. "April Cunningham."

Bryce bit back a curse. The Queen Bee of Central High School had been on his radar for months. After his first anti-bullying speech in the school auditorium, three different girls approached him about her behavior in the hallway. Now it seemed she'd taken up cyber-bullying too. "Girls like that aren't worth your time. They're definitely not worth your life."

"All I did was tell her I liked her haircut." Tears streamed down Michael's face. "She posted a picture of me eating at lunch with the caption, 'This fat bastard thought he was good enough to talk to me. He should go jump off a building and spare us all from looking at his lard ass.'"

His jaw clenched. "She's a bully, Michael. She's not worth it." He unhooked his foot from the desk and eased out onto the ledge. A few inches more and he'd be able to reach the kid, if he didn't pass out from the adrenaline first. *Note to self: next time, skip the coffee.*

"Everyone saw it. You should see the other kids' comments. They're just as bad. Everyone hates me." He shuffled farther down the ledge.

"Not everyone." Icy wind whipped through Bryce's hair, stinging his eyes. He gritted his teeth and inched closer to his neighbor. *Please let this cable hold.* "I don't hate you. I think you're a pretty cool guy. So does Sam."

"Sam." He looked at Bryce, making eye contact for the first time. "I'm supposed to walk him this afternoon."

"I know he's looking forward to it. He always tells me about your walks when I get home."

Michael shook his head. "He's a dog."

Bryce shrugged. "Maybe not in words, but I know he loves you. So does your mom."

He gasped. "My mom."

"Think about how she'd feel if you did this."

His bottom lip trembled. "I can't leave her all alone."

"No, you can't." He reached for the boy. *Almost there.*

Michael leaned toward him. He was nearly in his grasp. "But what else can I do?" He jerked away, and Bryce let out a hard breath.

"You can come with me. I can help you through this."

The kid peered over the ledge and squeezed his eyes

shut. "What do you know about being bullied, besides what they taught you at police school?"

His heart ached at the pain Michael must have been going through. "I know a lot more than you think. I was bullied too."

Michael let out a dry laugh. "Yeah, right. Look at you. You're a big, buff white guy. No one would ever mess with you."

His throat thickened. He'd known when he'd taken this job that his embarrassing past would come to light eventually, and he'd gladly share a little bit about himself if it meant saving a family from experiencing what he'd gone through. "I wasn't always this good-looking, kid. When I was your age, I weighed about a hundred and twenty pounds. I was a scrawny little nerd. In order to keep the bullies off my back, I had to do their homework for them."

Michael furrowed his brow. "I don't believe you."

Bryce sighed. "All right. You're the only person I've ever told this to, and I've *never* shown this to anyone." He reached for his wallet and pulled out a small photograph. "This was me at seventeen." He turned the picture toward Michael.

"I can't see it."

"Come closer then. If I get any farther away from this window, I'm going to vomit."

Michael inched closer, shuffling his feet along the ledge. Reaching out, he snatched the picture from Bryce's hand. Bryce glanced inside at Johnson and nodded as he slid back toward the window. He almost had him.

"You wore glasses," Michael said.

"Thick ones. I was nearly blind."

"And now?"

"Surgery."

"Well, that's not so bad. So you had to do some people's homework. At least they didn't publicly humiliate you."

"Well, now." He took a deep breath and cringed inwardly. He was going to have to say it. This kid's life was worth more than his shameful secret. "That's not entirely true. Once, I didn't do Aubrey Taylor's homework. He was beyond pissed."

"What did he do?"

"Our water wasn't running at home for a while, so I got to school early every day to shower in the locker room. When Aubrey figured that out, he followed me in and took all my clothes. When I came out of the shower, I didn't have so much as a towel to cover myself with. So, there I was, buck-naked and dripping wet in the boys' locker room when the first period bell rang."

Michael's eyes widened. "What did you do?"

"The other kids chased me into a stall. I barricaded myself in until Coach finally found me and gave me some sweats to wear home." His face heated, the shame of the memory adding to the nausea churning in his stomach.

"Ouch."

He laughed dryly. "Tell me about it. Can I have that picture back?"

"Why do you carry it around anyway?" Michael slid toward the window to hand the picture to Bryce. As soon as the kid got within arm's reach, Bryce grabbed him and yanked him inside.

All two-hundred-fifty pounds of Michael landed on top of him, knocking the wind from his lungs—a small price to pay for the opportunity to save a life. He regained his breath and pulled Michael to his feet.

His neighbor threw his arms around his neck and sobbed into his shirt. “I’m so sorry, Sergeant Samuels. I don’t…I don’t know what I was thinking. I don’t want to die.”

“Hey, you’re fine now. The paramedics are going to take you to the hospital. We’ll get your mom to meet us there, okay?”

“I’m scared.” He clutched his stomach, his lips paling to a light grayish-pink.

Bryce grabbed his shoulders. “Did you do something else?”

“Vicodin.” He doubled over, vomiting down the front of Bryce’s shirt. Two paramedics took his arms and eased him onto a stretcher. “I’m sorry.”

“It’s okay.” Bryce peeled the sticky, wet fabric away from his skin, the sour reek of stomach acid making him want to vomit himself. Johnson tossed him a box of tissues, and he wiped the muck from his shirt. “How many did you take?

“Twelve.”

Bryce let out a slow breath through his nose. “You want me to ride in the ambulance with you?”

He looked at him with frightened eyes. “Please?”

Alexis’s eyes fluttered open and adjusted to the fluorescent lighting. A small TV hung from the ceiling in the corner of the white room. Thin sheets and a scratchy blanket covered her achy body up to her chin. A metronomic beeping sound drew her attention toward a humming machine and a set of monitors, and as she turned her head, she focused on an IV drip and a tube that led down under the blankets, into her arm.

Oh, no.

Werewolves healed a hundred times faster than humans. Alexis even more so. After a fall like that, she should've been dead. Would've been if she didn't have extra healing abilities. How would she explain her recovery?

She'd rather have died from the fall than face the wrath of the congress if she exposed their secrets. Closing her eyes, she inhaled a deep breath, and sharp pain stabbed at her lungs. Why hadn't she thought this through?

She shoved the covers down and yanked the oxygen tube from her nose. Bruises mottled her arms in varying shades of red and purple. She moved her legs. Yesterday, the bones were broken. Or had it been two days? How long had she been out? She reached for the IV, ready to yank it from her arm, when a cheerful nurse with fiery red hair and pale green scrubs entered the room.

"Oh, good. You're awake." She shuffled to the bed and adjusted the blankets on Alexis's lap before placing the oxygen module back into her nose and lacing the tubes over her ears. "You're in New Orleans General Hospital." Her fingers flew across a keyboard, and she squinted at the screen. "Well, that can't be right."

Alexis stared at the woman. Thoughts scrambled through her brain as she tried to devise an escape plan. Eric must have thought she was dead, or she wouldn't be breathing. At least that part of her plan had worked.

The nurse tapped a manicured nail on the table. "According to this, your face was swollen beyond recognition a few hours ago. But I don't detect any edema now."

She pressed her icy fingers against Alexis's cheek bones. "Does this hurt?"

She held back a wince. "No."

"Well, you're lucky to be alive. That was quite an accident you had." She returned to the computer. "What's your name?"

"Alexis." She clamped her mouth shut. She'd said too much.

The nurse typed on the keyboard. "Last name? You weren't carrying ID."

She scratched the back of her neck. "It's…um… Sinclair." If Eric thought she was dead, she was safe for the moment. Macey was safe. She could lay low for a while and figure out what to do about stopping Eric's cockamamie plan—if she could get out of the hospital.

"Is there someone I can call for you? A relative? Friend?"

It felt like her brain slammed against her skull as she shook her head. It was best if no one knew where she was.

The nurse gave her a warm smile and patted her hand before hanging a new bag of fluids on a hook and connecting it to the IV tube. "I'm going to give you a little something for the pain. It might make you sleepy." She picked up a syringe and reached for Alexis's hand.

She jerked it away. "No. I'm not in pain. I don't want the medicine."

"Oh, nonsense. I can't even see your real skin color through all those bruises."

Alexis covered the IV with her hand and glared at the nurse. "No medicine." No way in hell was she spending another second in this place. "I want my clothes. I want to leave."

"I can't let you leave until a doctor dismisses you. The

police need to talk to you too." She squinted at the computer screen. "Something's not right about the details of your accident. It says you fell a hundred feet. Do you remember what happened to you?"

She cringed inwardly. Talking to the police was the last thing she needed. "Where's my stuff?" She could put on a show to convince them she was well enough to leave, but it was a matter of time before they figured out she'd given them a fake name. She had to get out before they started asking questions.

"Your things are somewhere safe, and you'll get them back as soon as you're released. Until then…" She reached for her hand. "Please…this will help you feel better."

"I feel fine."

The woman sighed and laid the syringe on a tray. "I'll go get the doctor."

As soon as the nurse shuffled out the door, Alexis sat up. Sharp pain ricocheted through her abdomen as if she were being stabbed by three knives at once. Clutching her side, she gingerly lay back on the mattress. Her enhanced healing abilities weren't healing her fast enough. She closed her eyes and breathed through the pain. As soon as she was capable of standing, she'd be out of there.

Bryce changed into a set of hospital scrubs and shoved his soiled clothes into a plastic bag. Michael would survive. They'd pumped his stomach, and the doctor seemed to think his liver would recover. Hopefully his mom would get him some counseling. Something. Anything to intervene in the downward spiral that had tempted him to the ledge. Bryce wouldn't give up until the kid got the assistance he needed. This was one cry for help that would not go unanswered.

He knocked on the door to Michael's hospital room. "How's it going in here?"

Karen, Michael's mom, sat on the edge of the bed, holding her son's hand. Her dark-brown hair was mussed, as if she'd raked her hands through it too many times, and tear stains streaked her cheeks. "He's going to be okay." She wiped beneath her eyes, smearing makeup across her face. "Thank you for saving him."

Bryce used his thumb to turn the ring on his right hand…the symbol of the life he couldn't save. "Any time. And you know I'm right upstairs if you ever need anything. Both of you." He squared his gaze on Michael. "I mean it."

Tears pooled in the corners of the kid's eyes. "I'm sorry I can't walk Sam today."

"Don't you worry about that old fur bag. He'll have to settle for walks with me for a while, but he'll survive." He looked at Karen. "You've got my number. Don't be afraid to use it."

She nodded. "Thank you."

"I'll see you soon, kid." He gave Michael a soft punch on the shoulder and then swallowed the lump from his throat as he stepped into the hallway and headed for the elevator. Michael was a good kid. No one deserved that kind of treatment, especially a kind-hearted soul like him. So far, Bryce hadn't been able to bring any charges against the bully, but this time…he was going to get through to that girl one way or another.

The fact that she could get under his skin the way she did presented another set of issues, though. To consider suicide as a viable option to solve his problems meant the kid needed professional help. Bryce knew how to recognize the signs…now that it was too late for his own family…but he'd be damned if he'd let it happen to another one.

As he made his way down the hall, he spotted Lauren, a red-headed nurse with brown eyes and freckles, and he ducked his head, hoping to pass by unnoticed.

"Sergeant Samuels." Excitement raised her voice an octave. She trotted over to him and batted her eyelashes. "Nice scrubs." Her gaze raked up and down his body.

He held up his bag of soiled clothes. "Occupational hazard. Have a good evening, ma'am." He tried to step around the nurse, but she caught him by the arm.

"I think we're beyond '*ma'am*.'" She grinned. "Congratulations on the promotion, Sergeant."

He flashed her a tight-lipped smile. "Thanks. It was a long time coming."

"You know…" She stepped closer, resting her hand on his shoulder. "My shift ends in a few hours. If you want to come over, I could give you a *proper* congratulations."

"Lauren…" He tried to make his voice firm and compassionate at the same time.

She pouted her lower lip. "My bed's been awful cold without you."

"That was one time, six months ago, and I told you I wasn't looking for a relationship." He removed her hand from his shoulder and gave it a squeeze before dropping it. "I thought I made that clear." This was exactly why he did his best to steer clear of women. He wasn't the settling-down type of guy, but they never seemed to understand that…always wanting to *get to know him*. They may have liked the package, but there was nothing on the inside they'd really want to know.

She sighed. "You did. I just thought…" She shrugged. "Anyway. Before you go, there's an alleged suicide attempt in room two-eleven. Jumped from a transmission tower. They pronounced her dead at the scene, but she woke up in the ambulance on the way to the morgue. The details of the accident seem…off. Not a single broken bone."

He looked at his watch and blew out a breath. His shift had ended two hours ago.

"There's a detective coming to talk to her about it, but I thought…since you're into rescuing people now and all…that you might want to see her."

Another suicide attempt? His shoulders sagged as the weight of her words pressed down on him. "Show me the way." He followed Lauren into the room and found a woman lying on her side, her back to the door.

Her short blonde hair stuck out in every direction, and she grumbled as they approached the bed. "I don't want the medicine."

"That's okay." Lauren rested a hand on the woman's shoulder. "This is Sergeant Samuels. He needs to ask you a few questions."

The woman rolled over gingerly, grimacing in pain from whatever had happened to her. Her arms were mottled with bruises, and a ring of dark purple encircled her left eye.

Bryce's pulse thrummed. She was battered, and her hair was shorter, but he would have recognized that face anywhere.

His breath caught in his throat. "Alexis?" He stepped closer to the bed and took her hand in his. "What happened to you?"

Her eyes widened, and she squeezed his fingers. She gave a tiny shake of her head and furrowed her brow. His heart wrenched at the sight of her, but the imploring look in her eyes stopped him from saying more.

"Oh, you know her?" Lauren typed something on the computer. "She didn't want me to call anyone for her."

He glanced at the nurse. "I do. I can take it from here."

Alexis released his hand and let out a long breath.

"Okay. I've got other patients to check on, so go ahead and do your thing, Sergeant." She swung her hips as she sauntered past him, stopping to rub her hand up his arm. "If you change your mind about this evening."

He stiffened. "I won't." And with Alexis back in town, he never would. She was the one woman he wouldn't mind getting to know.

"Well, if you do, you know where to find me." Lauren winked and slipped into the hallway.

As soon as the door clicked shut, he squared his gaze on Alexis. She closed her eyes and rubbed her forehead like she had a headache. From the looks of her, everything probably ached. His chest tightened. Even battered and bruised, she was the most beautiful woman he'd ever laid eyes on. The moment he'd met her, some long-dormant part of his heart had opened up, and he hadn't been able to get her off his mind since.

Meeting his gaze, she flashed a half-hearted smile. "Hi, Bryce."

She'd seemed fine at the wedding a few months ago. What could have caused her to spiral down so quickly? "What happened to you?"

"I...got in an accident."

He narrowed his gaze. "The report says you jumped from an electrical tower, trying to kill yourself. They pronounced you dead." Simply saying the words aloud caused the weight on his shoulders to press down harder, threatening to crumble him. First his neighbor, and now Alexis. He couldn't handle losing anyone else he cared about.

"No, the report is wrong. I didn't fall from that far up, and I was conscious the entire time. I..." She ran a hand down her face. "It was stupid, and I never should have tried to climb it, but I swear I wasn't trying to kill myself."

The urge to take her in his arms and hug away the hurt overwhelmed him, so he shoved his hands in his pockets. "You're gonna have to give me more than that."

She gazed at the IV in her hand and shook her head. "I got into a little bit of trouble and had an accident."

He could think of one kind of trouble that would leave a woman this beaten and scared, and his hands curled into fists as he pulled them from his pockets. "What's going on? I can help you."

"No, you can't. I'm about to be released; it's no big deal." She gripped his hand, and his fist relaxed. "Please, Bryce. Promise me you won't tell Macey." Determination offset the fear in her eyes.

He sank onto the edge of the bed. "Alexis, if this wasn't a suicide attempt. If someone did this to you, I can help. You need to get the police involved."

"No one did this." She folded her hands on her stomach. "It was an accident, and I'm going to be fine. I feel better already. Macey's got enough on her plate now; I don't want to worry her."

"She's your sister. She would want to know." He knew his ex-partner well, and if there was anything she could do to help her sister, Macey would do it. As strained as their relationship was, she loved her.

"Everything will be fine." She blinked up at him, her emerald eyes pleading. "Please don't tell her."

He chewed the inside of his cheek. Her bond with Macey was rocky at best, so who was he to insist she confide in her? His brother had been his best friend, and look at what had happened. He took a deep breath and let it out in a huff. This was going to come back to bite him in the ass somehow.

"All right. I won't say anything." *Yet.* For some reason, he believed her story that the report was wrong. Eyewitness accounts were often inaccurate and conflicting, and his gut told him to trust her that it wasn't a suicide attempt. He'd bet his left nut the bruises hadn't been put there by accident though. "Can I do anything for you? Tell me what you need."

"I need my stuff." She picked at the lint on the blanket. "They took my clothes and put me in this stupid gown, and the nurse keeps saying she'll give them to me, but she hasn't. Can you get them for me? I want to be ready when they release me." She laid her arms by her sides. "I hate hospitals."

"I can get your stuff." He put his hand on hers, and her gaze flicked to where they touched. "Where will you go when you're released? Where do you live? I can give you a ride." Anything to make sure she didn't go back to the man who'd done this to her.

"I…nowhere right now. I'll figure something out."

"Nowhere? You're homeless?"

She smiled, but it didn't reach her eyes. "I'm resourceful. I'll find somewhere to stay until I can go back to work."

He didn't doubt her resourcefulness; she'd been taking care of herself since she was a kid. But there was no reason for her to be homeless when she had people who cared about her. "If you don't have anywhere to go, stay with me."

She pulled from his grasp. "What? No."

"I've got plenty of room at my place. You can stay with me until the trouble blows over. I won't say a word to anyone."

She pursed her lips and gave him a quizzical look. "That's very sweet, but you don't need to be involved in this."

"I already am." And, damn it, he *wanted* to be. She may not have needed a knight in shining armor, but she did need a friend, whether she wanted to admit it or not. He could be that for her. He could be anything she needed him to be.

"Thank you. But getting my clothes will be enough. I can take care of myself."

"You sound just like your sister." Macey had been his partner for seven years. She was independent and stubborn as a mule. It appeared to run in the family.

He slipped out the door and made his way behind the nurse's station. Alexis's personal effects sat in a plastic bag on a shelf. He tucked the parcel under his arm, grabbed a pen and a sheet of paper, and strode toward her room.

Ducking into a bathroom across the hall, he examined the items in the bag. A pair of jeans, a dirty, black T-shirt, a car key, and a matching set of blue satin unmentionables. His cheeks flushed with warmth as he shoved them back into the bag.

He scribbled his address and phone number on the paper and slipped it, along with his house key, into the pocket of her jeans. The temperature would be near freezing tonight, and she'd have to go somewhere. He'd sleep better knowing she was safe and warm. Shoving everything into the bag, he took it to her room.

She sat up when he walked in, a smile lighting on her lips as she eyed the bag. The bruise around her eye was already fading. Or maybe her smile made it less noticeable.

He tossed the package onto the bed. "My offer stands." Plastering on a fake grin, he winked. "Most women would jump at the chance."

She rolled her eyes. "Keep telling yourself that."

He paused as the ache in his chest grew stronger. "I can stay with you until you're released."

Clutching the bag, she shook her head. "That's okay."

"Are you sure? I don't—"

"Go home, Bryce."

Inhaling deeply, he held her gaze. The logical part of his brain barely overruled his intense desire to scoop her into his arms and carry her home with him so she'd be safe. But he recognized the stubborn set of her jaw. Like her sister, when she set her mind to something, there was no use arguing. If the woman didn't want his help, all the charm and wit he could muster wouldn't be enough to change her mind. "You just…be careful." He turned and left the room.

CHAPTER FOUR

BRYCE PARKED HIS CAR ON THE CURB AND CLIMBED the steps to his half of the two-story duplex on the outskirts of the Garden District. Growing up, his family had barely scraped by in their three-bedroom rental on the wrong side of the tracks. He'd always dreamed of owning one of the big mansions in the area. While sharing a split-level with another family didn't exactly count as owning a mansion, at least he was in the right neighborhood.

A single massive oak tree filled the small front yard and shielded most of the yellow and white house from the street. Karen and Michael had wrapped the thick trunk with twinkling white lights for the holidays. That was as festive as Bryce was willing to get.

He lifted a fake fern out of a clay pot on the landing and grabbed his spare key from the bottom. Sliding it into the lock, he pushed the door open.

"Sam, I'm home." He stepped into the living room and braced himself for impact. His eighty-pound Siberian husky leapt from the couch and barreled toward him. He bent his knees to receive the goofball of a dog with open arms, and Sam showered his face in kisses, whining and wagging like he hadn't seen his owner in days.

"All right, boy. Calm down. You missed your walk today, didn't you?"

Sam woofed.

"You go do your business in the back yard, and I'll walk you after dinner. Deal?"

The dog licked his hand and darted to the back door.

"Out you go." Bryce flung open the door, and Sam raced onto the terrace and scrambled down the steps into the small back yard. He left the door open a crack and watched through the window as Sam chased a squirrel into a tree. "Crazy dog."

He grabbed a beer from the fridge and leaned against the counter, appreciating the peaceful silence of his home as he took a long drink. The effervescent liquid cooled his dry throat, and the quiet calm soothed his frazzled nerves.

The events of today had hit way too close to home, and while most of the guys on the team liked to let off steam at a crowded sports bar or night club, Bryce sought refuge in the solace of stillness. Michael would be okay, and Alexis…

He was done being the badass cop for today.

As soon as Sam came back inside, Bryce popped his last frozen dinner into the microwave and sighed. A trip to the dreaded grocery store was in order.

As he finished his last bite of Salisbury steak, he rinsed the plastic container and tossed it in the recycle bin. His favorite book sat on the end table, begging him to read it, but he'd promised Sam a walk after dinner. It was the eighth time he'd read *The War of the Worlds,* anyway. The Martians probably wouldn't change their plan of attack while he was out.

He picked up the leash, and Sam wagged his tail so hard his hind end could have fallen off. "Let's go, boy."

Sam darted out the door, dragging Bryce down the steps. The husky's tongue lolled from his mouth as he pranced down the street, sniffing and hiking his leg on every tree and bush he could find.

Normally, a cold, crisp night like this would clear Bryce's mind, but Alexis clouded his thoughts tonight. The official report said attempted suicide. A sickening feeling formed in his stomach. He couldn't live with himself if he'd left her there alone to enable another attempt. He twisted his brother's ring.

Stop second-guessing yourself. She'd sworn she wasn't trying to kill herself, and he believed her. In all his years as a detective, he'd gotten good at spotting a lie. This wasn't one. She had gotten into trouble though, and damn it, he promised he wouldn't tell her sister. Macey would want to know if someone had hurt Alexis. Now he was stuck between a boulder and a brick wall.

Macey trusted him explicitly. If he didn't tell her, she'd never forgive him if something happened to Alexis. But if he did tell her, who knew what kind of mess he'd stir up between the sisters? Alexis would probably never speak to him again. He hardly knew the woman, but based on the way his heart raced when she was around, he wanted to know more of her. A lot more.

Alexis double-checked the address Bryce left in her pocket and climbed the stairs to the second floor. Sharp pain shot through her knees with each step as she clutched the wooden railing and dragged her aching body up. She hesitated on the landing, toying with the key in her hand. This was a bad idea.

But what else could she do? Her sister would've been happy to help, but she couldn't get Macey involved. Eric was right. The Crescent City pack couldn't help her stop his sadistic plans. Their territory ended where Eric's began. All they could do was report it to the congress, and nobody listened to a rogue.

She had to handle this herself. Her life depended on it, and going to Macey would put her in danger too. Worse than that, Alexis would have to admit she'd gotten herself in over her head.

No, she'd figure something out. She needed a safe place to lay low for a while, at least until she recovered enough to shift. Then she could get her car from the parking lot in Pearl River and at least have her clothes and her phone back. After that… Eric's father might listen to her. If anyone could put an end to his scheme, it was David.

She put on a mask of resolve and knocked. No answer. She chewed her bottom lip. Bryce wouldn't have given her a key if he didn't want her to use it, so she slipped it into the lock and opened the door.

Warm air enveloped her as she stepped inside, relaxing the tension she carried in her shoulders. She expected the place to be a pigsty, typical of the cocky smartass type Bryce appeared to be, but this was no standard bachelor pad. The countertops gleamed like they'd been freshly polished, and the furniture looked brand new. The living room smelled of lavender with a slight undercurrent of dog fur so faint she could barely detect it. The place had such a homey feel that she found herself standing in the entry, brow scrunched, unable to move for a moment.

"Bryce, are you home?" Soft carpet squished beneath her boots as she tiptoed through the living room and down the hall toward the bathroom. A bedroom door hung open, and she resisted the urge to peek inside to see where he slept. Her mouth went dry. She'd imagined him in the sack plenty of times since she'd met him, and seeing his actual bedroom would add fuel to the fire she was trying to extinguish.

A second door stood shut, and curiosity got the better of her. She gave the knob a twist and found it locked. What secret was he hiding in there? As long as it wasn't another soundproof room, it didn't matter. As soon as she recovered, she'd thank him for his help and be out of his life. Let the man have his secrets.

Avoiding the bathroom mirror, she stripped out of her blood-crusted clothes and stepped into the shower. Warm water cascaded from the showerhead, the droplets stinging as they pelted her bruised skin. The purple marks were already fading to a greenish-yellow, but they hurt like hell. Everything hurt.

She turned off the water, stepped out of the shower, and stared at her reflection in the mirror. What the hell was she doing here? Bruised and broken, she'd barely escaped from one arrogant male, and she'd run straight into the home of another one.

Sure, Bryce was handsome. Smoking hot. She'd felt something stirring deep inside her soul the moment she'd met him, but she'd squashed the sensation like dead bug as soon as she'd caught it wriggling its way into her mind. A rogue couldn't be tied down to a human. Especially to a cop. She had a hard enough time following supernatural laws; being near Bryce would force her to consider human ones too. It would also force her to face her feelings for him.

If he really had lost most of his family like Macey said, he'd have deep emotional scars. Wounds like that hardened men, and every time she scratched away the sexy, self-assured surface, she found an asshole underneath. Maybe Bryce would be different, but…

She sighed. It didn't matter. Getting close to him would end in heartache. Either she'd leave like she always did when she started getting comfortable somewhere, hurting him, or he'd turn out to be an asshole like all the other men she'd fallen for. It would never work.

Still, she couldn't deny the spark she'd felt when she shook his hand over Macey's hospital bed last year. It wasn't the spark of magic that she always felt when she touched someone with supernatural abilities—Bryce was all man—but looking into his bright, hazel eyes had made her heart stutter and her wolf howl.

And when Macey was hurt, he'd stayed by her side like she was family. He seemed to genuinely care. Macey trusted him, and that was the reason she'd come to his house for refuge. But he was a man, and Alexis was done with men…no matter what her wolf—or fate—had in mind.

She chewed her bottom lip. Speaking of fate…a vague memory of waking up in the ambulance rattled through her mind. She remembered clutching the EMT's hand and feeling a buzzing, supernatural energy seeping from her skin. The rhyming rhythm of a healing spell knocked around in her brain, but she couldn't remember the words. It was no coincidence she'd ended up in a witch's ambulance.

She grabbed a towel and wrapped it around her chest.

She didn't need to justify her decision to come here—to herself or anyone else. Once she could shift, she could run back to Pearl River and get her car. This arrangement was temporary—like the rest of her life.

Bryce paused on the terrace with his hand on the doorknob. He remembered locking it when he left. His pulse quickened as he gazed in through the window. Light illuminated the hallway, but he always turned them off. Keeping Sam close by his side, he slipped inside and took his pistol from a drawer in the kitchen. It could've been Alexis, taking him up on his offer of refuge. It also could've been an intruder, and he wasn't taking any chances.

He padded into the hallway to find the bathroom door ajar, the scents of soap and shampoo wafting out with the dissipating steam. Widening his stance, he held the gun by his side. "Come out where I can see you."

The door opened fully, and he couldn't help but focus on the pair of shapely legs stepping through. He dragged his gaze up, over the midnight blue towel that covered her torso, and regarded the most disarming set of green eyes he'd ever seen. "Alexis." His posture relaxed, and a strange mix of relief and hope fluttered in his core.

A sly smile curved her lips as she raised her hands. "Don't shoot."

Sam lunged, yanking the leash from his hand. The dog whined and barked, shaking his whole body in excitement as he danced around her feet.

She grinned and reached down to pet him. "Some guard dog you got here."

"Sorry. He's not used to visitors." He picked up the leash and pulled Sam away, ducking into his bedroom to set the gun down.

"It's okay. He's sweet."

He returned to the hall. "Anyway, a badass cop like me doesn't need a guard dog." He winked and unhooked the leash. "Go to the living room, boy. Go."

Sam whimpered and looked at Alexis.

Bryce raised his voice. "Sam…Go."

The dog reluctantly sulked away, and Bryce focused on Alexis.

Damn. His chest tightened. Even the mottled bruises covering her body couldn't take away from her beauty. She stood about five foot ten, and her legs had to be a mile long. The towel barely covered the important parts. Heat flushed through his body, probably turning him ten shades of red. He was staring, but his brain couldn't seem to form a coherent thought to break the trance.

Resting her hands on her hips, she shifted her weight to one side. "You act like you've never had a naked woman in your house before."

He forced the words over the lump in his throat. "You're the first."

"Yeah, right." She stepped into the bathroom and came out with a wad of clothes. "Do you have a washing machine?"

"Yes." His mouth worked, but the rest of his body hadn't processed the shock.

She arched an eyebrow. "Can I borrow it?"

"Oh. Yeah. Here, let me take that." He took the laundry from her hands and padded to the washing closet. "Mind if I throw some of mine in with it? I had a rough day at the office."

"Fine with me." Her voice came from right over his shoulder.

He tensed. Her close proximity had his arms aching to hold her, and the scent of his soap on her body turned him on way more than it should have. He'd given her his key so she'd have a safe place to sleep, but he hadn't thought about what having her here would do to him.

He groaned inwardly. He had to get her out of that towel and into something more modest before he exploded. "Do you want to borrow some clothes while you're waiting on these?" Flipping on the washing machine, he turned to face her.

"Would it make you more comfortable if I did?" Amusement lilted her voice.

"It would, unless you…" He clamped his mouth shut before the automatic smartass comment could slip out. After what she'd been through, asking her if she wanted him to get naked too would be a dick move.

"Unless I, what?"

"Nothing." He sidestepped around her.

"Okay then." A muffled chuckle slipped from her lips as she followed him to his bedroom.

Pausing at the door, he considered saying it anyway. She seemed amused by the effect she had on him, but he wasn't lying when he'd said Alexis was the first naked woman he'd had in his house. Now she'd be the first one in his bedroom too. His home was his sanctuary. His quiet place to relax and recharge his batteries. He'd never been big on guests, especially overnight ones. He'd make an exception for Alexis, though. She needed him, and something about being able to provide for her had him aching with his own need.

He dropped the leash on the dresser and moved his

service weapon to the drawer next to his personal firearm before pulling out a pair of sweatpants. "Here." He handed them to her. "They have a drawstring, so you should be able to keep them up."

In his closet, he reached for a white T-shirt, but the thin fabric would've been more revealing than the towel. He handed her a dark green one instead. She took the clothes and looked around at his bedroom.

"What?" he said.

"Nothing." She shrugged. "It's not what I expected."

"My room?" He turned off the closet light and crossed his arms. How many times had he imagined having Alexis in his bed? And now here she was, nearly naked and standing three feet away from him.

"Your whole house."

"What did you expect?" And why did her answer matter so much to him?

"A pigsty. Tough guy. Lives alone. No time for cleaning since he's always out fighting bad guys and seducing women."

He flinched. "You don't know me."

"I know your type." She turned and headed for the bathroom.

Her statement stung, though it didn't surprise him. He'd worked hard to build up his no-bullshit reputation. To make sure no one saw the scrawny little nerd who'd had to do other people's homework to avoid getting his head shoved in the toilet. He'd created his confident, tough guy persona with a purpose. But for some odd reason, he didn't want Alexis to view him that way.

He shuffled into the living room and dropped his keys into a bowl near the door. Turning around, he found Alexis there in his baggy sweatpants and T-shirt. Thankfully, the garments hung shapeless on her body, hiding her curves. Then again, seeing her wearing his clothes was another kind of sexy entirely.

"Why are you wearing scrubs?" She gestured to his shirt.

He glanced at his clothes. "That rough day at the office I told you about? I got puked on."

"Ew." She wrinkled her nose. "That's what I smelled."

"Yeah. I'm going to shower real quick." He started down the hall, but he paused. "Are you going to be here when I get out?"

She winced as she lowered herself onto the couch. "I'm not going anywhere."

Sam jumped onto the sofa and licked her face. Bryce was about to scold his dog, but she laughed and scratched the fleabag behind the ears.

Warmth spread through his core. "If he's bothering you, I can put him in the back yard."

"He's fine. Mind if I turn on the TV?"

"Go for it." He hurried down the hall and showered and changed as fast as he could, tossing the scrubs into the wash with the other clothes. He even brushed his teeth just in case. Not that he was planning on kissing her—or even getting that close to her—but better safe than sorry, right? Holding his breath, he padded back to the living room. Fear that she'd be gone when he entered the room had his stomach in knots.

But there she sat, in the same place on the couch, Sam curled up next to her with his head in her lap. *Lucky dog.* "Can I get you anything? Water? Tea?"

She grimaced as she shifted her position. "Got any whiskey?"

"I've got a bottle of Jameson, but should you really be drinking in your condition?"

She stiffened. "In my condition, I could use a little pain relief."

"Do you want some ibuprofen?"

"Just the whiskey."

What a woman. "Yes, ma'am." He opened the bottle and poured two glasses. Offering her the drink, he settled onto a chair next to the sofa.

She sipped the whiskey and closed her eyes. "*Mmm.* That's better." As her lids fluttered open, her gaze locked with his. "What?"

Damn it, he was staring at her again. "Nothing. Are you hungry?"

"Starving."

Setting his glass on the coffee table, he shuffled to the kitchen and rummaged through the cabinets and the fridge. He'd eaten his last frozen dinner that evening. He had nothing with sustenance to offer her. "All I've got is a tube of Pringles and some Snickers bars. I can run out and pick something up for you."

"Chips and candy are my favorite." She grabbed the book from the end table. "*The War of the Worlds*? I didn't take you for a sci-fi nerd."

"I'm not." And he planned to make damn sure she never found out he was. Yanking the book from her hand, he set the food on the coffee table. Sam raised his head. "None for you, boy. You know what it does to your stomach."

She raised an eyebrow. "Junk food doesn't agree with him?"

"You thought *I* smelled bad. We'd need gas masks if he ate any."

She smiled and shoved a chip into her mouth. "This beats hospital food any day."

He slipped the book between the cushion and the arm of the chair, thankful he'd been able to change the subject. He'd prefer to talk about his farting dog any day over his love of science fiction. Alexis didn't seem like the type of woman who went for geeks.

She polished off half the tube of Pringles before moving on to the Snickers. Any woman who was happy with chips and candy for dinner was a keeper in his book. He sipped his whiskey and smiled. He could get used to this kind of company.

Aside from Macey's occasional visits, the only other woman who'd been in his house was Karen, and he usually tensed up when his neighbor overstayed her welcome. But something about Alexis being here added to the calm of his sanctuary rather than detracting from it.

She brought the chocolate to her lips and paused. "You're staring at me."

"Sorry." He set his glass on the table and yanked his head down from the clouds. "When are you going to tell me what really happened to you?" Nobody climbed a hundred-foot electrical tower unless they had a death wish or they were being chased.

Alexis sipped her whiskey and eyed him warily. "I'm not."

It figured. He'd have to be delicate with his interrogation if he wanted to get anywhere with her. "Whatever it is, I can help you."

She let out a cynical laugh and took a bite of the Snickers bar. "No, you can't. Believe me. You don't want to get involved."

"I already am, and I think I already told you that." He

held her gaze, and for a moment, her eyes softened. Her lips parted slightly, and she inhaled as if she were going to speak.

She shook her head.

"Look, I'm going out on a limb here by keeping this a secret. Macey may not be my partner anymore, but she trusts me. And she's my friend." He sighed. "She'd expect me to tell her if I knew you were in trouble. You've gotta give me something. Let me help."

She stroked Sam's fur, and he nuzzled into her lap. What Bryce would have given to be in that dog's place. "You are helping. Letting me stay here tonight is all I need. Tomorrow, I can go get my car back, and everything will be fine."

"Where's your car?"

"Pearl River."

He furrowed his brow. "That's forty miles away. How'd you end up in a New Orleans hospital?"

Drawing her shoulders toward her ears, she looked into his eyes. "Fate?"

He chuckled. "There's no such thing. Try again."

She paused and pressed her lips together, as if considering her words, and cut her gaze to the left. "Then, I have no idea."

"Okay." He'd let her hold on to this lie. It didn't matter how she ended up there; he was involved now, whether she wanted him to be or not. "Let me drive you to your car."

"Oh, I don't think so." She bit her bottom lip and focused on the dog.

"What are you going to do? Walk there?"

She shrugged. "Maybe."

Stubborn. Independent. Like her sister, she didn't

know how to accept help. "Let me take you. I've got nothing better to do."

She arched an eyebrow. "I highly doubt that, but, okay. I'll let you take me to Pearl River and drop me off at my car. That's it, though. No more questions and you stay out of my business."

"Deal." He crossed his arms and leaned back in the chair. There was no way in hell he was staying out of it. But at least if he drove her there, he might be able to pick up a few clues as to what was going on. Then he'd decide if he needed to get Macey or the police involved.

She stretched her arms over her head and cringed. "Ow. I should probably get some sleep. Can I borrow a blanket?"

"You can sleep in my bed."

She raised her eyebrows, and he could practically see the thought forming in her mind.

"Not with me in it. I'll take the couch. You're too sore to sleep out here."

"I'll be fine."

Man, she was beyond stubborn. "No, you won't. You need a good night's rest. You're sleeping in my bed."

She paused and regarded him, a tiny, heart-melting smile curving the corners of her lips. "Well, if you insist."

"I do. And if you need anything at all…ibuprofen, water, more whiskey…whatever…let me know. I'll be right here if you need me."

Her brow furrowed, a look of confusion clouding her eyes. "Thanks, Bryce. I appreciate that."

CHAPTER FIVE

SUNLIGHT FILTERED THROUGH THE BLINDS, CASTING a golden glow in the bedroom. The softness and warmth of Bryce's bed enveloped Alexis as if she were sleeping in a cloud. The last time she'd been this comfortable, she'd spent the night in a hotel room before Macey's wedding. After scrounging together enough money to buy her bridesmaid dress and pay for one night in the lush hotel, she'd been broke ever since. She needed to find a job fast.

Rising onto her elbows, she spotted her clean clothes sitting on the nightstand, folded into a neat stack. The house key she'd left in the living room last night lay on top.

She rolled onto her side and pressed her face into the pillow. As she inhaled deeply, a masculine, woodsy scent with a hint of citrus danced in her senses. She pulled the pillow on top of her head, allowing herself to get lost in the magnificent scent of Bryce. He'd been nothing but kind to her all evening. She'd fully expected him to try to climb into bed with her. No man was that nice without expecting something in return.

But Bryce had told her goodnight and left her alone all night. Maybe he really was different. Maybe not. She hugged the pillow tighter.

A knock on the door roused her from her thoughts, and she flung the pillow away from her face. Bryce stood in the doorway wearing nothing but a pair of gray sweatpants. His light brown hair was mussed on one side, making a sort of wave on top of his head. Just enough scruff peppered his jaw to give him a rugged look, and glorious muscles rippled down his stomach to disappear into the waistband of his sweats. Her own stomach fluttered, and she had to tear her gaze away.

He grinned and stepped into the room. "Were you smelling my pillow?"

Her ears burned. "No. Why would I do that?"

Grabbing a shirt from the closet, he slipped it over his head. "Yes, you were. You were sniffing it. What's it smell like?"

She ground her teeth as the heat from her ears spread across her cheeks. "It smells like you, dumbass." She chunked the pillow at his head, but he caught it in his hands.

His smile faded. "Dumbass? Is that what you think of me?"

She opened her mouth for another sarcastic answer, but the hurt in his eyes made the words stick in her throat. "I don't know what to think."

He set the pillow down and looked at her quizzically. Sinking onto the edge of the bed, he took her hand in his and ran a finger up her forearm. His gentle touch lit a fire in her core and sent shivers running down her spine. She wasn't used to gentle.

"The bruises are gone." His fingers grazed her forehead

as he brushed the hair away from her face, and her breath hitched. "Even your eye. How is that possible?"

She pulled from his grasp and slipped her arm under the blanket. "I'm a fast healer. Always have been."

He held her gaze. "You fell a hundred feet."

"No, I wasn't up that high. I told you, the report was wrong."

"Why were you up there?" So much concern emanated from his voice that she almost believed he cared about her.

She inhaled deeply. Something about Bryce made her want to open up and tell him everything. Maybe it was his kind eyes or his open posture. Possibly the smolder in his gaze. Her wolf insisted on another, much stickier reason, but she intended to ignore that instinct like she'd been doing since she met him.

It was probably a trick he learned in police school to get people to confess their crimes. If she told him about Eric, she'd have to leave out the supernatural part. Then the testosterone would kick in, and Bryce would insist on going after him. Cop or not, he was no match for a werewolf.

She faked a smile. "I'm starving. Got any more Snickers?"

He sighed and pressed his lips into a line. "There's a café a few blocks away. I'll go grab some breakfast while you get dressed. Then we can get your car." Rising to his feet, he pulled a pair of pants from a drawer. "Will you be here when I get back?"

"I will."

Nodding, he hesitated in the doorway before turning on his heel and striding out of the room.

Alexis lay in bed until the front door opened and closed and the key turned in the lock. Taking one more deep inhale of Bryce's masculine scent on the sheets, she sat up and stretched her arms over her head. A mild ache replaced the excruciating pain from yesterday.

Would it be wrong to stay in bed and invite Bryce to join her when he returned? The stirring she'd felt in her soul when she first met him was back in full force, and if she wasn't careful, her wolf would try to claim him. A low growl rumbled in her chest. Who was she kidding? Her wolf was already trying.

Would that be such a bad thing?

Yes, it would. She was a rogue, and he was a human. Her wolf was wrong about this. She wouldn't be bound to any man.

Slipping out of bed, she got dressed and padded into the kitchen to open the fridge. A six-pack of beer, a half-empty carton of two-percent milk, and what was left of a loaf of bread. His fridge screamed typical bachelor, but nothing else about him fit the stereotype. A whine from the living room pulled her attention to the goofy dog on the couch. He rested his chin on a cushion, and his bright blue eyes stared at her with intensity.

"I'm sorry, Sam. I forgot to tell you good morning."

The dog jumped off the sofa and bounded toward her. She scratched him behind the ears, and he licked her face before wagging his entire body and prancing around her feet.

"Maybe we can play later, okay?" She scanned the kitchen countertops for a coffee maker. Her head hurt from the fall, and a little caffeine might fix it. She found a bag of coffee and some filters in the cabinet—at least he had all the essentials—but when she filled the machine and flipped the switch to run it, nothing happened.

"Damn it. I need my caffeine." She unplugged the

machine and rummaged through the drawers to find a screwdriver. The back of the contraption popped off, and she turned it around to examine it. A wire had come loose from a terminal. A simple fix. With a few turns of a screw, she reattached the wire and tightened the connections of the others. She replaced the cover, plugged the machine in, and flipped the switch again. The little red light blinked on as the coffee started brewing. "Thank God."

"We've got a problem," Bryce said as he stepped through the door. "Their coffee machine is down, and mine broke—" He inhaled deeply. "Wait. Do I smell coffee?"

She took two mugs from a cabinet and set them on the counter. "It had a loose wire. I fixed it."

"Fantastic." He grinned and dropped a white paper bag on the table. "I got sausage kolaches. I thought you could use some protein to build up your strength."

"Thanks." She poured the coffee and carried it to the table.

"I got some beignets too." His gaze locked with hers, and her breath caught.

Why did he have to bring this up now? "I'm sorry about that. I lost track of time, and I had to be somewhere." She sank into a chair and lowered her gaze to her mug.

Dropping into a seat, he pulled a French doughnut from the bag. "No big deal. I found someone else to go with me."

Something in his tone said that her leaving the wedding without saying goodbye had hurt him more than he wanted her to know. "Who'd you go with?"

He narrowed his eyes briefly before focusing on the

beignet. "Best to eat them while they're warm." He shoved it into his mouth. "So good."

A thin layer of powered sugar dusted his lips, and she could almost taste the sweetness on her tongue. Her mouth watered. Why did he have to be so damn hot?

She always found herself attracted to the same type of men: muscular, good-looking assholes with tragic pasts. She'd convince herself that their cocky, abrasive attitudes were simply masks covering their wounded, softer sides. The softer sides didn't exist, though. Not in her experience.

Bryce seemed different. Sure, he was full of himself—most good-looking men were—but an undercurrent of kindness laced his actions. And she couldn't help but notice the fire that coursed through her veins when his tongue slipped out to lick the sugar from his lips. Oh, the places she'd like to feel his tongue. She shook her head to chase away the thoughts. "Thanks for taking me to get my car."

"My pleasure." He sipped his coffee. "What are you going to do once you have it back?"

"What do you mean?" She took a bite of the beignet and savored the sugary flavors dancing on her tongue.

"Are you staying in Pearl River? Do you live there now?"

She stopped chewing, clamping the mushed-up dough between her teeth. The thought of what to do next, where to go, hadn't crossed her mind. What *would* she do? She swallowed the beignet and took a sip of coffee. "I told you. I don't really live anywhere. I'm a wanderer." She forced a smile.

"You like living out of your car?" No judgment laced his words, simply curiosity.

She shrugged. "It suits me." Hell no, she didn't like it. But she'd spent her entire life on the run, first moving from foster home to foster home, then living on the streets. She didn't know how to stay in one place. Didn't know if she *could.* Every time she got comfortable somewhere, anxiety would get the best of her, and she'd run away. A rogue could never have an easy life, and that was all she'd ever be.

He shook his head. "It's too cold to sleep in your car. You can stay with me as long as you like."

Her stomach tightened around the butterflies attempting to take flight. Why was his offer so damn appealing? After she'd left Eric more than a year ago, she'd sworn off men all together. Then she'd met Bryce, and her wolf had been protesting her decision ever since.

Going back to Eric when he'd called her to do the sound-proofing job should have solidified her decision that men were bad news. Then again, if she hadn't done the job and gotten into trouble with him, she wouldn't have been sitting across from the sweetest, sexiest man she'd ever met. Fate had led her to this moment, but…

She shook her head. "Thank you, but I'm not going to steal your bed another night."

"If it means you're safe and have a warm place to sleep, I will gladly take the couch. Plus, you fixed my coffee maker. Saved me from buying a new one, so I owe you." He winked. "Think about it."

There he went with that kindness again. "I'm sure your red-headed nurse would be jealous if I stayed."

He stopped mid-swallow, choking on his coffee. Setting the cup down, he gave his head an adamant shake. "Lauren? She's just a friend."

The words "back off" had nearly slipped from Alexis's lips when the nurse had come on to Bryce in the hospital, but that would have been her wolf talking. As a woman, Alexis knew better than to get involved with him. *Yeah, right.* "Seemed like more than that to me. I may be injured, but I'm not blind. I saw the way she looked at you."

He straightened his spine, a cocky grin lifting the corners of his mouth. "I am easy on the eyes."

See, she wanted to tell her wolf. *He's no different from all the others.* She leaned back in the chair and crossed her arms. "And you're proud of it."

"So? I've worked hard to look this way. Don't tell me you don't know you're beautiful. You've probably got men tripping all over themselves to be with you."

"It's different for a woman."

"How so?"

Being with the man wasn't the issue. What happened afterward always proved to be the problem. Men didn't want to love her; they wanted to conquer her. It was either wham, bam, thank you ma'am, now get the hell out of my house, or they wanted to dominate every part of her life and treat her like an object rather than a person. She shrugged. "It just is."

His gaze locked with hers. "Lauren was a one-and-done deal. Don't worry about her."

"I'm not worried, but maybe you should have informed her of that. Women don't like to be used."

His posture deflated as worry knit his brow. "I did. We both agreed before it happened. I don't know why she keeps it up."

Because he was smoking hot. No woman would be

satisfied having him once. Alexis sure wouldn't. "It's not her fault if she's fallen for a womanizer."

"Womanizer?" His gaze hardened, and he straightened his spine. "Let's get one thing straight. I *never* use people. Never." He snatched the empty doughnut bag from the table and chunked it in the trash. Then he yanked a wet wipe from a plastic dispenser and cleaned the table. Every muscle in his body tensed as he furiously wiped the wooden top.

Maybe the name-calling was a little harsh. "Hey, I'm sorry." She stood and placed a hand on his arm to still him. "I was out of line. Your love life is none of my business."

He inhaled deeply and straightened to face her, his body mere inches from her own. Heat radiated from his skin, and his woodsy citrus scent made her head spin. She looked into his unreadable hazel eyes and fought the urge to press her lips to his. They looked soft, the scruff on his skin around them rough, masculine. Her comment had sparked a passion in him she'd never seen before. Would it be wrong to kiss him now?

He leaned in, his face drifting toward hers. No sugar remained on his lips, but she could imagine the taste on her tongue. Sweet, with a hint of coffee. She parted her lips, and her pulse thrummed in her throat.

He bypassed her mouth and hovered near her ear. "Damn right it's none of your business. Let's go get your car." He stepped past her, grabbed a jacket from the coat rack, and tossed it to her.

She caught it and stood there watching as he turned and bounded down the stairs. Slipping her arms into the sleeves, she pulled the jacket tightly around her. She'd barely scratched the surface with Bryce, and a hint of that mythical softer side had already been revealed. How could she convince herself he was like all the other men she'd dated, when his actions repeatedly proved otherwise?

Bryce gripped the steering wheel and focused on the road. Neither of them had spoken since they'd left his house, but it was just as well. His mind couldn't have formed a coherent sentence if his life depended on it. The woman had him so riled up he didn't know if he wanted to kiss her or take his key back and never speak to her again.

Alexis stared out the window and toyed with the buttons on his jacket. His chest tightened. Something about seeing her wearing his clothes turned his insides to mush and his outsides rock hard.

But she thought he was a womanizer. A dumbass. He could see why she would think those things. In his quest to rid himself of the nerd he used to be, he tended to come off as aloof at times. Stoic. He'd rather people saw him as detached than a geek.

But not a womanizer.

"I really don't use women." He glanced at her and focused on the road. "I told Lauren I wasn't interested in dating anyone. She said she felt the same, so I didn't think any harm would come of it."

She looked at him, her expression hard, distant. "You don't have to explain yourself to me. It's none of my business."

"I don't want you to think poorly of me." More than that, damn it, he wanted her to like him. To feel the same heat he felt every time he touched her.

"It doesn't matter what I think." She lifted a shoulder and returned her gaze to the window.

He gripped the steering wheel tighter. "It matters to me."

Letting out a sigh, she shifted in her seat to face him. "I don't think poorly of you. But I do have a terrible habit of being attracted to the wrong kind of men, so you'll have to excuse me if I keep my distance."

His pulse quickened. "You're attracted to me?"

She grinned and mussed his hair. "Who wouldn't be? Take a left here. My car's in the lot on the right."

He turned left and rolled into the parking lot. Her gaze darted around like she was looking for something. Possibly for the reason she climbed that damn electrical tower in the first place. Seemingly satisfied, she looked at him and smiled.

He let go of the steering wheel and fisted his hands in his lap. "What makes you think I'm the wrong kind of man?"

"You all are." She offered him the house key.

"Keep it. My offer stands. If you get too cold, or…if you need a shot of whiskey, my door is open."

She slipped the key into her pocket. "Thanks, Bryce. For your help and for not asking too many questions." She leaned across the console and pressed her lips to his cheek.

Electricity shot through his core as her mouth hovered near his face. He turned toward her, their noses brushing, her breath warming his skin. Her gaze landed on his lips, and she swallowed. His pulse thrummed. He hesitated, giving her plenty of time to move away, but she didn't.

Leaning in, he tentatively brushed his lips against hers, fully expecting her back away or slap him. Instead, she returned the kiss, parting her lips as her breath hitched in her throat. She tasted like sugar and coffee, and as he slipped out his tongue, a slight moan resonated from her chest.

He moved closer, reaching across the console to slid his fingers into her hair, deepening the kiss. Her lips were soft, her skin warm, and as her fingers grazed his neck, he closed his eyes and lost himself to the moment.

With a shuddering breath, she pulled away and cupped his cheek in her hand. Though her eyes held passion, her brow knit with worry. "Thanks again." She slipped out the door before he could respond.

His oversized jacket nearly swallowed her, the slight horizontal motion of the fabric the only indication of her hips swaying as she walked to her car. His mouth tugged into an involuntary grin as he imagined what her curves looked like beneath the coat. He sucked his bottom lip into his mouth and ran his tongue over the surface, savoring the last hint of Alexis on his skin.

As she reached her car and stuck the key in the door, a burly, dark-haired man carrying a doughnut box called her name. Alexis spun around, and fear flashed in her eyes. The man's brows lifted briefly in surprise before he hardened his gaze and marched toward her, stepping so close that her back pressed into the car as he set the box on the top.

Bryce flung open his door and stomped toward them.

"I thought you were dead, baby." The man reached a hand toward her face.

She slapped it away. "You thought wrong."

"Is this guy bothering you?" Bryce stepped next to her, trying to create some space between Alexis and the man, but the guy wouldn't back off.

Alexis glanced between them and focused on the dark-haired man. "Everything's fine. Isn't it, Eric? *Sergeant* Samuels was nice enough to bring me to my car once I got out of the hospital."

He didn't miss the emphasis she placed on his title, like she was warning Eric not to make a move. This guy must have been the reason Alexis fell from that tower. Was he her boyfriend? The "wrong kind of man" she'd said she was attracted to? He had to wonder if some of the bruises mottling her skin yesterday were there before she fell.

"Oh, yes, Sergeant." Eric's voice oozed with false charm. "I'm so happy to see my *girlfriend* alive after that tumble she took." He reached for her hand, but she yanked it away.

"I'm not your girlfriend."

"Hey, man." Bryce put a heavy hand on Eric's shoulder. "Back off."

Eric took a swing. Bryce jerked away, the man's fist narrowly missing his jaw. Bryce moved forward to return the favor, but he stopped short as Alexis stepped between them.

"Boys." She held up her hands. "There's no need for this."

"You're right," Bryce said. "There's not. Get in the car, Alexis. Let's go home."

"She's not going anywhere with you." Eric shoved Alexis out of the way and lunged at Bryce. His fist connected with the side of his head, sending him careening to the ground, and an explosion of pain ricocheted through his skull.

He blinked away the kaleidoscope dancing in his vision and got to his feet. Alexis clung to Eric's arm, but he jerked it away and charged Bryce again. He took another swing, but Bryce ducked and rammed a shoulder into his stomach, knocking him off his feet. He tried to pin him to the ground, but the guy had superhuman strength. He flipped Bryce onto his back and landed another punch square in his jaw. Eric grabbed him by the shirt, and Bryce could've sworn the guy started to shimmer and vibrate. He squeezed his eyes shut to chase away the wavering vision, and the pain in his head made his stomach turn. How hard had he been hit?

"Stop it, Eric," Alexis said. "There's people. Cameras."

Bryce turned his pounding head toward the strip center, where a crowd of patrons had gathered to witness the fight. Several people held their cell phones out, recording the incident. *Shit.* Just what he needed.

Eric glanced at the crowd and growled before rising to his feet and dragging Bryce up with him. "Sorry about that, officer." He smoothed the front of Bryce's shirt.

Bryce grabbed his arm, wrenching it behind his back before snatching his cuffs from his belt and slapping them on his wrist. "You're under arrest for assaulting a police officer." He cuffed the other hand and shoved Eric to his knees.

Eric laughed. "Looks more like battery to me, dude. I beat your ass."

Ignoring the jibe, he phoned the local police to make the official arrest. Within five minutes, an officer arrived and put Eric in the back seat of the squad car. Bryce gave his statement, and the officer turned to Alexis. She told him everything that happened in the parking lot, but she didn't elaborate further.

"Tell him what he did to you, Alexis," Bryce said. "If you want this guy to stay locked up, you need to tell him how he hurt you."

Her eyes widened as she shook her head. "He didn't hurt me. I'm fine."

He would never understand why so many women defended the bastards who beat them. Stepping closer to her, he lowered his voice. "It's for the best. Please tell him."

She chewed her bottom lip and stared hard into his eyes, as if she were pleading with him to understand. "That's it, officer." She looked at the uniform. "That's all I have to say. Am I free to go?"

The officer cut his gaze from Alexis to Bryce and nodded. "We'll be in touch."

As soon as the patrol car left the parking lot and the crowd dispersed, Alexis turned to him with panic in her eyes. "You have no idea what you've done."

"I put an abuser in jail where he belongs."

"Eric's more than an abuser. He's…Oh, forget it. I have to go." She reached for the door handle, but he grasped her hand. Her fingers felt like ice, and the color had drained from her cheeks.

"He's what, Alexis? What aren't you telling me?" He winced as a new flush of pain throbbed through his head. His eye pounded, his vision narrowing into a slit. No one had beaten him this badly since high school.

"Nothing." She took a deep breath and searched his eyes…or eye. He could only see out of one. "Oh, Bryce." She swept her fingers across his cheek and placed a soft kiss on his brow.

The throbbing in his head subsided, replaced by a dull ache. How could a simple touch from this woman ease his pain? "Let me help you. Unless someone posts bail, he'll be locked up for a few days. After that…" He shoved his hands in his pockets. After that, the usual would happen.

If she wouldn't press charges, Eric would find her. Abusers always did. "I can protect you."

She smiled and brushed her thumb across his lower lip. "I don't need protection. But thank you."

He let her open the door this time and watched as she climbed inside. "You have my key. I hope you'll use it."

CHAPTER SIX

After making a few stops on his way home from work, Bryce pulled into his driveway and stared at the file folder on the passenger seat. He'd run the scumbag's information, and Eric had a Mississippi driver's license, with a home address in Biloxi.

A quick search of the database had revealed another address in Pearl River and a criminal record. Mostly assaults, bar fights, evading arrest. The guy obviously had a temper. Unfortunately, he didn't have any outstanding warrants. Nothing to guarantee a lengthy stay behind bars, so he could get out on bail.

He might get six months for assaulting a police officer, but if Bryce could get Alexis to admit Eric hurt her —if she would testify—then he could lock the son of a bitch away for a nice long time. But she was protecting him, and something in his gut told him the reason ran deeper than thinking she deserved whatever he gave her.

A glance in the rearview mirror revealed a small, yellow bruise beneath his eye. No swelling. No blood. He looked again. Maybe Eric hadn't hit him that hard after all.

He climbed out of his car and shuffled up the walkway to the first-floor apartment. Karen opened the door as he approached. Her smile didn't mask the worry in her eyes.

"How is he?" Bryce asked. "I stopped by the hospital, but they said he'd been released."

"He's in the living room. Come on in."

He wiped his feet and stepped through the door. The floorplan matched his own upstairs: kitchen and dining area straight ahead, living room and hallway to the right. A bathroom and two bedrooms lay down the hall, though Bryce used his second bedroom as an office.

Michael sat on the pale-blue sofa, his gaze glued to the television. His skin still held an ashen tinge, but the puffiness encircling his eyes had eased.

"How ya feeling, buddy?" Bryce sat on the couch and put a hand on his shoulder as Karen turned off the TV.

Michael stared into his lap. "Better."

"Hey, look at me." He waited for the kid to return his gaze. "There's nothing to be ashamed of. We all go through rough patches."

Michael nodded, tears brimming in his eyes.

"The important thing is that you're alive. You're home with your mom. She loves you. Sam loves you. Hell, even I love you, kid. We're all glad to have you back." He wrapped his arms around him as Michael sobbed on his shoulder, and his heart wrenched. This was why Bryce did what he did. Everything he'd worked for from the day he graduated high school led him to this moment. Saving lives was all he'd ever wanted to do.

"Thank you, Sergeant Samuels." Michael wiped the tears from his cheeks. "I don't know if I said that before."

"I'm sure you did. So, what's the plan now?"

"He'll be seeing a therapist twice a week," Karen said. "And he's supposed to get back to his 'normal' routine as soon as possible." She made air quotes with her fingers. "Though I don't think going back to school right away is a good idea."

Michael fiddled with his hands in his lap. "It's almost winter break anyway. I can go back in January."

"When does therapy start? Not in January…?"

Karen sank into a chair. "His first appointment is tomorrow."

"That's good." He closed his eyes for a long, relieved blink and nodded. "And when you do go back to school, you won't have to worry about April Cunningham. She'll be spending the rest of the year at an alternative campus."

Michael's eyes widened. "Because of me?"

"You aren't the only one she's bullied. More kids are stepping forward with their own stories of harassment, and lucky for us, your school has a zero-tolerance policy when it comes to bullies."

His posture relaxed. "If it's okay with you, I'll start walking Sam again tomorrow."

Bryce smiled. "He'll be happy to hear it." He rose to his feet. "If there's anything you two need, I'll be right upstairs. Just give me a holler."

Karen walked him to the door. "How's your mother doing?"

He shoved his hands in his pockets. Karen and Michael had been his neighbors for five years. They knew his mom when she was functioning. His dad when he was alive. "Oh, you know. Same ol' same ol'. Sometimes she knows who I am. Sometimes she doesn't. She's progressively getting worse."

"I'm so sorry. I know she's all the family you have left, and I…" She shook her head.

And when she was gone, he'd have no one. But choosing to take on this tough cop persona and not letting anyone know the real him had been his decision. He may have been living a lie, but at least he could help people this way. A familiar ache tightened his chest. "She's seventy-five, and it runs in the family. It was bound to happen sooner or later."

She pulled him into a tight hug. "Thank you. I can't say that enough. Michael is my life. How can I ever repay you?"

"You being here for him is payment enough. I'm pretty fond of that kid." He patted her back, and she released her hold. "That's a pretty Christmas tree." He nodded to the sparkling fir standing in the corner.

"Thank you. Michael helped me decorate it last week. I can't…" Her voice cracked, and she cleared her throat. "I can't imagine what Christmas would have been like if he…"

"You don't have to imagine it. He's sitting right there. Go be with your son. I'll be upstairs if you need anything."

"Thank you, Bryce."

"You're welcome, ma'am." He stepped through the door and trudged around the building to the stairs. Christmas was a joyous time for people who had a family to share it with. He'd visit his mom on Christmas day, like he visited her every week. If he was lucky, she'd remember his name. Other than that, he'd be spending his holidays alone with his dog, like he had the past three years.

Sam greeted him at the door, doing his famous full-body wag. The tension melted from Bryce's shoulders, and he stooped to pet his dog. The house already felt too quiet.

Like a piece of it was missing. Sam looked expectantly at the front door and whined when no one else stepped through.

"She's not here, buddy. I'm sorry."

The dog sat and tilted his head.

Bryce scratched him behind the ears. "You like her, don't you?"

Sam let out a soft *woof* and continued looking at the door.

Bryce sighed. "I do too."

He plopped onto the couch and ran a hand over his face. Where could she have gone? Temptation to call Macey had him reaching for his phone, but he thought better of it. Alexis had been adamant that she not know she was in any kind of trouble. She wouldn't run to her sister now.

Hopefully she found somewhere warm to spend the night. He shuddered at the thought of her huddled in her car somewhere in the cold. The temperature wouldn't drop below freezing tonight, but it wouldn't be pleasant either. Would she go back to that scumbag's house? Bile lurched into his throat. Surely, she wouldn't. Even with the bastard spending the night in jail, the image of her taking refuge under his roof had Bryce reaching for his car keys.

He had Eric's address, but what would he do if he found her there? She was a grown woman, and if she didn't want his help, he wouldn't force it on her.

Instead, he closed his eyes, and the image of her leaning toward him filled his mind. He could still taste her lips on his, the soft, velvety feel of her skin lingering in his memory like a warm summer day. She wore his jacket. She'd smelled like his shampoo. He had no claim on her, but the idea she had something of his with her—wherever she was—made him smile. Hopefully it would make her smile too.

Alexis pulled into the parking lot at the Barataria Nature Preserve and dialed David Anderson's number. She hadn't spoken to Eric's father in months, and her stomach turned as it rang once, twice…three times. Would her call be a welcome one?

"To what do I owe the pleasure, Alexis?" His powerful voice held a hint of wariness. It always did when she'd made her weekly reports.

"It's about Eric."

"Your relationship with my son was your choice. I paid you to get keep an eye on him for me. No bonuses for sleeping with him."

She gripped the phone tighter. "I'm not sleeping with him."

"Not anymore. But you're off my payroll, so why are you calling?"

Chewing the inside of her cheek, she took a few slow breaths before speaking. "Eric's in jail. He assaulted a police officer." She told him how he attacked Bryce in the parking lot.

"Goddammit. That little shit got in trouble with the law again." He sounded more tired than angry. "I sent him to that Podunk town to stay out of trouble. His ass can sit in jail. I'm not sending bail."

She closed her eyes and leaned her head against the seat. She'd be safe for a few days at least. "That's not all. That sound-proof room he begged you for wasn't so he could start a metal band. He wanted it built so the neighbors wouldn't hear the screams of his victims."

He paused. "His victims?"

"I know it sounds crazy, but I witnessed it first-hand. He's trying to start his own pack by attacking humans. He thinks they'll turn into werewolves if he tears them up enough and they survive." She crossed her fingers that he'd believe her story. Pack members trusted the word of a rogue about as much as they'd trust a life boat made from papier-mâché.

David let out a long sigh. "Has he been successful?"

"Not yet. He says he's trying to find the right balance of blood loss and werewolf venom."

"Werewolves aren't venomous. The idiot has no idea what he's doing."

Silence hung on the line as she waited for him to continue. "Looks like I'll be making a trip to Pearl River," David finally said. "Thank you for the information, Alexis. We'll be in touch."

The last visitors exited the parking lot, leaving Alexis alone. She moved her car behind a dumpster and shut off the engine before turning off her phone and locking it in the glove box. Eric had been happy to move to the tiny Louisiana town to get away from his controlling father. Hopefully David would enforce some of that control and whisk him back to Biloxi. Then she'd never have to deal with the jackass again.

A twenty-pound weight lifted from her shoulders as she climbed out of her car and strolled into the woods. She'd done all she could do.

She climbed over a game fence and slipped into the trees. Though mostly made up of wetland, the twenty-three-thousand-acre Barataria preserve held plenty of dense forest. A wolf could easily spend the night in the brush unnoticed.

Curtains of Spanish moss cascaded from the leafless branches of bald cypress trees, creating a canopy around the thicket, and dry grass crunched beneath her boots as she made her way deeper into the forest. A wooden boardwalk led off the right, winding through the trees before jutting out over the marsh. Alexis turned left, away from the trail.

Wrapping Bryce's jacket tighter around her shoulders, she inhaled his scent. Memories of his warm bed flooded her mind. The feel of the soft cotton sheets sliding across her skin. The way his pillow cradled her head. The way his scent lingered in the blankets like it did in his jacket. She'd much prefer Bryce's bed over the forest floor, especially if he were in it.

But she couldn't go back to him. She definitely shouldn't have kissed him. Her lips still tingled every time she thought about it. A peck on the cheek was all she'd meant to give him, but once she'd gotten close, she couldn't pull away. Everything about that man drew her in. Made her want to stay.

Part of her craved companionship. She wanted to have a real relationship with Macey—and with Bryce—but so far all she'd managed was a brief visit once a month. If she was going to settle down somewhere, New Orleans would be the place. The city was alive with culture, music, food, magic. Her sister was there. Bryce was there.

She shook her head. What was she thinking? She hardly knew the man. He couldn't possibly be as kind and gentle as he seemed.

Then again, he'd shown her more kindness in twelve hours than she'd seen her entire life. The more she thought about him, the more she needed him. She slipped her hand into her pocket and toyed with his house key. Cold and hard against her skin, it contrasted the warmth and tenderness she felt from him.

Every fiber of her being screamed at her to go to him. To take comfort in the safety of his arms. But what could she offer him in return? She had nothing. No job. No money. She was a flake. A drifter. A rogue. He deserved so much more than she could ever dream of giving him.

She released the key and ran her hand along the coarse bark of a cypress tree. Rough, like her. Bryce deserved a woman more refined, educated, feminine.

Alexis needed to clear her head. Thinking about Bryce did her no good.

It had been ages since she'd hunted. Maybe a quick chase would do the trick. Hunt. Sleep. Get on with her life tomorrow. It sounded like a good plan. As she shifted into wolf form, everything she wore and carried in her pockets was absorbed by the magic. When she shifted back, everything would be in its place. She'd never given it a second thought until now, but she felt comforted to know that a part of Bryce—even if it was just his jacket—would be with her through the night.

CHAPTER SEVEN

BRYCE PUT THE FINISHING TOUCHES ON HIS ANTI-bullying PowerPoint and shut down his computer. Macey's shift would be starting soon, and he had to know if she'd heard from her sister. The temperature had dropped to forty-two last night, and the thought of Alexis shivering in her car, parked somewhere all alone, had him grinding his teeth in frustration. If he could get her phone number. If he could hear her voice to know she was okay, maybe he could relax.

He strolled by Macey's desk, but it sat empty. His promotion had earned him a coveted spot on the day shift; Macey worked nights. It didn't matter what time of day he went to bed, as long as he got to sleep, but working without his former partner had left an emptiness inside him he hadn't expected.

It had taken years of hard work and studying to earn his position as a negotiator, and saving lives and his work in community policing provided a satisfaction like nothing else. Though he'd never felt any kind of romantic stirrings for Macey, losing her as a work partner felt a little like losing a life partner. She was the closest anyone had ever gotten to actually knowing him. If Alexis would let him in, he wouldn't mind letting her get to know him too.

"Hey, Samuels." Lieutenant Johnson hovered in his office doorway. He kept his curly, dark hair sheared short, and the sprinkling of gray at his temples gave him that distinguished, senior officer look. A look he wore well. A series of fine lines etched into his forehead revealed the stress of the job.

Bryce made eye contact, and Johnson stepped back into the room and settled into his chair—his way of saying, "Come see me in my office." He was a man of few words. Bryce could appreciate that.

"What's up, LT?" He leaned against the door jamb.

"Sit down." His brow knit as he opened a file folder.

Bryce lowered himself into a chair and waited for the man to speak.

"I'm impressed with your work at the high schools. The kids are connecting with you. The principals are singing your praises."

A grin tugged at his lips. "Thank you, sir. Just doing my job."

"You're doing it well. But…" He pulled a photograph from the folder and slid it across the desk. Michael's red-rimmed eyes stared back at him. "You didn't tell me you knew him."

His throat thickened. "Oh. Yeah, he's my neighbor."

Johnson slipped the picture into the folder and let out a slow breath. "There's a reason we don't let friends and family talk to the jumpers when they ask for them. Do you remember why that is?"

He twisted his brother's ring on his finger. "More often than not, the loved ones will be a trigger. When emotions run too high, the jumper's more likely to go over the edge." *Shit.* He'd broken a rule. He was Michael's friend, and it hadn't even crossed his mind that he might be a trigger. He'd only been concerned with getting the kid off the ledge.

"Exactly."

"But, technically, he didn't ask for me. I happened to be there by coincidence."

Johnson pushed the folder aside and folded his hands on the desk. "It doesn't matter. You put that boy's life at risk by being there."

Bryce gripped the arms of the chair. "I saved that boy's life. You want to tell his mother I shouldn't have been there?"

"I know you did. That's why I'm giving you a verbal warning. Your record is nearly spotless. Not a single reprimand since you joined the force—aside from the cigarette incident."

When he'd first made detective, he'd dropped a lit cigarette onto a body, singing the skin a bit. It happened six years ago, but no one would let him live it down. "That was an accident." He hadn't had a smoke since.

"I know. I'll see you tomorrow." Johnson turned to his computer, ending the conversation.

Bryce grumbled as he left the office and turned down the hall toward Macey's desk. Thank God he'd gotten a verbal warning. He was proud of his nearly-untarnished record. He didn't need it blemished for saving a life. Rules and laws were made to be followed. His job was to enforce them. He couldn't go around breaking them; that would make him a hypocrite.

He stopped by the vending machine on the way to Macey's office—out of Snickers bars again—and he bought a Milky Way. Macey sat at her desk, examining a case report.

"How's it going, boss?" He stood in the doorway and took a bite of the candy bar.

"I think I should be calling you boss now, shouldn't I, Sergeant?" Macey smiled, her green eyes sparkling in the fluorescent lighting. He'd never noticed how similar they were to Alexis's eyes. They had the same hair color too, though Macey's golden locks flowed past her shoulders when she wore it down. Alexis had chopped hers into a short style that showed off her slender neck and heart-shaped face.

He sauntered into the room and plopped into a chair. "If I've learned one thing in all my years, it's that the woman is *always* the boss."

Macey rolled her eyes. "As long as she's cooking for you and keeping the house clean?"

He grinned. "You said it, not me." She knew damn well he'd never expect a woman to wait on him hand and foot, but it was fun watching her bristle when he joked about it.

She shook her head. "How's Michael?"

"Better. He's home now."

"That's good. I heard you pulled him in. Going out on the ledge like that? I don't know how you do it. It's amazing."

He shrugged. "Johnson doesn't think so. Seems I broke a rule."

She laughed. "You? That's a first."

"What can I say? I'm becoming a rebel in my old age."

"And mixing things up, I see." She nodded to his candy bar.

"Machine was out of Snickers." He shoved the last of

the chocolate in his mouth and dropped the wrapper in the trash can. "You working on anything important?"

She arched an eyebrow. "Nothing pressing."

He drummed his fingers on the arm of the chair. "I ran into your sister the other day. Have you talked to her lately?"

She picked up a bunch of papers and tapped them on the desk, evening the stack. "Not in about a week. Where'd you see her?"

Crap. He should've figured out a story before he brought it up. "Convenience store. Stopped to get gas. Where's she staying now?"

Macey sighed. "I have no idea. She comes and goes. I'm trying to give her space…you know, time to warm up to the whole family thing again. She's been on her own so long, I don't think she knows how to stay in one place."

"That's hard, having family you can't be close to." He knew that better than anyone.

"It is. But it's been twenty years. It's going to take time for us to have a real sisterly relationship again."

He wiped his sweaty palms on his pants and flashed her a grin. "You wouldn't happen to have her phone number, would you?"

She crossed her arms. "Seriously? How many women live in New Orleans? And you have to crush on my sister?"

"She's pretty." He shrugged and cringed inwardly. Alexis was so much more than a pretty face.

"So are ten thousand other women in this city."

"Please?" He couldn't explain it to her. The possessiveness he felt in his heart. The overwhelming need to keep Alexis safe. It didn't make sense for him to feel this strongly about a woman he hardly knew, but he couldn't deny it.

She let out her breath in a huff. "Bryce."

"C'mon, Mace. It's just a phone number. I'm not asking for a blood sample. Let me ask her out. If she says 'no,' then no harm done."

She licked her lips and narrowed her gaze. "I don't want to see either of you get hurt."

He raised his hands in a show of innocence. "I'm not going to hurt her." He wouldn't dream of it.

"I'm more worried about you."

Really? He scoffed. "Have I ever let a woman hurt me?"

"Have you ever dated one long enough to give her the chance?"

He leaned forward, resting his forearm on her desk. "If my memory serves right, a year ago you were scared to get that close to a man." He winked.

She sat up straight. "People can change."

"I know that's right."

Tugging on her bottom lip, she furrowed her brow as she considered his request. "Alexis can be…flaky. I don't know what her life was like for the past twenty years, but from what's she told me, it's been rough." She punched some numbers on her phone. "Be careful."

His phone chimed with the incoming message. Alexis's number lit up his screen, and the fist gripping his heart released its hold. "Thanks, Mace. I will."

Macey's phone beeped. "Lovely. Just fished a body out of the Mississippi." She grinned at him. "I haven't been assigned a new partner yet. Want to ride along for old time's sake?"

"I'd love to."

Bryce rode shotgun as Macey maneuvered the black SUV up Chartres Street in the French Quarter. This part of the city was built in the 1800s, and the narrow streets weren't made for cars this size...or any size for that matter. Two and three-story buildings in varying shades of red, beige, yellow, and blue lined the street. Wrought-iron railings wrapped around the balconies, and wooden shutters covered the windows, blocking the winter chill from creeping inside. Elaborate wreaths and twinkling lights decorated the terraces, giving the city a festive aura.

Everyone would be celebrating the holidays with their families soon, while he sat at home with his dog. He looked at Macey. She knew him better than anyone, and he trusted her with his life. Most of what she knew was the mask, but her comment about Alexis hurting him made him wonder if she didn't see a little more deeply into him than he'd thought.

She glanced at him. "What?"

"What makes you think Alexis is going to hurt me? Aside from what you said before?"

The corner of her mouth tugged into an almost-grin. "What is it that you see in her? And don't just say she's pretty."

"She's independent, capable, smart." He shrugged. "I know she doesn't stick around, but she seems to be there for you when you need her most. Like that time you were in the hospital."

Macey took a deep breath and let it out slowly. "And she left as soon as I recovered."

"She came back though. She was here for your wedding. She loves you." He smiled. "I admire her tenacity. I don't see why you think she's going to hurt me."

She narrowed her eyes. "You're a lot more sensitive than you lead people to believe, but you can't fool me. I'm psychic, remember?"

They hung a right on St. Philip and another on Decatur to pass Café Du Monde. Macey pulled onto the curb, got out of the car, and started up the steps toward the riverbank.

Bryce followed, mulling over what she'd said. "I thought you could only talk to dead people?"

She laughed and continued her climb.

He stopped on the sidewalk. "Go ahead without me. I'll be there in a second."

Macey turned around when she reached the top of the stairs and put her hands on her hips. "Tell my sister I said, 'hi.'" She shook her head and continued to the river.

He clicked Alexis's number and held his breath as it rang. Voicemail. Of course.

"Hey, Alexis. It's Bryce. I wanted to make sure you're okay…after what happened yesterday. And to remind you that you have my house key. I hope you'll use it." His stomach soured as he pressed end and jogged up the stairs to the scene.

The moon reflected off the river, causing the muddy water to sparkle like the stars, and lights from the Crescent City Connection bridge illuminated the water with a reddish glow. A massive white steamboat docked down to the right, and a crowd of uniforms stood in a semicircle around the body. Bryce caught up to Macey as she began to ask questions.

"What have we got?" she asked a man in blue.

"Male. Mid-forties. A couple found him floating face down a few feet out. Hasn't been in the water long, but it looks like something tried to eat him."

Bryce followed the man's gaze to the mangled body lying in the grass. Jagged tears covered the dead man's flesh from head to legs, and obvious teeth marks punctured his arms. Bryce's skin crawled. After seven years of working cases like this, he was happy to be saving lives rather than investigating deaths.

"What do you think, boss?" he said to Macey.

She slipped on a pair of blue latex gloves, snapping them at the wrists, and bent to examine the body. "Looks like an animal attack to me. Maybe a wolf or rabid dog." She gestured to his arms. "See the teeth marks here?"

"I don't know. The neck's clean. Seems like a wolf would go for the throat on instinct to kill its prey before eating it."

She yanked off her gloves and tossed them in a trash bag. "Then it was a dog."

"A dog dumped the body in the river?" Was she serious?

"Maybe he fell in while trying to run away. Anyway, I don't think a person did this, but we'll see what the autopsy says."

He followed her while she investigated the scene, though he hesitated to call what she did an investigation. A half-ass glance, maybe. She shined a flashlight on the ground in a few spots and walked along the bank where they'd dragged the body from the water for a total of two minutes and thirty-seven seconds. Then she nodded to a uniform. "I've seen enough. Pack it up."

"What about your spirit sensors?" Bryce asked as she made her way toward the street.

She shrugged. "No objects to touch. Let's go."

"Yes, ma'am." Bryce may not have had psychic abilities, but his cop sensors screamed murder. Macey had never been one to overlook evidence, but the way she dismissed this as nothing more than an animal attack seemed downright strange. It was her case, though, so he'd let it go. For now. "Hey, can I buy you a cup of coffee or a beignet? It's been a while." He slid into the passenger seat and clicked his seatbelt.

"I would love that, but I've got a lot of work to catch up on." She turned onto Decatur and headed back to the station. "Besides, your shift ended an hour ago. Don't you want to go home and get some rest? Leave the night shift to us lowly detectives?" She playfully punched him on the arm.

"Yeah. That's fine."

"Rain check. I promise. Hey, maybe you can come to dinner with me and Luke sometime. I cook a mean pot of gumbo."

"Sure. That sounds great." He stared out the window.

She stopped in a parking space and shut off the engine. "I guess Alexis didn't answer?"

"Voicemail."

"That's not surprising."

He got out of the car and walked around to Macey's side. "Need any help with your paperwork? I remember how to investigate a murder."

She cast him a sideways glance and shook her head. "This wasn't a murder, but no thanks. I've got it."

He shoved his hands in his pockets. Her answers didn't sit right with him. She was hiding something, but he knew her well enough to know she wouldn't share it until she was ready.

"Go home, Bryce. Tell Sam I said, 'hi.'"

"Will do, Mace. Take care." He got in his car and headed out of the French Quarter, through the Central Business District, and into the grandness of the Garden District. The "American" part of New Orleans. Massive Victorian, Greek Revival, and Italianate homes built on generous lots populated the neighborhood along St. Charles. A streetcar chugged along the track as he made a left into the neighborhood and pulled into his driveway.

Karen sat on her front porch, sipping a mug of coffee. Light from the television flickered in the window behind her, and she waved as Bryce trekked up the sidewalk.

"Evening, ma'am." He stopped and rested a hand on the railing. "How's he doing?"

Her smile didn't reach her eyes. "Shaky, but better. Sam's a good stress reliever."

"That he is." He nodded to her mug. "Careful. That stuff'll keep you up all night."

"It's decaf."

"Good deal." He tipped an imaginary hat and started toward the stairs.

"I made you dinner," she called after him.

He stopped and turned around. "You didn't need to do that. A man can be sustained on candy bars and potato chips."

"It's just to say thank you. Again. I can't say it enough."

"You don't have to say it at all." Rules be damned. Seeing Michael safe at home with his mom trumped any kind of reprimand Bryce could have received, verbal or not.

She folded her right leg beneath her left and gripped the mug with both hands. "You worked late, so I left it in your fridge. I hope you don't mind."

He smiled. "I would never be opposed to finding a home-cooked meal in my fridge. Thank you."

Once inside, he gave Sam a good scratch behind the ears and headed straight for the refrigerator. A large plastic container occupied an empty shelf. A handwritten note on pink stationary sat atop the blue lid.

Thank you for saving Michael's life. You're a hero. –Karen.

He set the note on the counter and scooped out a generous helping of jambalaya. Covering the rice and sausage dish with a paper towel, he popped it in the microwave while he poured himself a glass of whiskey. The smooth liquid warmed his insides as he settled onto the sofa and flipped on the TV.

When the microwave beeped, he retrieved his dinner and found *Star Trek: The Next Generation*—the best TV series ever created—on Netflix. The herbs and spices of Karen's jambalaya danced on his tongue as he savored the tangy sausage. Sam sat on the floor, his snout resting on the edge of the sofa, his sorrowful puppy-dog eyes pleading.

"Sorry, buddy. You know the rules."

Sam let out a pitiful whine. Bryce took another bite as his front door swung open.

CHAPTER EIGHT

ALEXIS HESITATED IN THE DOORWAY AS BRYCE'S EYES widened. He fumbled with the remote, dropping it in his lap twice before he mashed the power button and turned off the TV.

She rested her hand on the knob. "I'm sorry. I should've knocked."

"No, no." He stood and wiped his palms on his pants. "I gave you a key. I wanted you to use it."

As she stepped into the living room, she slipped out of his jacket and hung it on the coat rack. She immediately missed its warmth and woodsy scent. It had been like a permanent hug from Bryce over the last couple of days. "I got your message."

His Adam's apple rose and dipped as he swallowed. "Good."

Sam bounded toward her, his tail wagging like a tornado, and she bent down to pet him. "What were you watching?"

He ran a hand through his hair and cast his gaze to the TV. "Oh, uh…football."

She suppressed a grin and ran both hands over the dog's shoulders, giving him a good scratch as his left leg thumped the floor. "Who's playing?"

Bryce chuckled. "The Saints, of course."

"The Saints?" She straightened and put her hands on her hips. "Didn't they play last night?"

He scratched his head and looked at his dog. "I DVR'd it."

"Right." What was he up to, and why didn't he want her to know what he was watching?

He picked up a plate from the coffee table and rushed into the kitchen. "Are you hungry? Karen made some amazing jambalaya. Want some?"

Her heart dipped into her stomach to swim through the jealousy boiling there. He had a woman cooking for him? "Sure. Who's Karen?" She shuffled into the kitchen and picked up the pink stationary lying on his counter. It would be her luck if he had a girlfriend he'd neglected to tell her about. "She have the hots for you?"

He stopped and looked at her, and the corner of his mouth tugged into a crooked, kissable grin. "She lives downstairs. Read it." He gestured to the paper.

She scanned the note. "Who's Michael?"

"Her son. I talked him down from an eleventh-story window ledge. That's why I was in the hospital that day. When I found you." He locked eyes with hers, and her stomach fluttered. When he'd *found* her…like she'd been lost.

Maybe she had.

"You…Wow." Her chest warmed as if her wolf were saying *I told you so*.

He shrugged. "It's my job."

"You act like it's no big deal." Of all the things for him

to be proud of himself for, saving lives should have topped the list. She set the stationery on the counter.

He took a deep breath and twisted the ring on his finger. “I know it is a big deal, but I have to play it down. Ultimately, it was his decision to let me grab him and pull him to safety, like it would have been his decision if he jumped. If I go around saying *I* saved his life, then what will I have to say if I lose someone?” His hazel eyes held a deep sadness, as if the safety of the world rested on his shoulders.

Having that kind of responsibility was unimaginable. She sank into a dining chair as he put a plate of food in front of her. What a stressful job that must have been. “I never thought of it that way. Have you ever lost anyone?”

He hesitated, his gaze growing distant before he blinked and shook his head. “No, but I’ve only been doing this for a few months. I know people who have.” He settled into the chair next to her.

“Still, it’s amazing what you do.”

“Thanks.” He held her gaze, the look in his eyes somewhere between a smolder and curiosity. He was either going to drill her with questions or pull her into his arms and kiss her, and she couldn’t handle either at the moment.

Focusing on the food, she took a bite of jambalaya. The overwhelming heat of the spices burned her tongue, but she couldn’t seem to stop eating. She shoveled it in and had cleaned her plate before she realized it.

The corners of his eyes crinkled when he smiled. “Hungry?”

She took a sip of whiskey. “I can’t remember the last time I had a home-cooked meal. Tell Karen I said it was delicious.”

Bryce cleared the dishes from the table and washed them in the sink. Alexis watched his backside as he dried the plates and returned them to the cabinet. He was meticulous in his ways, putting each dish in its proper place before wiping down the counters and the table and pouring two more glasses of Jameson.

He was a walking, talking contradiction. Cool and cocky on the surface, but inside he was so much more. He saved lives for a living, dedicated his life to helping others. Her initial perception of Bryce had been all wrong, and her wolf was gloating in her soul.

"Shall we?" He gestured to the living room.

She followed him to the sofa and sat next to him, shifting her knees toward his so she faced him. The intensity in his gaze held her as he pressed the glass to his lips and took a sip. A tiny drop of alcohol dripped onto his lower lip, and his tongue slipped out to retrieve it, sending a warm shiver cascading down her spine.

He set the glass on the table, never taking his gaze off hers. "What made you decide to come back?"

She rubbed the goose bumps on her arms. "It's pretty cold out tonight. Didn't want to sleep in my car again."

"I see." His eyes searched hers, penetrating her soul, making her want to open up to someone for the first time in her life. Could he really be the one? Was she ready to listen to her wolf?

"That's a lie." Her body involuntarily drifted toward him.

"I know." He didn't move away.

"I came to see you. I couldn't stop thinking about you." She reached behind his head and pulled his face to hers. Their lips met, and warmth spread through her body like a wildfire consuming a forest. She closed her eyes as her tongue brushed his, and he slid a hand to her hip. She wanted him. To feel his hands on her body, his bare skin pressed to hers. Taking his face in her hands, she kissed him harder, trailing her lips across his jaw and down his neck.

"Alexis." He gripped her shoulders gently and pushed her away.

His eyes swam with emotion, the greenish-gold irises almost molten, the brown flecks seeming to shimmer as he blinked. He looked at her with desire, but his mouth pressed into a hard line. "As much as I enjoyed that. I need answers before it happens again."

She slumped her shoulders. Of course he needed answers. He deserved them. He deserved so much more than she could give him.

He released his hold and leaned back on the couch. "This Eric guy. He your boyfriend?"

She stared at her hands folded in her lap. "I used to date him a long time ago, before I met you. I guess he still thinks there's something between us, but there isn't. I swear." She raised her eyes to meet his gaze. "It's kinda like you and that red-headed nurse."

"Not even close." His jaw clenched, the tendons in his neck tightening like wires. "Is he the reason you climbed that tower? Was he trying to hurt you?"

She swallowed. "Yes."

"Why did you lie to the police?" He stared at her, his silence willing her to continue.

She held her breath as a hundred different lies flitted through her mind. There were a thousand ways she could spin this story, but in her heart, she didn't want to lie to Bryce. "I did a job for him."

He arched an eyebrow.

"Not like that. I do construction work. I fix things. It's how I make a living. I soundproofed a room for him, so he could start a heavy metal band and not disturb the neighbors." That wasn't a lie. She never would've done the job if she'd known the real reason he needed the room.

He let out a dry laugh. "That sounds about right for a guy like that."

"When things didn't work out between us the first time, I left him. Then he called me a few months ago to do the job, and I needed the money so I agreed, but he never paid me. He gets an allowance from his dad, and he said he was late on the deposit, so I waited. When I went back to collect, he still didn't want to pay, but he *did* want me to stay."

Bryce's hands balled into fists. "And he hurt you."

Her gazed drifted to the floor, and she forced the word over the lump in her throat. "Yes."

His eyes softened. "Why won't you press charges?"

This was the hard part. She couldn't tell him the real reason, but he could obviously spot a lie. She'd talked to Eric's dad and done all she could to stop his idiotic plan.

"I want it to be over. I don't want to deal with all that, and I never want to see him again. Please." She reached for his hand, and his fist relaxed under her touch. "Can we let it go?"

The sound of his teeth grinding told her the answer. "He's the 'wrong kind of guy' you always go for?"

She clutched her hands in her lap. "I guess so."

He leaned away from her. "And that's what you think I'm like?"

"No. I…I don't know."

He rose and shuffled behind the couch. "Well, you're

not doing a very good job of keeping your distance if I'm the wrong kind of guy."

She twisted around to face him. "I'm trying to figure out what kind of guy you are. You're cocky one minute, and then you're the kindest person I've ever met the next. You care about people, but you act like nothing bothers you. I can't stop thinking about you, though I honestly don't know who you are."

"Who do you want me to be?"

"I want you to pick one. Either be the sweetheart or be the jerk, but don't keep me guessing which one is real."

He crossed his arms and studied her. His gaze narrowed as he chewed his bottom lip and drummed his fingers against his forearm. "You want to know who I really am?"

"Yes."

"I'll show you the real me, but you're not going to like him." He hesitated then slowly moved around the sofa and took the remote from the coffee table. "You wanted to know what I was watching? Here you go."

He pressed a button, and the TV flickered on. A bald man in a futuristic red and black shirt filled the screen. "*Star Trek*. I was watching *Star Trek*." He picked up the book from the end table. "I've read *The War of the Worlds* eight times. You accused me of being a sci-fi nerd, remember?" He lowered his gaze to the book and sighed. "Well, you were right."

Why didn't he want her to know he'd been watching *Star Trek*? "Just because you like science fiction, it doesn't make you a nerd." She grinned, trying to lighten the mood. "Eric likes *Star Wars*. You can still be a jerk."

He sucked in a breath like he planned to say more, but then he clenched his jaw shut. He tossed the book onto the table and dropped into the chair. "Yeah, I guess you're right. I'm a jerk."

"That's what I thought." *Not even close.* She stood and paced around the couch.

Bryce stared at the TV screen. "Get me a beer while you're up." Though he'd tried to make it sound like an order, the inflection on the final word lifted, turning his attempted command into a request.

She stifled a laugh and continued to the front door. "Nice try." He was too sweet to bark orders. Turning the knob, she pulled it open.

Bryce shot to his feet, a hint of panic tightening his eyes. "Hold on, now. You don't have to leave."

She straightened. "Maybe I want to."

He let out a defeated sigh. "It's too cold to sleep in your car. Stay here. Please?"

"That's not a very jerk thing to say." She suppressed a grin.

"Even an asshole wouldn't want you to freeze to death."

He had no idea. "All right. I'll stay. I'm going to get some clothes from my car." She stepped through the threshold before he could respond and slammed the door to keep in character.

Crossing her arms over her chest to ward off the cold biting at her skin, she trotted to her Ford she'd parked on the curb. Opening the back door, she glanced at Bryce's apartment and found him peering through a slit in the curtains.

That man couldn't pull off asshole if he tried. The more time she spent with Bryce, the more she saw through his smartass exterior, and that conversation proved it. There was a lot more to Bryce than met the eye, and now she was determined to know the man beneath the mask.

She shoved some clothes and toiletries into a backpack and shut the door. As she turned toward the window, the curtains fell shut, and when she returned to the living room, she found Bryce sitting in the chair, beer in hand, staring at the television.

If he wanted to pretend he was a jerk, she'd let him. If he'd admitted to being the sweetheart she knew he was, she might not have been able to resist him tonight. She had no clue what she was going to do about her blossoming emotions for the man, but sleeping with him wouldn't be the best place to start. First, she needed to get to know him. The mask would have to come off sometime.

"Mind if I use your shower?"

He didn't look at her. "Whatever you want to do."

"Okay then." She shuffled to the hall and glanced at him.

He flicked his gaze toward her, and his eyes held so much confliction, she almost apologized for calling him a jerk. Instead, she turned and headed for the shower.

Fifteen minutes later, she emerged from the bathroom to find Bryce sprawled out in his bed, his arm draped over his eyes. Lamplight seeped into the hall from the living room, but all the other lights were off.

She stood in his doorway. "I'm not climbing into bed with you." No matter how tempted she was.

"I didn't invite you." He folded his hands on his chest and met her gaze. "There's a pillow and blanket on the couch."

"What happened to you gladly giving up your bed if it meant I was safe and warm?"

"You can be safe and warm in the living room. I'm a jerk, remember?"

She rested a hand on the door jamb. "You're not a jerk, and your couch is actually pretty comfortable. I've been treated a lot worse."

He rolled onto his side and propped his head on his hand, and her chest tightened. Her wolf wanted her to climb into bed with him and end this ridiculous charade, but pride kept her feet glued to the floor.

"If you want to talk about it, I'm happy to listen." He paused, pinning her with a heavy gaze as he waited for her to respond. When she didn't, he rolled onto his back.

Would it be so wrong to talk to the man? In her heart, she trusted him. In her soul, she wanted to share everything with him. And that was the problem, wasn't it? If she allowed herself to fall for Bryce, she'd want to stay. Rogues never stayed, and people never changed. "Goodnight, Bryce."

CHAPTER NINE

Eric squinted against the bright headlights streaming through the windshield. His asshole of a father had made him spend two nights in that damn cell before bailing him out. He'd remember that when he became alpha of his own pack.

Neither man spoke on the drive from the jail to Eric's house. He stomped inside and tried to slam the door behind him, but his old man caught it with his meaty hand.

"I drove an hour to bail your sorry ass out of jail. The least you can do is thank me." David stepped through the threshold and let the door shut behind him.

"Thanks." Eric plopped onto the couch and rested his feet on the coffee table. "Now leave."

"You assaulted a police officer. What the hell were you thinking, son?"

"I caught him making out with my girl. What was I supposed to do?" His insides burned as the image of his woman pressing her lips to the pig's face flashed in his mind. They were both going to pay for that little display of affection. Alexis would learn not to cheat, and Sergeant Samuels would learn to stay away from his property.

David shook his head like he was disappointed. The man was always disappointed. "Alexis hasn't been your girl since you beat the shit out of her for denting your car." He crossed his arms over his chest and stood over him. Trying to intimidate him.

It wouldn't work this time. Eric put his feet on the floor and sat up straight. "How'd you know I was talking about Alexis?"

"She called me. If she's *your girl*, why'd you try to kill her?"

"I didn't mean…Wait. Why'd she call *you?*"

David narrowed his eyes as a reptilian smile curved his thin lips. "How do you think she ended up in this God-forsaken town? I paid her to keep tabs on you."

Eric tried to take a breath, but it got caught in his throat. "You…paid her?"

His old man shrugged it off. "She got into some trouble with the pack in Biloxi. I got her out of it and sent her here to watch you."

Eric fumed with anger. No wonder she'd turned down his offer to be mates. She was nothing more than a prostitute, and his own father was her pimp. "I didn't try to kill her. It's not my fault she fell off the electrical tower. She tried to kill herself."

"But she survived, even though you left her for dead."

"I thought she *was* dead." He should've known she'd survive. He'd seen her healing powers first-hand, and they obviously worked on herself too.

"Come on, son. You wanted her dead. She told me about your cockamamie plan to build your own pack out of humans. Are you trying to get yourself killed?"

He crossed his arms, tucking his fists beneath them to stop himself from punching the bastard. He hated the old man with a passion, but he needed his money. He had to play it cool. "Build my own pack?" He forced a laugh. "Alexis told you that? She was probably trying to squeeze more money out of you. She seemed destitute when she came here. She practically got on her knees begging me for some cash." He rose to his feet. "She's good on her knees, if you know what I mean, but I didn't give her the money."

His dad cocked an eyebrow. "Who knows what you've been up to? She hasn't worked for me since she left you."

"Exactly, Dad." He put a hand on the old man's shoulder. "She's broke. She'll do anything for a few bucks."

His dad eyed him warily. "Let me see your music room."

"Yeah, sure. No problem." He led his father down the hall and pushed open the door. A drum set sat on a raised platform in the corner, and several guitars hung from a rack on the wall. The tile floor had been hosed down and cleaned with bleach after his last unsuccessful attempt at turning a human, and thankfully the bodies were in a freezer at Trevor's place. David wouldn't find a lick of evidence in this house. After Alexis had shown up unannounced, Eric had made sure he wouldn't be caught off-guard again.

His father may have thought him a stupid loser, but he took plenty of precautions. He'd even taken care of the Jane that Alexis had set free. Now, he had to take care of Alexis.

David scanned the room, running his hand along the wall and fingering the strings of the bass guitar. Eric held his breath, hoping the old man wouldn't ask him to play it. He hadn't touched the instrument since he hung it up. His dad opened the closet door and peeked inside. It was empty. He stepped in front of Eric and stared him hard in the eyes. "Where are the bodies?"

Eric let out an exasperated breath. "There are no bodies. I told you she was lying. She's desperate, Dad, and she's just a rogue. Believe me."

"Why do I smell bleach?"

Shit. Would he ever let up? "I got a little crazy on a guitar solo and knocked a six-pack off the table. It shattered on the tile. You smell floor cleaner. That's all."

David sighed and walked to the front door. "I don't understand why she'd make this up, but your story checks out, son. If there is something unethical going on here, I will find out."

"There's not. Everything's legit. I swear. And I'm sorry about getting in a fight with that cop. When I saw him with Alexis…you know how I feel about her. Jealousy got the better of me. It won't happen again."

"You're damn right it won't. You've embarrassed the family name enough. I'd like you to come back to Biloxi one day, but not until you've gotten your act together. The pack won't tolerate miscreants."

"I understand, Pops. I'm trying." No way in hell would he step foot in Biloxi again. He'd go completely rogue before he'd be under his old man's thumb.

His dad stepped through the door, and the new motion-sensor camera he'd installed on the doorbell made his phone chime. "All right. I'll see what I can do about getting you out of this assault mess if you promise me you'll stay out of trouble."

"You have my word." He closed the door and marched into the living room.

That bitch. He rammed his fist through the sheet rock. White powder rained onto the floor as he jerked his hand from the wall. Alexis could fix the hole. She could fix everything. He hadn't been successful in turning a human into a werewolf a single time. The bodies were piling up, he was no closer to having his own pack, and now he had his dad on his back.

At least she'd run to a human for help and not her sister's pack. Cops he could handle. His old man he could handle. Starting a war between Biloxi and New Orleans he could not. Luckily, Alexis didn't catch on to the hollowness of his threat to harm her sister. If he could hang that over her head, he had leverage.

Her sister was a cop. He had enough bodies in the freezer to easily pull her in without getting the pack involved. Trevor had already dumped the first one in the river, and there were plenty more to keep her busy. Samuels would be easy to find too. Alexis was bound to turn up on one of their doorsteps sooner or later, and then she'd be his for the taking. She'd come back to him on her own once he was done.

CHAPTER TEN

Bryce rolled out of bed and stood still for a moment, listening for a sound that Alexis might have actually stayed the whole night. Sam's soft snoring filled the otherwise silent house. He fought the urge to tiptoe into the living room to see if she was there and shuffled to the shower instead.

After the way he'd treated her last night, he'd be surprised if she stayed. *Asshole.* What had he been thinking?

She'd convinced herself he was just like her dipshit ex-boyfriend, and instead of proving her wrong, he'd given her exactly what she wanted—a dickhead.

He groaned as he shut off the water and toweled off. Jabbing the toothbrush into his mouth, he scrubbed his teeth, and then he stomped to the bedroom to get dressed. He shoved his legs into his pants and struggled with the buttons on his shirt.

Taking a deep breath, he let it out slowly, hoping to calm the anger making his heart pound like a hammer. If her opinion of him mattered so much, why the hell had he acted like an asshole?

After fumbling with his belt for half a minute, he finally got the damn thing buckled and pulled on his shoes. He'd make it up to her—if she ever spoke to him again.

He shuffled to the living room and found Alexis curled up on the couch next to Sam, stroking his fur as he snored away happily. Her boots sat next to her backpack by the front door, and she'd folded the blanket and stacked it with the pillow on the chair.

Shoving his hands in his pockets, he nodded. "Hey."

She looked at him, and her green eyes sparkled in the early-morning sunlight streaming through window. "Hey."

"I...didn't think you'd be here."

She glanced at her stuff by the door. "Do you want me to leave?"

"No." He sauntered into the room and sat on the arm of the couch. "I'm glad you're here. I want to apologize for the way I acted last night."

She narrowed her eyes and studied him, the seconds stretching into an eternity. "Why *did* you act like that last night?"

He let out his breath in a huff. "I was childish. There's no excuse for my behavior, but..."

Sam raised his head and peered at Bryce sleepily before sliding off the couch and walking to the back door.

"Hold on." He shuffled to the door and opened it, and Sam scrambled outside and down the steps. Bryce left the door cracked and turned to find Alexis on her feet, leaning against the back of the couch.

She crossed her arms, and the corners of her mouth twitched. "You were saying..."

"Here's the deal. I like you, and when you compared me to that jackass you dated..." He sighed. Why couldn't he spit it out? "Like I said before, I don't want you to think poorly of me, but you're not giving me a chance. I got frustrated and acted like an ass, and I'm sorry."

She smiled. "Apology accepted. And I'm sorry for assuming the worst of you. You're nothing like Eric or any other man I know."

"Thank you." The tension in his shoulders loosened. Stepping toward her, he took her hand. "Let me make it up to you. If you'll stay here today, I'll make dinner for you tonight."

"You can cook?"

"I can learn."

She gazed at their entwined fingers before blinking up at him. "I don't know, Bryce. I..."

"Where else are you going to go?"

She drew her shoulders toward her ears. "I was thinking about seeing Macey."

"One more night. Please? Have dinner with me, and then if you don't want to see me anymore you can leave. I won't bug you to stay." He held his breath, waiting for her answer.

"I guess dinner won't hurt." She smiled. "I'll go see Macey this afternoon, and I'll be back in time for dinner. Does that work for you?"

The knot in his chest unfurled in a flush of warmth. He still had a chance. "Be home by seven?"

"Sure."

He could have lost himself staring into her emerald eyes. Her irises sparkled like actual jewels, and they held so much depth he felt as if he could swim through her soul, if she would let him in. As she held his gaze, a strange energy passed between them, and he could have sworn he felt a piece of her wall crumble. He leaned toward her. "Is this the part where we kiss and make up?"

She laughed and pulled her hand from his. "Don't push it, mister."

He held up his hands. "Okay. Okay. I have to go to work. I've got a school visit this morning."

"Michael's school? Is he going back already?"

He grabbed his keys from the bowl and dropped them in his pocket. "The bully's been removed, but Michael's not going back until January. I need to check on the other kids. Make sure things are running smoothly."

She caught his gaze, and her smile held so much warmth the entire world seemed to pause for a moment. "Those kids are lucky to have you looking out for them."

He cleared his throat. "You're welcome to stay here as long as you want. Sam enjoys your company."

A knock sounded on the door, and Bryce tore his gaze from hers to answer it. Michael stood on the landing, holding a metal pan.

Alexis moved behind Bryce and rested her hands on his shoulders. His stomach tightened at the casual way she touched him. It felt way more intimate than it should have.

"Do you always have your meals delivered?" She moved a hand to his bicep and peered into the dish. White icing melted on top of four giant, fluffy cinnamon rolls.

The kid's gaze cut back and forth between Alexis and Bryce. "I…uh…Sorry. I didn't know you were busy. My mom wanted me to bring you these."

Bryce smiled and patted her hand. "No problem, man. I'm never too busy for your mom's cooking. This is my friend, Alexis Gentry."

She offered him her hand to shake.

"Hi. I'm Michael."

Alexis glanced at Bryce, and he gave a small nod of confirmation as he took the cinnamon rolls.

"Well, I'm going to go. Have a nice day, Sergeant Samuels." He raised his hand in a timid wave. "Nice to meet you, Ms. Gentry."

Bryce closed the door and carried the cinnamon rolls to the table. "I'll have to take mine to go." He snatched a plastic container from the cabinet and pulled a roll from the tray. Gooey icing dripped down the sides onto his fingers as he dropped it into the container.

He stuck his finger in his mouth to lick off the frosting, and Alexis bit her bottom lip. Her gaze slid from his eyes to his mouth and back again, and his knees nearly buckled beneath him.

She sank into a chair. "Sweet kid."

Bryce blinked away the memory of the way her lips had felt pressed to his. "Yeah, he is." He grabbed a plate and a paper towel and set them in front of her. "Help yourself. They're best when they're warm."

"Thanks."

He poked his head out the back door. "Sam." The dog stopped and looked at him for a second before lowering his nose to the ground and ignoring him. "C'mon, Sam, I've got to go to work."

"You can go. I'll watch him." She took a bite of her breakfast, and icing dripped onto her lip.

He couldn't help but stare as she flicked out her tongue to lick it off. Blood rushed to his groin, and a shudder ran down his spine. Watching a woman eat shouldn't have affected him this way, but he'd never met a woman like Alexis. Everything she did had sex appeal. "I appreciate that." He sauntered to the door, fighting the urge to adjust his crotch. "I'll see you at seven?"

She stood and padded toward him. "I'll be here." Leaning in, she placed a soft kiss on his cheek. "Thank you. For everything."

He nodded and opened the door. "My pleasure, ma'am."

Warmth filled Alexis's core as she watched Bryce through the window. He had a slight spring in his confident gait, and she hoped she'd put it there. She let the curtain fall shut and sank onto the sofa. Maybe nice guys did exist after all.

She checked her phone. Nothing from Eric or David, so hopefully that debacle had been taken care of. As second in command of the Biloxi pack, David should have been able to keep control of his son. He just needed to tighten the leash.

A high-pitched whining noise sounded from the kitchen, and she turned around to find Sam sitting by the back door, licking his front paw. She shuffled toward him, and he whined again.

"What's the matter, buddy?" She reached for his leg, and he shied away, flattening his ears against his head. "I can't help you if you won't let me look."

She gently took his paw and examined the underside. A huge bur wedged between the first and second pads, so she pinched it between her thumb and forefinger and pulled it out. Sam licked his paw one more time and jumped to his feet, doing his adorable full-body wag.

Alexis laughed and tossed the bur in the trash. "You're welcome."

She closed the back door, and the sound of a key turning in the front lock sent her heart racing. The door swung open, and a woman in her mid-forties stepped into the living room. She had medium-length, dark hair styled into a classic mom-cut. High-waisted jeans and a button-up blouse completed the look.

The woman closed the front door and fisted her hands on her hips as she turned to face Alexis. "Who are you, and what do you want from Bryce?"

Whoa. She got right to the point. "You must be Karen, right? My name is Alexis. It's nice to meet you."

Her eyes widened, and her aggressive posture relaxed slightly. "Yes, I'm Karen. I live downstairs." She crossed her arms. "How do you know Bryce?"

Alexis mirrored her posture and tried to ignore the territorial instinct that had her wolf wanting to growl. How many women had a key to Bryce's home? "We're friends. Macey, his ex-partner, is my sister."

Karen dropped her arms to her sides and let out a slow breath. "Is that your car on the curb?"

"Yes. I can park somewhere else if it bothers you."

She nodded. "I know your type."

"Excuse me?"

"Everything you own is in the back of that car, isn't it? You drift from man to man, sleeping with whomever will take you in, using him until you get tired of him or he stops spending money on you."

"You don't know a thing about me." How dare this woman force her way in here to corner her? She had no right to make accusations like this. Alexis didn't use men.

If anything, her life had been the exact opposite, and Bryce…she wouldn't dream of hurting him.

What kind of person waltzed into a man's house and started spouting insults at the woman he *had* invited over? She ground her teeth to fight the rumble trying to roll up from her chest.

Karen raked her gaze over Alexis's cargo pants and sweatshirt. "I know enough. Bryce is a great guy. He deserves someone who's going to treat him with respect, not someone who's using him for a free ride."

Alexis straightened her spine. "I'm not using him. I care about him." *He's mine.*

Whoa. Where did that thought come from? She'd dealt with plenty of territorial women in the werewolf community, and her wolf was standing her ground. That's all it was. She hadn't *actually* claimed him.

She took a deep breath and let it out slowly. "Karen, I appreciate that you want to protect Bryce. He is an amazing man, but you have to understand that he's an adult, and who he invites into his home is his business. Unless you have some kind of claim on him?"

The muscles in Karen's jaw tightened as she turned for the door. She paused with her hand on the knob. "Please don't hurt him. He deserves better."

Alexis sank onto the couch as Karen shut the door and trotted down the stairs. Sam jumped onto the cushion next to her and made a whining sound in his throat.

She scratched his head. "I really do care about him." Way more than she should have. Karen was right, though. He did deserve better.

CHAPTER ELEVEN

Bryce's leg bounced beneath his desk as he scoured the internet for recipes. Alexis had been impressed with Karen's jambalaya, and he wanted to give her another home-cooked meal to prove he wasn't the jackass she'd thought. That he could be a provider. The kind of man she wanted.

He'd known Alexis for more than a year now, seeing her with Macey every now and then when she'd popped into town for a few days. She never seemed to stay in one place for very long, and from the way she talked, it sounded like she'd never met a man worth staying for.

Bryce wanted to be that man. He *would* be the reason she stayed this time. And if he had to learn how to cook to convince her he was the right man for her, so be it. He'd do anything.

His computer pinged with an incoming e-mail, and he clicked the tab to open it. His pulse quickened. The autopsy report on the body they'd pulled out of the river had finally come through.

He scanned the contents, and a sickening feeling

pooled in his gut. Macey had tried to write it off as an animal attack, but the body temperature had been seven degrees below the ambient temperature of the Mississippi in that area.

If the body had been colder than the atmosphere they'd found it in, it must have been refrigerated—or possibly frozen—before the killer dumped it in the river. He didn't know any wolves that had access to freezers, let alone opposable thumbs and the brains enough to put a body in one. Let Macey try to dismiss this as an animal attack now.

Johnson knocked on his office door, his expression grim. "Jumper on the CCC. Let's go."

A brick settled in Bryce's stomach. The Crescent City Connection, the bridge between the Mississippi's East and West banks, hosted a couple of suicide attempts annually. This would make number three for this year.

He followed Johnson out of the station and climbed into his SUV. Flipping on the siren, he high-tailed it for the bridge and said a silent prayer they'd make it in time.

When he approached the bridge, the uniforms already had the westbound lanes closed, and a line of cars blocked his access. He cut the wheel right and took the shoulder the rest of the way before killing the engine and sliding out of his seat.

Adrenaline made his nerves hum as he paced up the street toward the bridge entrance. Frigid wind whipped into his face, biting at his skin, and a thick blanket of clouds covered the sky, masking the sun. A harbor police boat chugged through the murky water below, and a chill wound up Bryce's spine. He zipped his jacket.

A uniform approached, shaking his head, and a heaviness pressed on Bryce's shoulders as if he were Atlas, trying to hold the weight of the world. A fist of dread yanked his heart into his stomach, and he quickened his pace.

The uniform put up his hands. His name tag read Blanchard. "Dude already jumped. Harbor police are searching the water to see if he's alive, but you know how this goes."

"Goddammit!" Bryce clenched his jaw so tight a sharp pain shot through his temple. If he'd been five minutes earlier, he might've been able to save that man. He *would* have saved him.

"Hey." Blanchard slapped him on the shoulder. "At least he's out of his misery now, right?"

Bryce's nostrils flared as he inhaled the stifling odors of car exhaust and muddy river water, and the corner of his mouth twitched. Misery? He had no idea the kind of misery this man had left behind for his loved ones. Pain. Guilt of not doing enough to help. Remorse for not paying attention to the signs. The suffocating agony of never having an answer to why. Drowning in a sea of a thousand regrets, unable to break the surface to simply breathe…

Blanchard shook his head. "I don't know why we try to stop them, honestly. If they want to die—"

"Walk away, Blanchard." His anger morphed his words into a growl. That man probably had a family. Parents. Friends. *A brother*. People who cared about him. His suffering may have ended, but theirs was just beginning… and for what? Because of the screwed-up way society viewed depression? Because people thought it was something to be ashamed of rather than an illness that could be treated? People were all too willing to talk about their physical problems…cancer, heart disease, diabetes…they'd tell you all about the treatments and medications they took. But as soon as the problem had to do with the mind, people acted like it was a personal weakness. He curled his hands into fists.

"All I'm saying is, who are we to decide who lives and who dies?"

"You've got five seconds to get your ass off this bridge before I plant my fist in your face."

Blanchard raised his hands in surrender. "All right, I'm going. Man, all you negotiator guys got a chip on your shoulders." He shook his head and strode away.

"Chip on my shoulder, my ass," Bryce grumbled. Most of the guys on the team had witnessed firsthand the aftermath of a suicide. It wasn't a chip. It was a deep desire to stop it from happening to anyone else.

Another slap on his shoulder pulled him from his thoughts.

Johnson scowled. "Body's already on the bank." He nodded to the left, where a team dragged a corpse from the water. "Once we get ID, I'll handle notifying the next of kin. You can head back."

"Yeah." Bryce stared out over the water as a familiar numbness spread through his core and down his limbs. Too late to save him. If he'd only known sooner.

He closed his eyes and let out a slow breath. Internalizing would do him no good, so he wiped the emotion from his face and made his way down the riverbank. He'd save the next one. And the one after that.

Seeing the body wouldn't help, but he always had to look. Maybe one day he'd find a clue to the reason a person could slip into such a state of distress. Could feel so alone, even when he had people who loved him.

He peered at the body lying in the grass, and his heart stuttered. "I thought the jumper was a male."

"He was," an officer answered.

Bryce took a step closer. A series of jagged tears covered the woman's arms and legs. Her torn shirt revealed teeth marks in her shoulder, and the gash in her neck probably severed her carotid artery. He backed up as Detective Sharon Dupuis crouched to examine the body.

She shook her head. "Looks like another animal attack." She addressed a uniform. "Weren't there reports of wolves in the surrounding area last year?"

"Yes, ma'am. I believe so," the officer replied.

She stood. "We'll need to contact the park rangers and see if there have been any recent reports." She typed something into her phone and turned to walk away.

"Now, hold on a minute, Detective." Bryce strode toward her. "Have you seen the autopsy report on the other one?"

She crossed her arms. "Sergeant, what are you doing here?"

"I was on the bridge for the jumper. Have you seen the report?"

Her brow furrowed as she fought off a cringe. "Not yet."

"The first *animal attack* victim measured seven degrees colder than the river. Unless you know a wolf that keeps a deep-freezer in its den, I'd say it was more than an animal attack."

She tilted her head. "You're a negotiator. Why were you looking at the autopsy report?"

Damn it, why did it matter? "I was helping Detective Mason."

"I see. Well, I'll be sure to let her know if the case is the same with this one." She flashed an insincere smile, turned on her heel, and strutted away.

Bryce ground his teeth on his way back to his SUV. Something fishy was going on with these bodies, and though murder investigations were no longer in his job description, he'd be damned if he'd let any criminal roam free. He'd give Macey a chance to get up to speed with the inconsistencies in the autopsy report, and if she didn't start treating this case like the crime it was, he'd do it for her.

Alexis tugged Bryce's jacket tighter around her shoulders and pressed her nose against the collar. His warm, masculine scent filled her senses, stirring the strange feelings deep in her soul. What was it about this human that commanded her wolf's attention?

She strolled up Royal Street toward the Gumbo Place, absorbing the scenery and relishing the warmth Bryce provided against the cold. Two and three-story wooden structures rose on both sides of the street, their colorful facades reflecting a time long ago. Festive holiday colors decorated the wrought-iron railings that trimmed the balconies and galleries, and a three-piece band played an upbeat version of "Have Yourself a Merry Little Christmas" on the corner of St. Louis Street.

She passed Spellbound Sweets, and her witch friend Rain leaned her head out the door. "Hey, Alexis. I didn't know you were back in town." A gust of wind kicked up, whipping her dark curls into her face. "Do you want to come in for a minute?"

"Thanks, but I'm on my way to meet Macey for lunch."

Rain smiled and raised her eyebrows. "Have you seen Bryce lately?"

She paused, unaccustomed to talking about her feelings, and warmth unfurled in her chest. "I'm seeing him tonight." Was that giddiness bubbling from her stomach? No, it had to be heartburn.

"Good. Stop by if you have a chance before you leave town."

"I will." She grinned and hung a left on St. Peter. It might not hurt to stick around for a while this time. She hadn't heard a peep from Eric or his dad, so that mess had probably blown over. Knowing David, he tore Eric a new one the second he stepped out of jail and then hauled his ass back to Biloxi to keep a closer eye on him.

She had friends here now. Macey was here...and Bryce. Her stomach fluttered. It might be nice to see where things went with him. To explore these strange emotions stirring in her soul.

She opened the door to the Gumbo Place and found Macey and her sister-in-law, Amber, sitting at a table by the window. Macey smiled, and Amber waved her over. Zydeco music played through the speakers in the ceiling, and Alexis sashayed past a row of booths covered in red-checkered cloths.

Macey had pulled her blonde hair back into a ponytail, and it swished over her shoulder as she hugged Alexis. "I was wondering if you were ever going to call me."

Alexis hugged Amber and settled into a chair. "No visit to New Orleans is complete without seeing my little sister." She ignored the pang of guilt squeezing her heart. She was here now, and that was what mattered.

Macey opened her mouth to speak, but the waiter arrived to take their orders. Amber asked for a roast beef po-boy, and Macey ordered a muffuletta.

"I'll have a glass of water." Alexis pressed her lips into a tight smile.

As the waiter nodded and turned to walk away, Macey held up a finger to stop him. She lowered her voice. "I can buy your lunch. Go ahead and order something."

Alexis straightened her spine. "I don't need you to pay for me." She shrugged. "I'm not very hungry."

Macey put her hand on hers. "I don't want you to have to sit there and watch us eat."

Alexis let out a slow breath. Because she was a homeless rogue, everyone immediately assumed she didn't have a dime and couldn't be depended on. Macey may have been right about the money, but Alexis could take care of herself and anyone else that came along.

"All right. I'll get a little something, but I'm paying for it myself." She scanned the menu. "I'll have the half ham sandwich. Separate checks, please." At $5.99, after tax and tip, the half sandwich would eat up half her life savings, but it was better than admitting she was broke.

The waiter shuffled away, and Alexis picked at her unpainted nails, unable to look Macey in the eyes.

Amber broke the awkward silence. "What brings you into town, Alexis?"

"Oh, umm…" Heat climbed her neck and settled in her cheeks.

"I'm the one who gave him your number, remember?" Macey smiled, but it didn't mask the wariness in her eyes. "I'm pretty sure that's his jacket too."

Wrapping her arms around herself, Alexis stroked the soft fabric. The central heating in the restaurant provided enough warmth that she didn't need to wear the jacket inside, but it had become a sort of security blanket.

She deserved every bit of doubt her sister had about

her, but earning it didn't make it any less painful. If she'd have stayed last year, when they'd first reunited, things would be different. The alpha had given her a job. She'd had a place to live. Family. But as soon as she'd gotten comfortable, she'd gotten scared, and she'd left like she always did. Being a rogue, Alexis had learned the hard way that letting her guard down—getting comfortable—set her up for people to take advantage of her. To hurt her. She knew in her heart that Macey and her friends here weren't like that, but a lifetime of being on the defensive wasn't easy to change.

She popped in and out of town, but it didn't provide the kind of relationship her sister wanted. Hell, it wasn't the kind of relationship she wanted either.

This time would be different. "I'm seeing Bryce."

Amber looked at Macey. "Your old partner?"

Macey nodded.

"That's sweet." Amber tucked her light-brown hair behind her ear and folded her hands on the table. "I knew you'd get to keep him in your life somehow."

Alexis's breath hitched. As a second-born werewolf, Amber's psychic power was empathic premonitions. She felt things about the future that usually came true. "Have you seen anything about him? Or…me?"

"No, I meant that Macey and Bryce were too close to let a little promotion end their friendship. I only have premonitions about people I see on a regular basis."

"Oh." She slumped her shoulders.

"Maybe if you stick around a while this time." Amber grinned and raised her eyebrows.

"How long are you planning to stay?" Macey asked.

The waiter delivered their food—and an ounce of relief—and Alexis used the distraction to avoid answering the question. She took a bite of her sandwich. The earthy aromas of the whole-grain bread offset the sweetness of the ham, and the Cajun seasonings in the mayonnaise added a zip to the medley of flavors on her tongue. She mushed the food around in her mouth longer than necessary before swallowing and taking another bite.

The heaviness of things unsaid hung over them as they ate in silence. Macey flicked her gaze toward her, inhaling as if to speak several times, but she didn't. She didn't need to. The words were apparent in her expression.

Amber must have sensed the tension, because she focused on her po-boy, lifting her gaze from her food occasionally.

Alexis finished her sandwich and folded her hands in her lap. "I like Bryce. A lot."

Macey wiped her mouth with a napkin and dropped it on her plate. "He likes you too. More than I've seen him like anyone in the seven years I've known him."

Her lips tugged into a smile. Hearing those words from someone who knew Bryce well had her pulse racing.

Macey gave her a curious look. "Please be careful with him. He pretends he's a tough guy, but he's more sensitive than he'd like anyone to believe."

His sensitive side was the reason she was still in town, planning to have dinner with him in a few hours. The reason she was falling head over tail for a human. "I know you're worried about him, but I promise I don't plan to hurt him. I care about him."

Macey shook her head. "You care about me too, don't you?"

"Of course I do." How could she even ask such a thing? "After I ran away from foster care, I spent the next twenty years looking for you."

She swallowed hard, her gaze lingering on her crumpled napkin before locking with Alexis's eyes. "You hurt me every time you leave."

Her breath hitched. "Macey, I…"

"I don't know where you go. I don't know what you're doing. Half the time you don't answer your phone when I call. I…" She clamped her mouth shut and took a deep breath. "I guess what I'm trying to say is that you tend to hurt people without realizing it."

Did Alexis not realize it? Or had she been ignoring the pain she'd seen in her sister's eyes every time she'd said goodbye? Convincing herself she wasn't the cause because nobody cared about her enough to be hurt by her absence? "Why haven't you told me this?"

She shrugged. "Would it have made a difference?"

Fisting her hands on the table, Alexis inhaled deeply. "I started shifting on the first full moon after my thirteenth birthday. I had no idea what was happening to me, so I ran. Do you know *why* I ran?"

Macey held her gaze. "You were scared."

"That, yes, but I also ran because that's what Mom and Dad did. You were too young to remember, but we moved eight times before I turned six. It seemed like every time I got close to making a friend, we packed up and moved."

Amber's brow puckered. "That must have been hard."

"That's just how it was. I didn't know any better." She returned her gaze to Macey. "Then we went through four different foster homes after they died, and none of our foster families gave a damn about us. You had nightmares. You'd wake up screaming, and when an adult would come in to spank you for waking them up, I'd take the blame. I took the beatings, but I couldn't stop the nightmares. I couldn't fix you."

Macey's eyes shimmered. "I remember that. I remember when you were there for me."

"I failed you. No matter how much I tried to help, I couldn't fix the pain in your heart."

Her shoulders drooped as she slowly shook her head. "You didn't need to fix me. I just needed you to be there."

Alexis folded her hands on the table. "Me being there didn't seem to do anything for you. It never did. Our parents weren't the best role models for reliability. They never had any friends. I had zero social skills, and then I turned into a freaking wolf. I ran, and instinct led me to a rogue that I found hunting one night. He took me in. Promised to keep me safe. To take care of me." She swallowed the sour taste from her mouth. "He made sure I took care of him too."

Macey sucked in a sharp breath. "He didn't..."

"He did. And I didn't know any better, so I let it happen. I thought it was how werewolves behaved." She sipped her water, washing the dryness from her throat. "Now I know that's just how assholes behave, but...you're lucky you got adopted when you did because when I came back looking for you..." She didn't need to finish the sentence. The horror in her sister's eyes said she understood.

Amber shifted uncomfortably in her seat, casting her gaze to her lap.

"Eventually, I got away and started living on my own, but I was already broken. He made me think I was worthless, and I still struggle with that today. I've never had a healthy relationship. Nobody trusts a rogue. My life has never had a positive impact on anyone, so I'm not used to anyone caring what I do...or whether I live or die for that matter." Pressure built in the back of her eyes, so she blinked it away. She would not cry. Crying meant weakness, and she was anything but weak. “I’m sorry.”

Macey reached across the table and took her hand. “People do care. I care, and so does Bryce.”

Heaviness settled in her chest, squeezing her insides from her heart to her throat, making it hard to breathe. “I love you, Macey.”

“I love you too. I’m so sorry you went through that.”

She shook her head. “It’s over now. Bryce is a good man, and I don’t want to hurt him.”

Macey leaned back in her chair. “You need to understand that when people love you, your actions have consequences. If you get close to him…if you bring him into our world and tell him what we are, his life will turn upside down. Don’t do that to him unless you plan on sticking around.”

Alexis focused on her hands folded on the table. Things were different now. She had the beginnings of a romantic relationship with an amazing man, but the biggest difference resonated in her soul. Her wolf wanted to stay this time, and that was something she’d never felt before. It was time to stop fighting these emotions and go with her gut.

Lifting her gaze to Macey’s, she smiled. “Is Luke hiring?”

“You know you have a job here if you want it. We’ve got an extra bedroom too.” The hopeful look in Macey’s eyes tugged at her heart.

Could she stay this time? She opened her mouth to say she would, but fear clamped her throat, blocking the words from flowing. Her pulse sprinted, and nausea churned in her stomach. She wanted to stay. God, she *needed* to. Her wolf craved the companionship and comfort of the people she cared for, and Bryce… He wasn't like any man she'd ever met. She'd gotten a tiny peek behind his mask, and a hardened asshole didn't reside beneath it. He was kind and gentle.

She squared her shoulders toward her sister and straightened her spine. "I'm going to stay." She had to. She was done running.

Macey raised her eyebrows. "For how long?"

"For as long as you can stand having me around. It's time I put down some roots, don't you think?"

"I agree." Her smile finally reached her eyes.

Amber had remained silent during their exchange, but as she paid her tab, she took both their hands in hers. "I've got an extra room too, if you'd rather stay with another single lady." She winked and rose to her feet. "I have to get back to work."

"Yeah, I have things to do too." Alexis handed her last twenty to the waiter.

Macey paid her tab and stood. "I'll talk to Luke for you. And please…be careful with Bryce. He's a skeptic at best. Bringing him into our world won't be easy."

Alexis stayed at the table when Macey and Amber left the restaurant, her stomach tying itself into a massive knot as Karen's words echoed in her mind: *he deserves better.* Rising to her feet, she fisted her hands at her sides. She could do this. Bryce wanted to be with her, and she wanted to—she *would*—be the woman he deserved.

CHAPTER TWELVE

BRYCE FILLED A POT WITH WATER AND SET IT ON THE stove before washing a saucepan in the sink. His mom had bought him the cooking set when he'd graduated college and gotten his first grown-up apartment, but they'd sat unused in every place he'd lived since the day he'd moved in. How a layer of dust had managed to settle on the dishes in a cabinet he never opened, he wasn't sure, but he'd be giving his kitchen a thorough cleaning on his next day off.

He'd been a nervous wreck all damn day. First losing the jumper before he could get to the scene, and then witnessing yet another suspiciously mutilated body retrieved from the river. He'd left Macey a message about the autopsy, but she hadn't returned his call. She'd been acting so strange lately she probably wouldn't. He added getting to the bottom of her out-of-character behavior to his mental to-do list.

Rolling his neck, he stretched the soreness from his muscles and popped open a jar of tomato sauce. Pouring it into the saucepan, he set it on the counter and peeked inside the oven. A gelatinous mixture of flour, soda, and salt coagulated in another pan he'd never used until today. It didn't look much like bread, but it had another ten minutes to cook.

The saucepan clanked as he set it on the stove, and then he turned on the burner. Orange flames whipped out from the contraption, licking upward and nearly engulfing the small pan in fire. "Shit." He twisted the dial, making the flames fit beneath the pan, and pulled his buzzing phone from his pocket.

Alexis's name lit up the screen, and his heart raced as he pressed the device to his ear. "Hey there, beautiful."

She missed a beat in her response. "Hi, Bryce."

"Dinner's almost ready. Are you on your way?"

She took a deep breath. "If I told you I was leaving town tomorrow, would you want to see me tonight?"

His stomach tightened. Leaving tomorrow? Had she already made up her mind before she'd given him a chance? "Yeah. Of course I would. I mean…any time with you is time well-spent."

"Okay."

The crunching sound of a key sliding into a lock reverberated through the phone and in his living room. The front door swung open, and Alexis strutted in wearing skinny jeans, black lace-up boots, and an olive-green sweater that dipped below her collarbone, accentuating the delicate curve of her neck. She dropped her backpack and locked the door as Bryce slipped his phone into his pocket.

She turned to face him, and her brow furrowed, a look of determination falling across her features. She raked her gaze from his head to his toes, and when her eyes met his, their intensity stilled his heart in his chest.

The corner of her mouth twitched as she closed the distance between them in three purposeful strides. Without saying a word, she slipped one hand behind his neck and the other around his waist and planted her soft lips on his.

Fire shot through his veins. This wasn't the hello he'd been expecting from a woman who intended to leave town tomorrow, but he wasn't about to complain. Instead, he wrapped his arms around her, tugging her close, and deepened the kiss.

She tasted like warm honey, and as he coaxed her lips apart with his tongue, a tiny growl rolled up from her chest. She pressed her body harder against his and opened for him, lapping at his tongue, brushing it with hers before catching his bottom lip between her teeth. With a gentle tug, she released him and glided her lips across his cheek to nip at his earlobe.

A moan rumbled in his chest, and he slid his hands down to cup her ass. "If I'd known this was the reward for making a woman dinner, I'd have learned to cook a long time ago."

Biting her bottom lip, she leaned back and ran her hands down his chest, stopping above his jeans. She gripped the hem of his shirt and tugged it up toward his head. He could've stopped her. Told her to slow down, take her time. But, damn it, he wanted this woman as much as she seemed to want him.

He helped her tug it over his head, and as his arm came down to hold her, he hit the saucepan handle, knocking the pot to the floor. Tomato sauce splattered across the tile, and Alexis had the common sense to jump out of the way. Bryce stood there in a daze as red goo plastered his pants and shoes.

"I'm so sorry." She grabbed the pot and dumped it in the sink before tugging the roll of paper towels from the rack. When he didn't move, she stopped and put a hand on his chest. "Are you okay?"

The warmth of her skin touching his sent blood rushing to his groin. Was he okay? He was half-naked with the woman of his dreams standing in his kitchen. He was a hell of a lot better than okay. "Yeah." He took the paper towels from her. "I'll clean this up; I knocked it down."

She pulled a string of towels from the roll and knelt on the floor. "You knocked it down because *I* tried to get you naked while you were cooking. I'll help."

"Wait…you were trying to get me naked?" He knelt beside her and wiped up some of the mess.

She grinned. "I didn't plan on stopping with your shirt."

Heat crept up his neck. "Oh."

She laughed. "You really haven't had many women over, have you?"

"I told you. You're the first." And if he got his way, she'd be the last. He didn't plan to leave a trace of doubt in her mind after tonight. She couldn't leave town tomorrow. She couldn't leave *him.* He gathered the mess of paper towels and tossed them in the trash. "We've got a problem."

"What's that?" Her gaze lingered on his chest, and she licked her lips.

Dear Lord, if she didn't stop looking at him like that he'd never be able to speak a coherent sentence again. "Umm…" He cleared his throat. "That was my only jar of tomato sauce. I've got nothing to put on the spaghetti now."

She sucked in a sharp breath and blinked before looking him in the eyes. "You've got ketchup, right? Isn't that tomato sauce?" Peering into the fridge, she pulled out a bottle of Heinz. "It's in a bottle rather than a jar, but the first ingredient is tomato sauce. This should work if we heat it up."

"I never thought of that, but I think you're right. Let's do it." He washed the pot in the sink and set it by the ketchup before grabbing the dried pasta from a shelf.

Alexis wrinkled her nose. "What's that smell?"

He paused and inhaled, and a faint, sweetly pungent odor with the sharp reek of something burnt greeted his senses.

She nodded to her left. "I think it's coming from the oven."

"Oh, crap. The bread." He yanked the oven door open, and cloud of black smoke billowed into the kitchen. It rose quickly, wafting toward the ceiling, and he fanned it out of his face as he chased it toward the smoke alarm.

Too late.

A high-pitched squealing sound filled his apartment and probably half the block. Grabbing a paperback, he fanned the book in front of the device to dissipate the smoke, but the damn thing wouldn't turn off. He mashed the reset button with his thumb and blew into the plastic cover. Nothing would silence the incessant screeching, so he tore it from the wall and yanked out the battery. Glorious silence filled his throbbing ears.

He took a deep breath and set his jaw. This was no big deal. He could save face. He'd go back in there, they'd laugh it off, let a restaurant cook them dinner, and maybe they'd finish the other thing they'd started this evening.

He sauntered to the kitchen and found Alexis with her backside pressed against the counter, her hands gripping the Formica so tightly her knuckles turned white. Sam sat at her feet, a ridge of hair down the center of his back standing on end.

Karen stood at the sink, fanning the smoke out the window. "If you're going to try to cook for him, at least figure out what you're doing before you burn our house down." Her voice held a venom he'd never heard from her before, and from the look on Alexis's face, Karen had done more than insult her lack of cooking skills.

He moved to stand next to Alexis and draped an arm across her shoulders. "Thanks for your concern, Karen, but we've got this under control."

"You obviously don't. Spaghetti with ketchup?" She picked up the bottle and curled her lip before setting it down. "You shouldn't be in the kitchen with your shirt off, especially with an inexperienced cook like her. You could have been burned."

He grabbed his shirt from the counter and yanked it over his head. "I had tomato sauce, but it spilled on the floor. And *I* am the inexperienced cook. I was making dinner for Alexis."

She flashed an unbelieving look. "And what is this supposed to be?" She gestured to the burnt mess she'd retrieved from the oven.

"I was trying to make bread."

Alexis slid her arm behind his back. "And it was a sweet gesture, Bryce. I appreciate the effort." She kissed him on the cheek and rested her other hand on his chest.

If he didn't know any better, he'd say it felt a little bit

like she was claiming him. He suppressed a grin. Something about the idea of Alexis feeling the need to fight for him warmed him from the inside out.

Karen ignored her comment. "What did you put in it?"

Bryce shrugged. "Just what the recipe called for. Flour, salt, soda…I used Dr. Pepper. Should I have gone with something clear?"

Karen laughed. "Soda means *baking* soda. Not the kind you drink." She shook her head. "You know what? I made a pot roast, and there is plenty for everyone. Why don't you come down and have dinner with Michael and me?"

Alexis tightened her grip on his waist, and he could've sworn he heard a growl rumble from her chest. "We'll pass."

He gave her shoulder a squeeze and stepped away to usher Karen to the door. "I do appreciate the invitation, ma'am, but this was supposed to be a date. I'll take her out somewhere for dinner."

He stepped onto the landing and closed the front door before lowering his voice. "What are you doing, Karen? You can't let yourself into my house when I've got company over and start insulting my girlfriend."

Karen crossed her arms. "She's your girlfriend?"

"With any luck, she might be some day. I'm working on it." He crossed his arms to chase away the chill in the air.

She glanced at the Ford on the curb and huffed. "She lives out of her car."

"She's going through a rough patch right now. It can happen to the best of us."

Her jaw clenched. "She's using you."

While he appreciated Karen's concern, her judgment of the woman he cared for grated on his nerves. He needed to nip this cat fight in the bud before it turned ugly. "She's not using me." He chuckled. "I practically had to beg her to come over."

"I know you like to save people, but believe me, this won't end well. You can't save someone like her. I tried once, and I ended up alone and pregnant."

He sighed. "She's not Bobby…and I don't have the parts to end up pregnant, so the worst she can do is break my heart. Cut her some slack, huh? She's Macey sister."

Karen swallowed and nodded. "You're right. I'm sorry I turned into a mother hen on you. I just…I need to protect my boys." She flashed an apologetic smile. "I'll give her a chance."

"That's all I'm asking. Tell Michael 'hi' for me."

"I will."

He stayed outside as she shuffled down the stairs toward her own apartment. Hopefully he'd seen the end of the turbulence with Karen. Convincing Alexis to stay was already hard enough; the last thing he needed was another woman driving her away. When he opened the door, Alexis stood in the living room with her arms crossed over her chest.

A fire burned in her emerald eyes, and as she arched a brow and drummed her fingers against her bicep, he fought off a smile. "Does she do that often?" she asked.

He shoved his hands into his pockets. "Do what?"

"Let herself in whenever she wants."

"She didn't mean any harm. I'm sorry about that." Damn, she was cute when she was jealous. "She heard the smoke alarm, and if my place burns down, hers does too."

She inclined her chin. "Is there something going on between you?"

"What? No." He moved toward her. "Karen is like… she looks out for me…like a second mom."

"A mom who would've been ten years old when she had you."

"Okay…how about an older sister? I swear, Alexis, there is nothing going on between me and Karen." The only woman he wanted to have anything going on with was standing right in front of him. If she didn't understand that by now, he'd have to do a better job showing her.

She narrowed her eyes, studying him. "Her pupils dilated when she looked at your chest. She finds you attractive."

He laughed. "Who wouldn't?"

Alexis rolled her eyes. "I believe there's nothing going on between you because I don't think you'd lie to me… and…you've got no game." She grinned.

His mouth dropped open. "I've got game."

"Do you?" She slinked toward him and ran her fingers up his chest before placing a soft kiss on his lips. Then she nodded toward the kitchen. "You call that game?"

His teeth clicked as he clenched his jaw. He wanted to argue…to defend his manhood, but what could he say? "I see your point. Let me get rid of that godawful science experiment and get cleaned up." Then he'd show her game. He strutted into the kitchen. "Would you have known baking soda wasn't the stuff you drink?"

She laughed. "Everyone knows that."

Not everyone. He grabbed the bread pan with both hands, and searing pain exploded across his skin.

"Godammit! Shit!" Dropping the pan on the counter, he peered at his palms. "Damn thing's still hot."

Bright-red marks covered his palms and fingers where he'd made contact with the heated glass. His skin warped, as if the top layer no longer connected to the skin beneath. His hands throbbed, and he bit the inside of his cheek to hold in a groan. "That's gonna blister."

"Let me see." Concern danced in her eyes as she gingerly took his right hand in hers. She tilted her head. "That's not so bad."

"If you say so." His voice sounded strained, and he took a deep breath to rein in the wuss and act like a man. The skin on his fingertips was already puckering, moisture building beneath the loose layer of flesh. He held in a whimper. Men didn't whimper.

Alexis gently ran her fingers over the burned areas of his hand, and he'd be damned if the woman didn't have a magic touch. The throbbing subsided, and as she brought his fingertips to her lips and kissed them, the pain ceased entirely. She did the same thing to his left hand, and just like that, the agony was gone.

"You bring kiss-it-and-make-it-better to a whole new level." He looked at his hands, and his eyes widened. "The burns are gone. How'd you do that?" He turned his hands over a few times and rubbed his palms together. No trace of the injury remained. His mind reeled. All she did was touch him. His skin should've been a blistered mess by now.

The woman had a way of making him feel better whenever she was near, but there was no way in hell she'd healed his wounds with a touch. It wasn't possible. "Alexis?"

He looked at her, and she closed her eyes, her body swaying as if she were on the verge of passing out.

"Are you okay?" He clutched her shoulders, steadying her.

With a deep inhale, she opened her eyes and nodded. "I'm fine. Those burns were pretty deep." She cupped his face in her hands, running her thumbs across his cheeks. "I'm okay. Why don't you put some clean clothes on, and I'll take the pan to the trash outside? That smell is horrible." She grabbed a dish towel from a hook and folded it over, using it as padding to pick up the mess. "I don't think the pan is salvageable."

"Yeah. Okay." He stood motionless as she walked to the door, his mind running in circles. *What just happened?*

She paused in the threshold. "Go change, goofball." She grinned and shut the door.

Goofball? Well, it was better than dumbass.

He dumped his dirty clothes in the washing machine and pulled on a pair of clean jeans and a black T-shirt. Sinking onto the edge of the bed, he stared at his hands. No matter how hard he wracked his brain, he couldn't come up with a logical explanation for what she'd done to him. How had the pain stopped instantly like that? And where were the blisters?

He took a deep breath and blew it out hard. Macey had her psychic ability to read spirit energy. Her friend Rain claimed to be a witch, and they both insisted she could cast spells. It was possible Alexis had the ability to heal, wasn't it? Hell, why not? Plenty of faith healers claimed to have powers like this. Maybe they weren't all scam artists after all.

He put on his shoes and padded to the living room, where he found Alexis on the couch, petting Sam. She looked so comfortable in his apartment, lounging with his dog like she belonged there. His heart couldn't decide if it wanted to race or skip a beat as he paused to look at her. Having her here felt almost too good to be true. Almost…magical.

He shuffled to the couch. "Are you ready to tell me what you did to my hands? Do you have some kind of weird power like your sister and her spirit sensors?" He sank onto the cushion next to her.

She bit her bottom lip in that oh so sexy way of hers, and her eyes tightened with uncertainty. "What I did… drains me. Can we get some food, and then I'll try to explain?"

He held her gaze, searching for a sign that she planned to avoid the issue, that she was concocting a lie to appease him. He only found fatigue. "Fair enough. There's an Irish pub a few blocks away. Good food. Great whiskey."

She smiled. "Sounds fantastic."

"Are you too tired to walk? I can carry you on my back if you are." He winked.

"Really?" Her musical laugh danced in his ears, adding warmth to the hominess she already brought to his apartment. What would it take to convince her she belonged here?

"Or we can drive."

Giving Sam one last pat on the head, she rose to her feet. "A walk would do me good, but…can I borrow your jacket again? I lost mine."

He sauntered to the door, took the one she'd worn a few times from the rack, and held it out to her. "How'd you lose your jacket?"

She slipped her arms through the sleeves and kissed him on the cheek. "I left it at Eric's."

The mention of her abusive ex stopped Bryce in his tracks. The fact that sorry excuse for a man had hurt Alexis fanned a fire of hatred in his heart so hot that he might not be able to stop himself from tearing into the asshole if he ever saw him again. A sour sensation burned in his stomach, and he caught her hand. "Have you heard from him lately?"

"Not a peep." She laced her fingers through his. "Let's go eat."

CHAPTER THIRTEEN

ALEXIS HELD BRYCE'S HAND AS THEY STROLLED through the neighborhood toward the tavern. Massive oak trees wrapped in twinkling white lights created a canopy over the sidewalk, and wreaths and tinsel adorned the homes along the path. Quaint, modest houses sat next to huge nineteenth century buildings with white columns and gas lamps for porch lights. The area had a cozy, welcoming ambience that she'd like to get used to.

Bryce remained quiet on the walk, giving her time to figure out how much to tell him. She wanted to spill it all. To tell him everything about herself, about her abilities. But to expose the werewolves to him would be a bigger step than she was ready to take.

Werewolves shared their secrets when they planned to make a serious commitment. While she knew, without a doubt, that she wanted to be with Bryce, the idea of settling down…of trusting someone…had her insides tied in knots.

If she could get out of her head and let her wolf take the lead, she'd be able to admit he was her fate-bound.

Hell, her wolf had been trying to convince her to make the man hers since the day she met him. It was time she started listening.

She clutched his bicep with her free hand and leaned into his side. He was warm, strong, kind. He deserved to know everything, but could he handle the truth? Would he believe her?

He patted her hand on his arm. "We're almost there. You doing okay?"

"I'm good." She caught his gaze, and the words *I'm a werewolf* danced on her tongue. She bit them back. "Why don't you have a Christmas tree?"

He laughed dryly. "I don't do much for the holidays anymore."

"Why not?"

"There's not much to celebrate when you're alone." A sadness she'd never heard before laced his voice. An ancient pain she didn't dare drag up for him to relive. Bryce was charismatic, friendly…everyone seemed to like him. A man like him wouldn't be alone unless he chose to be.

"Surely there are plenty of single guys at the station throwing parties, going to bars. Why don't you celebrate with them?"

"I do occasionally, but…" He stopped and faced her. "It may not seem that way, but I'm an introvert at heart. I enjoy hanging with the guys, but it drains me. I need my alone time to recharge my batteries." He opened the pub door and motioned for her to enter. "And speaking of doing things that drain you, I believe you owe me an explanation."

The wooden floor creaked as she stepped through the doorway, and she slipped out of Bryce's jacket, folding it over her arm. Dim, green-shaded lights hung from chains above the twenty or so tables scattered about the restaurant, and an impressive assortment of whiskey bottles lined the shelves behind the dark wood bar. A hostess seated them at a small table in the corner, and Alexis ordered the shepherd's pie, while Bryce went for an English breakfast. As the server scurried away to enter their orders, Alexis excused herself to the restroom. She hoped the extra time would give her a chance to come up with an easy way to explain to a skeptic that magic was real, but she returned to the table with nothing.

As she slid into her seat, Bryce leveled a heavy gaze on her.

Her stomach tensed. There was no easy way to say it. Bryce liked to deal with facts, so that was what she'd give him. "I healed you. I have…healing abilities."

He blinked at her, saying nothing.

"Like how Macey can read spirit energy, I can access my own healing energy and share it with others. It takes a toll on me, though, so I don't do it very often."

He shook his head. "That's impossible. You can't heal someone with a touch."

"I…" She paused as the waiter delivered their food. "I can, Bryce, and I did it to you. Twice."

The muscles in his jaw worked as he ground his teeth. "Twice? You mean both hands?"

"Also when Eric hit you."

He exhaled in a huff and scooped a forkful of beans into his mouth. She could practically hear the gears turning in his mind as he rolled over what she'd said. She'd had a hard time believing in magic herself in the beginning, even after she'd transformed into a werewolf the first time.

She gave him time to process and picked up her fork to break open the layer of mashed potatoes on top of her meal. Steam wafted out of the pie, and she swirled the utensil through the ground beef, picking up a scoop of meat, potatoes, and veggies and placing it on her tongue. The savory medley melted in her mouth, and she took another bite as she waited for Bryce to respond.

He finished half his plate before he spoke. "I'm a skeptic. Always have been. But what I saw you do today, and what you apparently did before…I can't explain it." He looked into her eyes with a gaze so intense it pulled the breath from her lungs. "I also can't explain the way I feel about you. The way *you make me* feel. But just because I can't explain it, that doesn't make it any less real."

He smiled and reached for her hand across the table. "You've got magical powers. I can live with that."

If he only knew the half of it. She smiled tentatively and gave his hand a squeeze.

"Since Macey has her own abilities, I take it this runs in the family?" He went back to eating like they were having the most normal conversation in the world.

"Something like that. You know Chase's wife, Rain?"

He nodded. "The witch."

"Her sister thinks we might be related, so that could be where it comes from."

He shrugged. "Makes sense."

"Does it?"

"Not really, but if I keep pretending it does, then maybe one day it will."

He'd taken it so much better than she'd thought he would. The way Macey had made it sound, she'd expected him to put his hands over his ears and refuse to listen the moment the idea of magic got tossed into the conversation. Maybe learning about the werewolves wouldn't turn his life *completely* upside down.

They finished dinner and walked hand-in-hand to Bryce's apartment, making a wide berth around Karen's front porch. She was nowhere to be seen. *Thank God.* That was another issue she'd have to address with him, but she'd save it for another day.

Once inside, they settled on the sofa, and she snuggled into his side as he draped his arm across her shoulders. She could get used to this feeling of belonging. Of finally being home.

He kissed the top of her head and held her tighter. "Are you really planning on leaving town tomorrow?"

She sat up to look at him, and the worry in his eyes tore at her heart. "Actually, I was planning on sticking around for a while, if that's okay with you."

The tension in his shoulders eased. "I'd like that very much."

"I will be out of your hair soon, though. Luke offered me a job on his construction team, and his sister has a spare room she's going to rent me."

"You're welcome to stay with me as long as you need to." He brought her hand to his mouth and kissed her fingers. "As long as you *want* to. What made you decide to stay?"

A warm shiver raced up her spine at the tenderness in his eyes, in his touch. "I'm staying for you, Bryce. I…" She looked at their entwined fingers as her heart beat at a hummingbird's pace. "Now that I've gotten to know you, I think I kinda like you."

A look of confliction furrowed his brow, and he let out a slow breath. "You don't really know me. Not the real me."

"I think I do. You're not the asshole I first thought you were." She sighed. "Actually, I never really thought you were an asshole. Most assholes have game, and you've got none." She winked and poked a finger at his stomach.

He shook his head. "There's a lot you don't know."

Not the reaction she was expecting. She leaned away, narrowing her gaze. "Then tell me. Tell me everything I need to know…to know the real you." She grinned slyly. "Because I'd like to know every inch of you."

"Come with me." His tone serious, he took her hand and pulled her off the sofa.

She followed him down the hall, past his bedroom, to a closed door. His hand rested on the knob. "You haven't looked in this room, have you?"

She shook her head. "You keep it locked."

"So you have tried?" He reached above the door and took a key from the trim.

Her pulse thrummed. Was it a sex dungeon? Or maybe a storage closet for his homemade taxidermy? She shivered. "I might have given the knob a twist the first time I was here alone. I figured it was an office or a home gym or something."

"It is my office, but no one has been in this room but me. No one knows about this side of me but my mom, and she rarely remembers who I am anymore." He squeezed her hand and pushed open the door.

Alexis held her breath as she stepped into the room. A large oak desk sat against the far wall beneath a window overlooking the back yard. Stacks of Sudoku puzzle books lay on either side of the laptop computer.

No torture devices. No dead animals. She released her breath.

Bookcases overflowing with paperbacks lined the walls

to the right and left. He must've had more than a thousand books crammed into the small space. She fought the grin that tugged at her lips. Who would've guessed this sexy cop was really a nerd? "I was expecting whips and chains. Why do you keep it locked?"

He shrugged. "Karen and Michael come in to bring me food and take care of Sam. Even they don't know this side of me."

She ran her hand along the spines and stopped on a copy of George R. R. Martin's *A Game of Thrones.* "I've seen this show. It's good."

"The book is better." He stepped behind her, so close his breath warmed the back of her neck.

She closed her eyes for a moment, the close proximity of his body making her nerves tingle. If he thought she wouldn't like him anymore after showing her his intellectual side, he was dead wrong. "Have you read all these?"

"Every one."

The wall opposite the desk held two large shelving units. Every type of *Star Trek* toy imaginable occupied the space. She stepped toward the toys, his heated gaze following her every move, and she pulled one from the shelf. "Why are the dolls still in boxes?"

He took the package from her hands and gently set it in its place. "They're action figures, and they're collectibles. They're worth more in the box."

"Why are you showing this to me?"

"If you're going to stay in New Orleans for me, you need to know what you're getting." He gestured to the room. "*This* is me. No matter how cool and tough I try to be, this is who I really am inside. I'm a fake." He dropped into the chair and rubbed his forehead.

"So you like to read. Big deal. I don't understand why

you think you have to hide it. And lots of people like *Star Trek*, obviously, or they wouldn't make the toys to begin with. Why are you ashamed?"

Why wouldn't he be ashamed? Why was he even telling her this? "It's not just the books and the toys. I'm a certifiable nerd. Always have been. I'd rather stay home and work math puzzles than watch a football game at a sports bar. Everyone thought I'd end up being a computer programmer or a rocket scientist or something. Hell, I probably should've been."

Her eyes held an emotion he couldn't read. Pity maybe? "Then why did you decide to become a cop?"

He'd told her this much. He might as well go all in. "Believe it or not, I was bullied in school. A lot."

"You? I don't believe it. Look at you. You're hot, and I know you know it."

He fished his wallet out of his pocket and pulled out the photograph. "I didn't always look this good." He passed her the picture.

Her brow furrowed as she looked at it. "This isn't you, is it?"

"I'm afraid it is."

She examined the photograph more closely, a tiny smile tugging at the corners of her mouth. "Huh. Once you see past the braces, glasses, and acne, you've got the same sweet eyes. You were kinda cute."

Yeah, right. He took the picture and slipped it into his wallet. "You wouldn't have thought so in high school."

"I never went to high school. You don't know what I would've thought. Why do you carry it around?"

"To remind me of who I was and why I do what I do. This was my junior year. The lowest point in my life. I had to do the football team's homework every week to avoid getting my ass kicked."

She grimaced. "That's awful."

"Tell me about it. I can't stand football. I made it through high school and decided I had two options: I could be a victim or I could do something about it."

"So you became a cop."

"I started working out. I went away to college and got a criminal justice degree. I decided to dedicate my life to fighting bullies. I changed the way I look. I changed the way I act. But no matter what I do or how hard I try, I can't seem to change the person I am on the inside. This." He gestured to his body. "This isn't really me. I will always be the kid in that photo."

She knelt by the chair and laced her fingers through his. The warmth of her touch tempered the chill running through his heart. Aside from his confession to Michael on the ledge, he'd never told anyone about his past. He did his job, followed the rules, enforced the law, and that was all anyone needed to know about him. But not Alexis. For some reason, he wanted her to *know* him. Everything about him.

Blonde lashes shielded her emerald eyes from his view as she stared at their entwined hands. How could she even want to touch him now that she knew his whole persona was nothing more than a mask?

She lifted her gaze to meet his. "You did change. I think this really is you. You're the kid in that picture, and you're the tough, sexy cop."

He shook his head.

"Why can't you be both?" She moved to the front of

the chair, keeping a firm grip on his hand and situating herself between his knees.

"When I'm Bryce the cop, I feel like I've got Bryce the nerd locked away somewhere inside me, and he's screaming to get out. It's almost like this persona is invading my body and taking over, but it's fake. You can't be two people. It doesn't work that way."

Her eyes tightened. "Sure it does. The bullied kid in that picture is the reason you're the person you are today. And this person you are on the inside…" She rested her other hand on his chest. "That you so desperately try to hide from the world. This is exactly who you should be. This is the part of you I've been getting to know. The part of you I'm falling for."

His heart slammed into his sternum. "So, you're okay with all this?"

"Well…" She leaned into his lap and traced the outline of his pecs with her finger. "It's a little intimidating, seeing as how I never finished eighth grade. But brains *and* brawn? You're the complete package. Incredibly sexy."

He took her hand and pulled her into his lap. "Why did you run away when you were so young?"

"That's a conversation for another day, but I will say this: I've been running my entire life because I've been scared. Now, I can't remember exactly what it was that I was afraid of."

He could live with that answer. She'd already opened up to him about her impossible ability, and she hadn't run away when he'd confessed to being a fake. But how could she find him attractive? "For some reason, it's easier to believe that you have magic powers than that you're falling for me after seeing all this."

"I've shown you my powers. Apparently, I'm not doing

a good job of showing you how I feel about you. Let's change that." She leaned in and pressed her velvet lips to his mouth. His heart seemed to stop for a moment, then stuttered to restart. Gliding her hands up his chest, she hooked them behind his neck and slipped her tongue into his mouth. A moan rumbled from his chest to his throat, and he took her face in his hands as he kissed her. Her skin smelled like his soap, and she fit in his arms like she was made for him to hold.

Shifting from his lap, she turned to straddle him, pressing her soft curves into his chest. His core tightened, his dick hardening beneath her, and he wrapped his arms around her, crushing her body to his. Kissing her here, in the room where he kept his true self locked away, in the midst of everything he hid from the world, was enough to send him over the edge.

This part of him…the real him…had never been with anyone before. He'd always donned his mask of machismo before he'd hopped in the sack. No one ever bothered to look beneath it.

But Alexis did.

Her hips rocked, sending a jolt of electricity from his dick to his heart.

He groaned.

She found the hem of his shirt and yanked it over his head. Her tongue slipped out to lick her lips as she trailed her fingers down his chest, over his stomach, to grip his cock through his jeans. *Holy shit.* She fumbled with his belt, and he reached out to still her hands.

She looked at him with uncertainty in her eyes. "You want me to stop?"

He laced his fingers through hers. "Oh, no. I want to keep going, but are *you* sure you want to do this?"

She rose to her feet, pulling him with her. "This is exactly what I want."

"Well, then." He cupped her face in his hand, rubbing his thumb across her smooth skin. "Let's slow down and do this right." Lifting her in his arms, he carried her to the bedroom.

Alexis lay on the bed, and Bryce climbed to his knees on the mattress. Soft moonlight filtered through the blinds, washing the room in a silvery glow. Mischief danced in his hazel eyes as a slow smile turned up the corners of his mouth, and anticipation tightened her stomach.

He shifted to the end of the bed and unlaced her boots. "It's kinda unfair, you know?" He slipped off her shoes and socks and dropped them on the floor.

"What is?"

He took her foot in his hands, massaging the sole. "That you know so much about me now."

"And I like everything I know." She started to sit up, so she could talk to him face to face, but his firm hold on her foot kept her in place. He rubbed his thumbs in circles on her arch, sending tingling warmth shooting up her legs.

"But I know so little about you." He stood on his hands and knees above her, his gaze traveling from her eyes to her lips. He kissed her mouth then trailed his lips along her jaw to nip at her earlobe. "And I want to know *all* of you."

He sat back on his heels and slipped her shirt over her head. She tried to sit up again to undo his pants, but he caught her hands in his. He kissed each palm and gently laid her back.

"You first," he said. "It's only fair." His gaze roamed over her body. "Where to start?"

He bent down and pressed his lips to her stomach. Her breath hitched as warmth spread below her navel, and he roamed his hands up her body to cup her breasts. He continued to kiss, working his way up her stomach, stopping at the clasp on the front of her bra. Tracing his fingers along the edge of the material, he grinned.

"This needs to go." He unclasped the garment and laid it open. "Much better." He took his time, tasting every inch of her body, his tongue slipping out to tease her nipples into tight pearls. Then he pressed his body to hers, trailing kisses up her neck to find her mouth once more.

His warmth enveloped her, his tender touch sending shivers from the base of her neck down to her toes. Never in her life had she been touched this gently. This unselfishly. Pressure built in the back of her eyes as she finally gave in to her wolf's demands. Bryce was the one. Her soulmate. Her fate-bound.

She squeezed her eyes shut and willed the tears away. She would not ruin this moment by crying.

"Now for the fun part." He shifted to the end of the bed and unbuttoned her jeans, slipping them over her hips. When he pulled her panties off, she sucked in a shuddering breath.

He paused. "Are we okay? Do you want to keep going?"

She nodded, swallowing the dryness in her throat. "Yes. God, yes."

He grinned and slipped out of his clothes. His body was lean and firm, his defined muscles sculpted to perfection. He stood beside the bed, and his dick, thick and rock-hard, had her mouth watering to taste it, her fingers twitching to touch it. She reached for him, but he caught her hand and brought it to his lips.

"Not yet. I'm getting to know *you* right now."

Good God. Who knew selflessness could be this hot?

Crawling onto the mattress, he trailed more kisses below her navel as he settled between her legs. Massaging her inner thighs, he explored her body with his tongue, kissing up one hip and down the other. His mouth hovered above her center, his warm breath teasing her skin. Anticipation knotted in her core as she gripped the bedsheets, and she arched her back, raising herself closer to his lips.

He slipped out his tongue and tasted her. Warm wetness enveloped her clit, and she gasped as he slid a finger inside her. Fiery electricity shot through her veins, setting every nerve on edge.

She knotted her fingers in his hair. Dear lord, the sensation was maddening. Her hips rocked involuntarily, and he dared to slip a second finger inside. Her core tightened, the orgasm coiling inside her as he continued the tortuous pleasure. She cried out as the climax ripped through her body, wave after wave of uncontrollable ecstasy rocketing through her core.

Panting, she tried desperately to catch her breath as the elation subsided into a tranquil hum. As her breathing finally slowed, Bryce looked up at her and grinned.

She sucked in a shaky breath. "I take back what I said about you not having game."

He chuckled and lay beside her, the length of his body warming more than her skin. This man lit her soul ablaze.

She gazed into his eyes, mesmerized as the tiny flecks of green and brown seemed to dance in his irises. He looked at her with an intensity that made her heart flutter, and a deep feeling of possessiveness stirred in her core. Her wolf had claimed him, and now it was the woman's turn.

Rolling toward him, she took his length in her hand and stroked him. He inhaled deeply, and his lids fluttered shut as he let out an aroused *mmm*. She pressed her lips to his, and he opened his eyes.

"Make love to me, Bryce."

He cocked an eyebrow. "My pleasure."

As he started to move, he let his head fall onto the pillow and rolled onto his back. "Okay, you win. I've got no game."

She trailed her fingers up and down his stomach, reveling in the way his muscles tightened and goose bumps rose on his skin. "You've got plenty. No one has ever made me feel the way you do."

He let out a heavy sigh. "I don't have a condom."

She cupped his cheek in her hand, turning his head to face her. "Go grab my backpack. I've got some."

With a grin, he hopped off the bed and returned with her bag. "At least one of us is prepared."

Unzipping the front pocket, she took out a condom and whisked off the wrapper. "I was hopeful."

"Nothing wrong with that." He took the rubber and rolled it on.

Positioning himself on top of her, he settled his hips between her legs and pressed his tip against her. She bit her lip as she gazed into his soulful eyes, and he filled her. An electric tingling sensation shot from her center to her chest, and she pulled his face to hers to take his mouth in an urgent kiss as they became one.

Rocking his hips, he slid in and out, sensuous friction making every cell in her body hum. She clutched his shoulders and hooked her heels behind his thighs, driving him deeper inside her with every thrust. She couldn't get enough of him. He trailed his mouth from her lips to her neck, searing her with kisses before nipping at her skin.

His woodsy scent. The salty taste of his skin. The warmth of his body on hers… She was on sensory overload and relishing every goddamn second of it. This man was made to be hers. It didn't matter that he was human. He belonged to her, and she belonged to him.

She found his lips with hers and drank in his essence, giving herself to him fully. As he moaned into her mouth, the vibration sent warm shivers running across her entire body. She held him tighter, the orgasm building in her core like a river behind a dam.

His rhythm increased, his thrusts growing harder and more determined. She gasped as the dam broke and a tidal wave of ecstasy crashed through her body, shattering her senses.

Tossing her head back, she cried out his name. He groaned in response, a shudder running through his muscles as he slowed his motion and relaxed on top of her.

He nuzzled into her neck and slipped his fingers into her hair. "I like your haircut. I don't think I've told you that."

"Thank you. I like…everything about you."

"That's good to know." He rose onto his elbows before sliding to his side. "I happen to like everything about you too." Rolling out of bed, he tossed the condom in the trash and settled next to her again.

She turned to face him, and he took her hands and entwined his legs with hers—a tangle of limbs and pounding hearts. Sleeping with Bryce was nothing like she'd expected. He was unlike any man she'd ever known, and he'd forced her to reconsider everything she believed about human nature. People *could* change. Bryce was living proof. He'd taken the hand he was dealt and turned himself into the most amazing man she'd ever met. If he could go from zero to hero by sheer force of will, a rogue could learn to settle down and stay in one place.

So many emotions coiled and twisted through her soul. Sensations she'd never felt before. For the first time in her life, she hadn't had sex—she'd made love.

"I'm glad you decided to stay." He kissed the back of her hand and gazed into her eyes like he was looking into her being.

"Me too." She had so many secrets, and at that moment, she wanted to share them all. To tell him everything about her—her past, her abilities, the werewolves. But she couldn't. Not yet. If he couldn't accept that his nerd side combined with his cop side to create his whole being, how could she expect him to accept that she was both a woman and a wolf?

"How was lunch with Macey? Did you talk about anything interesting?"

She grinned. "We talked about you. She warned me not to hurt you. All your friends seem to think I'm going to."

His brow furrowed. "I don't think you're going to hurt me."

"I don't want to hurt you."

"Well." He glided his fingers down her side to rest on her hip, leaving a trail of goose bumps on her skin. "I believe ours are the only opinions that matter in this case. Don't you agree?"

"I do."

His expression turned somber. "Did you tell her about your trouble with Eric?"

She drew her shoulders toward her ears. "It didn't come up in the conversation."

He arched an eyebrow. "You should tell Macey. She'd want to know."

"Tell her what? That I stupidly attempted to climb an electrical tower while trying to get away from an abusive ex-boyfriend? I'm her big sister. I should be taking care of her. She doesn't need to know I can hardly take care of myself. Anyway, that mess is over now." If he would stop bringing it up, maybe she could put her past behind her and focus on making a future with him.

He propped himself on his left elbow and used his thumb to fiddle with the ring on his right hand. "She's your family. You're lucky to have to that."

Alexis was damn lucky; she knew that. But she *didn't* know how to handle people who actually cared about her. This new life she was trying to make…staying in one place for good…would require baby steps. She was finally willing to accept that she could change, but he couldn't expect her to dive right in and act like she'd been here all along. "What about your family? Where are they?"

He let out a sigh, untwined their legs, and rolled onto his back. She immediately missed his warmth and scooted closer to rest her hand on his chest.

"My mom is at Autumn Winds Nursing Home. She has Alzheimer's." A mask of sadness covered his features, and his eyes grew distant.

She sidled next to him, pressing the length of her body to his side and propping her head on her hand to catch his gaze and keep him grounded in the present. "Do you ever see her?"

"I visit her every week." He stared at the ceiling. "Most of the time, she doesn't even know I'm there. She…" He inhaled a shaky breath. "She doesn't remember she has a son."

Her own mother had died when she was six, and she would give anything to see her one more time. To ask her the questions that had burned in her mind since she discovered she wasn't human. But for Bryce's mom to be alive and not recognize her own child… She could imagine the hole that must have left in his heart. "I'm so sorry. That must be hard."

"Yeah." He inhaled a quick breath. "How do your healing abilities work? Could you…?"

She smiled sadly. "No. I can only heal physical wounds. Diseases…" She shook her head. "I can't. I've tried." Her wolf made her immune to disease, so she had no need for the ability to heal them. "Is she all you have left?"

He looked at her and rested hand on top of hers. "My dad died of a heart attack three years ago. He was seventy-six. My mom started going downhill after that. She couldn't live without him. They had such a strong bond. So much love." A small smile curved his lips. "No matter what life threw at them, they always made it through because they had each other. And believe me, life threw some pretty wicked curve balls." He laced his fingers through hers. "Family is important. Don't shut your sister out."

Family. It was hard to believe she actually had one now. "I know you're right, but I don't want to be a burden on her. Luke's already giving me a job, and…"

"Family is never a burden." He swallowed. "I had a brother. He was six years older than me." He sandwiched her hand between his palms and raised their hands to his lips. "He killed himself when I was seventeen. Overdosed."

"Oh, Bryce. I had no idea." Her throat thickened. "And then you saw me in the hospital, and you thought that I…I'm so sorry."

His eyes began to glisten, so he blinked and shook his head.

"And then Michael… How do you do your job when it's so personal? How do you handle it?"

He laid her hand on his chest and rubbed his ring. "It's *why* I do it. The bullying is part of why I became a cop, but I became a negotiator so I could help people. So I could keep it from happening to anyone else."

"Because no one helped your brother?"

"I didn't know anything was wrong with him. He…" He paused and blew out a hard breath. "He had severe chronic depression, and he suffered in silence for years. Nobody knew. At least…*I* didn't know. I hadn't exactly mastered my people skills back then, so I wouldn't have recognized the signs if he'd broadcasted them. He put on a mask around his friends and family. Pretended to be happy. To be someone he wasn't." He laced his fingers through hers. "His smile never reached his eyes, though. I should've…" He pressed his mouth into a hard line. "Not a day goes by that I don't regret not knowing. Not helping."

Turning his head toward her, he pinned her with a heavy gaze. "If he had opened up and let me know what was going on, I might have been able to help him."

"But you didn't know."

"Doesn't make it hurt any less. Suicide doesn't stop the pain. It passes it on to someone else. Don't shut Macey out of your life because it isn't as perfect as you'd like it to be. She loves you no matter what."

She snuggled into his side and draped her arm across

him. If only her healing powers worked on broken hearts. "That ring isn't yours, is it?"

"It was my brother's college ring. He'd just graduated when…" He let out a hard breath. "I wear it to remind myself why I do what I do."

"And because it keeps him close to you."

He wrapped his arms around her, pulling her even closer to his side. "That too."

A familiar ache expanded in her chest, and she closed her eyes. "I used to have my mom's wedding ring. It was a simple, gold band, but it meant a lot to me."

"What happened to it?" His chest vibrated against her cheek.

"I pawned it." She buried her face in his neck, the shame of losing her connection to her mother twisting a knife in her heart. "I was broke. Hadn't eaten in days. I used to steal people's junk that they'd thrown to the curb and pawn it, but the broker wasn't interested in the busted bicycle I tried to sell him. He offered me fifty bucks for the ring and gave me a month to buy it back."

"You didn't make it in time?"

"No, I did. I came back three weeks later, but he'd already sold it. I lost the one thing I had of my mom's for fifty bucks."

"I'm sorry. I guess he wasn't willing to track down the buyer and try to get it back for you?"

She laughed dryly. "No, he wasn't, but I hear you about family. I'm going to do my best to repair my relationship with Macey. She's all I have left."

CHAPTER FOURTEEN

Bryce woke and reached for Alexis, but the bed was empty. Panic fluttered in his chest. He'd dumped so much on her last night…his fake persona, his family, his brother's death. Had she changed her mind about staying? Decided he carried too much baggage? He rose onto his elbows, and light shining from beneath the bathroom door eased his fear. When he put his hand on the bed where she had lain, her warmth remained in the sheets.

Her sweet scent lingered on the pillow, and he pressed his face into the fabric, inhaling deeply. The bathroom door swung open, and Alexis stepped into the room, wearing nothing but a towel. His mind flashed back to the first time he'd seen her in a towel, and he smiled. Not a single bruise marred her skin now, and she was finally opening up to him. Letting him into her world.

"Now you're doing it." She strode across the room and sat on the edge of the bed. The towel slid up until it barely covered the important parts, and heat pooled in his groin.

"Doing what?"

"You're sniffing the pillows. And smiling about it."

He swung the pillow behind her back, clutching it with both hands and pulling her to his chest. "You smell good." He nuzzled into her neck and took a deep breath. The scent of his soap mixed with a sweetness that was all Alexis, making his mouth water to taste her.

She laughed. "I smell like you. What's with the citrusy shower gel?"

"I like it. Especially when it's on you." He trailed kisses up the curve of her neck to take her earlobe between his teeth.

She shivered. "Don't you have to go to work?"

He tossed the pillow onto the bed and lay back, lacing his fingers behind his head. "Not for a few hours. It's six a.m."

Her gaze traveled the length of his body before settling on the tent he'd made of the sheets. She grinned. "I don't start my new job until Wednesday. Mind if I do a little exploring?" Her fingers brushed his stomach as she slid the sheet down. "Or do you have something you need to be doing?"

His core contracted, and his dick twitched beneath the sheet. "The only thing I need to be doing right now is you, darlin'."

"Darlin'?" She unknotted the towel from her chest and tossed it on the floor. "I've never let anyone call me that before."

Damn, she was gorgeous. All fair, flawless skin and delicate curves. He'd call her anything she wanted him to if she'd crawl into bed and press her supple body against his. "Would you like me to stop?"

"I like it coming from you." She tugged the sheet from his legs and climbed on top him.

Every nerve in his body hummed as she lay against

him, coaxing his lips apart with her tongue. She tasted like mint toothpaste, and as he wrapped his arms around her, he couldn't seem to hold her close enough. He needed to be in her. To be one with her.

His home had always been his sanctuary. His place to be alone when the world became too much to bear. He'd never realized how lonely he'd been, isolating himself like he had. Now, with Alexis in his bed, her scent lingering on the sheets, her essence filling his space with promises of companionship, he couldn't imagine a life without her in it.

She glided her tongue down his neck toward his chest, and anticipation knotted in his muscles.

"You know," he said. "You don't have to move in with Luke's sister."

"I don't?" She trailed kisses across his right pec and flicked out her tongue to lick his nipple.

His stomach clenched, and he sucked in a sharp breath. "Not if you don't want to."

"Where would I live then?" She grazed his sensitive flesh with her teeth and sucked his nipple into her mouth.

Electricity shot straight to dick, his hips involuntarily bucking with the sensation. "You could stay with me."

"I could?" She kissed her way down his stomach, his muscles coiling tighter as her lips neared his groin.

He rose onto his elbows to look at her. "I like having you here, and I plan on spending every free second I have with you."

"Do you, now?" She grinned as she took his length in her hand and stroked him.

His lids fluttered, but he forced his eyes open. She knew exactly what to do. Where to touch. To lick. She was made for him, and he needed her to know exactly how he felt about her. "I don't know how to describe it, but there is something about you. I felt it the first time I met you, and it's gotten stronger the more I spend time with you."

She stroked him again, and a bead of moisture gathered on his tip. A moan rumbled up from his chest, and she stroked him again.

"Maybe I do know how to describe it. Alexis, I..."

She flicked out her tongue to lick him, and the thoughts evaporated from his mind like a fog burned away by the morning sun. He dropped his head onto the pillow and closed his eyes as she took him into her mouth. Warm and wet, her tongue massaged the underside of his dick as she sucked him deeper. Then she slid her head up until only his tip remained between her lips before taking his entire length into her mouth again. A shudder ran through his body as she repeated the motion again and again, pushing him closer to the edge.

He could barely suck in enough air to speak. "I need you. I..."

She rose to her knees and grabbed a condom from the nightstand, rolling it on before she straddled him. Gripping his cock, she guided him to her center and sheathed him before he could finish the thought. Her gaze locked with his, and she rocked her hips, sending searing electricity pummeling through his veins.

With her hands on his chest, she rode him, her gorgeous breasts swaying with her movements. She was sheer perfection, and the connection he felt with this woman ran deeper than he'd imagined possible. He belonged to her. Every part of him.

He licked his thumb and pressed it to her clit, and she gasped, straightening her spine and increasing her rhythm. His climax coiled like spring in his core, and has she tossed her head back and cried out his name, an explosion of ecstasy ricocheted through his system and sparks danced before his eyes.

Breathless and trembling, Alexis collapsed on top of him. She clutched his shoulders and showered him in kisses, and he glided his fingers across her sweat-slickened skin. Her hair was still damp from the shower, and he ran his fingers through it, brushing it away from her face.

"One of the perks of moving in with me?" He kissed her cheek. "Mornings like this."

She lifted her head and smiled. "I'll think about it."

His chest tightened, and three little words danced on his tongue. He bit them back. She said she'd think about it, and he didn't need to press his luck by saying more. He would give her all the time she needed to warm up to the idea of being his. Right now, he'd find satisfaction in the fact that she was staying in town.

He held her for another half hour before showering and getting ready for work. Alexis dressed and followed him into the living room, where she gave Sam a scratch on the head and let him out the back door.

"Mind if I make some coffee?" She kissed him on the cheek and padded barefoot into the kitchen.

A fluttering sensation formed in his stomach as she made herself at home, opening cabinets, taking out cups, and filling the machine to brew. He stepped behind her and slid his arms around her waist. "Will you be here when I get home?"

She turned her face toward him and kissed his cheek. "Do you want me to be here when you get home?"

"You know I do." Today and every day for the rest of his life.

"Then I will. Once my job starts, I'll have to figure out

this whole staying in one place thing. It's scary."

He released his hold and moved to face her. "The last thing I want to do is scare you away. If I'm coming on too strong, please let me know."

She put her hand on his face. "I'm not scared of you, Bryce."

"That's good to know, darlin'." He kissed her palm. "Do you like frozen waffles?"

"I prefer them heated."

He laughed and popped some Eggos into the toaster—a feat of cooking he could actually handle. They ate and cleaned up the mess together, the routine as effortless as if they'd already lived together for months.

She walked him to the door and kissed him on the cheek, and he paused to take in her beauty.

"You are an amazing woman, Alexis Gentry. I'll see you tonight."

She smiled. "Bye, Bryce."

He tugged the door open and stumbled over a heap of fabric blocking the exit. A brown envelope slipped from the pile and landed at Alexis's feet. The color drained from her face as she bent and scooped the fabric and the envelope into her arms.

"This is my jacket." Her voice came out as a raspy whisper.

Bryce's heart slammed against his ribcage. "The one you left at Eric's?"

She nodded, and he wrapped his arm around her, pushing her back inside before locking the door. He should have expected this. Abusers never let go that easily.

Standing utterly still, she stared at the envelope in her grip. "He found me."

Bryce took the envelope and carried it to the kitchen.

"I guess someone bailed him out of jail." He tore it open and dumped the contents onto the counter. A stack of glossy photographs slid across the Formica, and anger burned in his chest. "Bastard's been watching us."

Alexis peeked over his shoulder as he spread the photos out on the surface. Pictures of his car parked at the station, Alexis's Ford on the curb in front of his house. The two of them walking hand-in-hand beneath the oaks on their way to dinner last night. A shot of them embracing in the living room, taken through the open blinds.

She picked up an image of her and Macey having lunch in a restaurant. Dropping it on the countertop, she covered her face with her hands. "I'm so sorry. I really thought this was over."

"Guys like that don't take rejection well. I'm not surprised at all." But he *had* let his guard down. He'd been so caught up in his feelings for Alexis that he'd been careless. Sloppy. The bastard had been following him, and he hadn't even noticed. He was a detective, for Christ's sake; he should have caught on.

Her hands trembled as she stacked the pictures. "I'll go talk to him."

"No, you won't. This." He gestured to the photographs. "This is stalking. He's already hurt you once."

She dropped her gaze to the floor, and ice flushed his veins.

"At least once." He didn't need to know exactly what the asshole had done to her. The look on her face said enough. He ground his teeth. "You need to get the police involved. Get a restraining order, so if he does something like this again, I can arrest him."

She opened her mouth as if to argue, but she let out a

defeated sigh instead. "Okay. You're right. I'll get a restraining order." She fumbled with the pictures, nervously stacking them face-down on the counter. When she reached the image of the two of them embracing in the living room, she swallowed hard and shoved it into the middle of the pile.

He called Sam inside and locked the back door. "Put your shoes on, and you can come to the station with me. I'll take the day off and stay with you until we can get this sorted out."

She inhaled a shaky breath. "If you don't mind, I think I'd like to get Macey's help with this." She glanced into his eyes before lowering her gaze again. "After our talk last night, I feel like she would want to help."

Hooking a finger under her chin, he raised her eyes to meet his. "You won't regret that." He tugged her into a firm hug. "I'll follow you to her house to be safe."

"You don't have to do that." Her face was pressed against his chest, muffling her voice.

"I want to." If he didn't trust Macey with his life, he'd insist she go to the station with him. Macey would keep her safe, though, and this might be exactly what they needed to mend their rocky relationship.

She sighed and pulled from his embrace. "Okay. Let me get my things from your room. I'll just be a minute."

Alexis gazed at Bryce through her rearview mirror on the way to Macey's house. Even at a distance, his clenched jaw and furrowed brow were unmistakable. His concern for her safety warmed her soul, and part of her actually considered his suggestion of letting the police handle Eric.

Maybe another run-in with the law would convince his bully of a father to take him back to Biloxi. Then again, if he hadn't bothered this time, he'd probably washed his hands of his delinquent son.

She pulled to a stop on the curb in front of Macey's house and said a silent prayer thanking whatever god was responsible for ensuring that cars lined the rest of the road so Bryce had nowhere to park. He stopped in the middle of the street and rolled down his passenger side window.

Alexis slipped out of her car, lightly shutting the door to avoid bringing any attention to her presence. Resting her hands on the door, she stuck her head through his SUV window. "Thanks for the escort, officer."

He pressed his lips together, his brow knitting as he held her gaze. "I know Macey can protect you, but…if you need anything, please call me. I—"

"I will." She couldn't let him finish the thought. Not if it was the same thing he'd tried to tell her this morning. He might change his mind after what she was about to do.

A car stopped behind him and honked.

"You better get out of the road. I'll see you later." She straightened and wiggled her fingers. "Bye, Bryce."

He nodded. "Be careful."

"I will."

He hit the button to roll up the window and slowly drove away.

Alexis spun around and made her way toward Macey's front door, but as soon as Bryce turned the corner, she got in her car and sped off in the opposite direction.

Eric wouldn't stop until Alexis was by his side or dead, and being anywhere near Bryce put him in danger. A restraining order would do nothing to stop a werewolf. She had to handle this herself.

She turned onto Interstate 10 and headed to Pearl River. Maybe she couldn't beat Eric in a fair fight, but she could outsmart him again. She'd take care of this problem for good, and then she'd come back to New Orleans and settle down with Bryce like her wolf had been begging her to do.

And once her sadistic ex was no longer a threat, she'd tell Bryce what she was…tell him everything. She'd bring him into her supernatural world once it was a safe place for him to be.

Her stomach soured as she pulled into the driveway and parked behind Eric's Mustang. She shoved some clean clothes into her backpack and slung it over her shoulder as she paced up the walk. A new video doorbell hung beside the frame, and she pressed the button before smoothing her hair into place. A red light blinked beside the camera, and a few seconds later, the lock disengaged.

Eric crossed his arms and leaned against the jamb, a smug smile contorting his features. "I knew you'd come back to me."

"You didn't give me much of a choice."

"You always have a choice, baby. You finally made the right one."

She clenched her jaw, trying to keep her expression neutral. "If I help you, you *will* leave Bryce alone. Macey too."

His grin widened as he drew a cross over his chest. "You have my word."

"Like that means a lot." She pressed her hand against the small of her back—where Bryce's gun fit snugly into the waistband of her jeans—and pushed past Eric to enter his home.

CHAPTER FIFTEEN

BRYCE SET HIS PHONE ON THE DESK AND STARED AT the blank screen. Two hours had passed with no word from Alexis. She hadn't shown up at the station to report the bastard yet, and anxiety had him wound up so tight his muscles ached. His knee bounced incessantly beneath his desk, and he popped a piece of peppermint gum into his mouth, clenching it between his teeth.

He'd called her half an hour ago and gotten her voicemail. She was doing exactly what he'd suggested: getting Macey involved, building the bond with her sister. And he trusted Macey with his life. She could handle whatever that bastard threw at them, but damn it, not knowing where Alexis was made him crazy.

He'd almost told her he loved her several times that morning, and now he was cursing himself for not forcing the words from his lips. She'd had a hard life. Wasn't used to people caring about her. She didn't understand how profoundly her actions could affect the people who loved her. If she changed her mind and went after Eric on her own…

Shit. Why hadn't he told her?

His computer chimed with an e-mail, and he clicked it open—the autopsy report on the female they'd retrieved from the river. He scanned the document and squinted at the body temperature. That couldn't be right. Bryce rubbed his eyes and looked again. Thirty-eight degrees.

He scrolled down to the examiner's comments. *Evidence of freezing after death.*

What the hell? He pulled up the other case. Nothing new since Macey suggested an animal attack. Had she even seen the autopsy? Or was something else going on that she was trying to cover up?

A sour sensation crept from his stomach up the back of his throat. Had Macey gotten involved in something sinister? No way she'd voluntarily participate in something like this, but if she were being forced…and he'd sent Alexis to her for help.

He mashed the button on his phone to dial Macey's number.

"Bryce? Is everything okay?" Her voice was raspy, and the sound of rustling sheets filled the silence.

His heart sank. "Were you asleep?"

"It's not even ten a.m. What's wrong?"

He swallowed the thickness from his throat as icy tendrils of dread wound their way up his spine to grip his neck. "So you haven't seen Alexis today?"

"No. What happened?"

"Nothing. I'm sorry I woke you." He pressed end and slammed his phone onto the desk. How could he have been so stupid? Alexis never had any intention of asking her sister for help. She was stubborn and overly confident, and he'd let love blind him to her faults. He should have known.

Assholes like Eric couldn't be reasoned with. Bryce had been on his fair share of domestic abuse calls, and these guys never quit.

He dialed Alexis's number. Straight to voicemail. A quick search of the database gave him Eric's address, and he grabbed his jacket and stormed out of the station.

His mind reeled on the drive to Pearl River. What exactly was he going to do when he got there? He had no warrant. No legal reason for busting in and beating the shit of the dude. Alexis went there of her own free will, so as a cop, his hands were tied.

But as a man…

He yanked his badge from his belt and tossed it on the passenger seat. If he'd have been thinking straight, he'd have stopped by his house to grab his personal firearm, but he didn't plan on needing to use it. He was simply there to talk. *Right.*

Pulling into the grass on the side of the road in front of Eric's house, he tightened his grip on the steering wheel. Alexis's car sat behind a Mustang in the driveway, and Bryce closed his eyes, gritting his teeth until pain shot through his jaw.

He wasn't breaking any laws. Yet. He'd knock on the door and ask for Alexis. If the bastard wouldn't let him talk to her, then…he'd cross that bridge when he got to it. Prying his fingers from their death-grip on the wheel, he opened the door and slid out of the car.

Sunlight glinted off his badge lying on the seat, and he slammed the door. If he did cross any bridges today, the emblem wouldn't shine so brightly as his boss confiscated it. His career would end. He squared his shoulders toward the house and marched to the door. He'd choose Alexis over his job any day.

Ignoring the doorbell, he pounded his fist against the wood. A muffled shout sounded from somewhere inside, and a tiny red light blinked beside the camera on the bell. The sound of something hitting the floor resonated from the other side of the door, and Bryce's heart rate kicked up.

He clenched his hands into fists, ready to defend himself if the asshole tried to catch him off guard, and he took a step back as the lock disengaged. Alexis's face appeared by the jamb, and his breath caught in his throat.

She glanced over her shoulder before stepping through the doorway and shutting it. "You shouldn't be here."

"Like hell I shouldn't. I told you not to try to talk to him." He took her hand. "C'mon. We're going home."

She pulled from his grasp. "This is my home, Bryce, and you don't get to tell me what to do."

"No, Alexis, this isn't…you don't have to stay here. We'll get the restraining order, and if he tries anything else, I'll throw his ass in jail. I will take care of you."

"I don't need you to take care of me." She crossed her arms and lowered her gaze to the ground. "I don't want you to."

"What?" He blew out a breath. "What are trying to say?"

The muscles in her throat worked as she swallowed and lifted her gaze to his. "I'm saying I *want* to stay here. With Eric." Her lip curled as she said his name. "This is where I belong, and I'm sorry for leading you on. I…" She cut her gaze to the side before making eye contact again. "I was using you until the heat blew over. He forgives me now, so you should go."

As she held his gaze a moment longer, a tiny shard of doubt wriggled into his mind before he slammed the door on it. After everything they'd shared last night and this morning, there was no way. "C'mon, darlin'. You don't mean that."

"I do."

She didn't. The rapid blinking, cutting her gaze to the left, holding eye contact longer than was natural when she did look at him…they were all classic signs of lying. And the way her brow knit as she glanced over her shoulder at the window, she couldn't hide the fear in her eyes if she tried.

The red light on the doorbell camera blinked, indicating Eric was watching every move she made. Bryce stepped toward her, lowering his voice and resting his hand on her elbow. "Did he threaten you? Is he making you say this?"

"No, Bryce." Her gaze hardened, and she whispered, "Look, we had sex, okay? It doesn't mean I want to move in with you. Just…go home and forget about me."

"That's enough, babe. Time to come inside." Eric's massive frame darkened the doorway.

Alexis's shoulders tensed.

Bryce clenched his fists. "Please, Alexis. Come home with me. I love you."

She locked eyes with him, and a thousand emotions played across her features. As she opened her mouth to respond, her lower lip trembled. "I could never love a man like you. Go home, Bryce."

Eric grabbed her arm, but she yanked from his grasp and stomped inside. He turned to Bryce. "Whatever you thought you had with my girl is over. I don't want to see your pig face again."

He didn't move as Eric slammed the door. Not a word of truth had spilled from Alexis's lips, but what else could he do? Bust the door down and drag her away? If she wouldn't listen to him, he'd call in backup.

Turning on his heel, he ground his teeth and strode to his SUV. This was far from over.

Alexis leaned against the kitchen counter, careful to keep her back toward the wall. Eric hadn't let her out of his sight since she'd knocked on the door, and she needed to stash Bryce's gun somewhere she could get to it later.

A fissure tore through her chest as pressure built in the back of her eyes. Bryce had said the words, and they'd nearly crumbled her. Fate had bound her heart to his, and hearing him confirm it had her wolf howling with joy.

And then she hurt him.

Lying to Bryce had been the hardest thing she'd ever done, but she'd had to do it to keep him safe. If he thought he didn't have a chance with her, surely he'd give up long enough for her take care of Eric. Then, with the threat extinguished, she could crawl back to Bryce on her hands and knees and beg for forgiveness.

What else could she do? The man held her heart in his hands, and Eric would tear Bryce's throat out if he knew.

"Don't look so sad, babe." Eric adjusted his crotch and sauntered toward her. "He's a human."

She blinked back her tears and nodded. "You're right. I don't know what I was thinking running to him. I was stupid."

"Damn right you were." He slid a hand up her shoulder, and she recoiled.

Clutching her chin between his thumb and forefinger, he forced her gaze to his. "I think I need to fuck you 'til you forget him." He grabbed the back of her neck with his other hand. "What do you say?"

She shrugged out of his hold and paced toward the couch. "I'm on my period."

Following, he leaned toward her and sniffed the air. "I don't smell blood on you."

"I wear tampons, dumbass. Of course you don't."

His lip curled in disgust. "Nasty bitch."

"Wow, Eric." She hung her backpack over her shoulder. "If you're trying woo me, you might want to watch your language."

He shuffled around to block the front door. "Where do you think you're going?"

"To the bathroom to change my tampon."

"Hold on." He jerked the bag from her shoulder and opened it. "What you got in here?" He stuck his hand in the bag and rummaged around.

She rolled her eyes and unzipped a side pocket before yanking out a handful of feminine hygiene products.

He wrinkled his nose and shoved the bag toward her. "Make it fast."

She shook her head. What kind of alpha male was afraid of a little period blood?

Padding down the hall, she slowed her stride as she passed *the room*. The stench of bleach assaulted her senses as she peered inside the pristine area. All the musical instruments hung seemingly untouched on the wall, and the tile floor shone like it had been freshly polished.

Her stomach turned. How many people had he killed in that room?

Ducking into the bathroom, she turned the lock on the knob and pulled the gun from her waistband. She shoved it into her backpack and covered it with clothes before opening a tampon and tossing the wrapper in the trash. She flushed the rest of it to hide the evidence—she wasn't due to start her period for another two weeks—and looked at her reflection in the mirror.

The bruise Eric had given her had thankfully faded right before Bryce arrived. She'd taken the beating like the "dutiful girlfriend" Eric expected her to be, but she was biding her time. All she needed was a little evidence to show the council, and she'd be justified in what she planned to do.

With the gun hidden in the bottom of her backpack, she crept into the living room to find Eric lounging on the couch with a beer in his hand.

He grinned and unzipped his pants. "Come on over here, darlin'."

Her skin crawled hearing Bryce's name for her spilling from that meathead's lips. "Don't call me that."

"Since I can't fuck you for a while, why don't you come suck me off to show me your appreciation for taking you back."

The Eggos she'd had for breakfast threatened to make a reappearance as she set her bag against the wall and crossed her arms. "I'm not in the mood."

He narrowed his eyes. "You will be. You'll learn to love me again."

Looking at him now, with a beer in one hand, the other hand in his pants, she couldn't recall an ounce of positive emotion that she'd ever felt for the man. He had a muscular body, strong jaw, and symmetrical features. All the things a woman was supposed to find attractive in a man. But the hatred and idiocy that spilled from his mouth overshadowed any amount of physical appeal he possessed. "I never loved you, dickhead."

He laughed. "I like it when you're feisty."

A chime sounded from a speaker in the hall half a second before his phone buzzed. The back door opened and slammed shut, and a male called, "I got one, boss. Better make it quick, though. The chloroform is wearing off."

"All right." Eric stood and zipped his pants. "Let's get to work then."

Bryce parked on the curb in front of Macey's house and chewed the inside of his cheek. His stomach had tied into a knot on the drive over, and his heart flipflopped between aching for Alexis and burning in rage for the man who was holding her captive. She may not have wanted her sister involved, but she'd left him no choice.

He strode to the front door and pressed the bell. Laughter resonated from inside, and light footsteps sounded on the floor. He let out a breath. At least he hadn't woken her.

The door opened a crack, and Macey peeked through the slit. "Hey, Bryce. This isn't the best time." She wore her police uniform, though the shirt was untucked and the top four buttons hadn't been fastened.

"It's important. It's about Alexis."

Macey sighed and opened the door. "What did she do this time?"

He tilted his head as he stepped through the threshold. "Why are you wearing your uniform? Did you pick up an extra shift?"

Her husband, Luke, padded in from the hallway, wearing unbuttoned jeans and no shirt, and examining a pair of handcuffs. His light-brown hair hung loose, nearly brushing his shoulders. "You're sure you've got the key for these, babe? I'd hate to have to break them when we're done."

Heat crept up Bryce's neck as he cut his gaze between Macey and Luke. This was a sight he could not unsee.

Macey plastered on a fake smile. "We've got company, dear."

Luke lifted his gaze. "Oh, hey, Bryce." He glanced at the cuffs in his hand. "This…" He looked at Macey apologetically. "Isn't what it looks like?"

She laughed. "It's exactly what it looks like. Come sit and tell me what my sister has gotten herself into." She buttoned her shirt and led the way to the living room.

"I'll leave you two to it. Good to see you, Bryce." Luke nodded and shuffled down the hall.

Bryce followed her and sank onto the sofa, trying to ignore the images of the scene he'd interrupted that his brain kept projecting behind his eyes. She wasn't kidding when she'd said this wasn't the best time, but what he had to say was too important to wait. "Alexis went to her abusive ex-boyfriend's house, and he's holding her there against her will."

Macey lifted an eyebrow. "Abusive? How do you know?"

He hesitated. Breaking the trust of the woman he loved wasn't the best way to start out a relationship, but damn it, she needed help. "Hear me out." He told her about finding Alexis in the hospital and how she had been staying with him on and off for the past week. "He's been stalking us. He left a stack of photos on the doorstep this morning. Alexis told me she was coming to you for help, but she went to him instead. She lied to me."

She folded her hands in her lap, and her eye twitched as if she fought to keep her expression neutral. "Wow. You must really like her. It's not like you to miss a lie."

He scrubbed a hand down his face. Did she even care that her sister was with an abuser? "Mace, I'm in love with her."

"Oh, Bryce." She shook her head, sympathy softening her eyes. "I warned you not to do this. She's not the settling down type."

His chest tightened. "She is. She was. We talked about it last night. She said she was starting work with Luke on Wednesday and that his sister offered her a room in her apartment. She was making plans to stick around until her jackass ex left that package on my doorstep." He shifted toward her. "Her first instinct was to go talk to the dude. Try to get him to stop. But I convinced her not to."

He stared at his hands in his lap. He *thought* he'd convinced her not to.

Macey put her hand on his. "What do you want me to do?"

"Talk to her. See if you can get the truth out of her. Get her to let you file a report." He raked a hand through his hair. "He's hurt her, Mace, and when I tried to get her to leave with me, she refused. If she won't press charges, I don't…" He could go back, beat the shit out of the guy, and drag Alexis away. But then he wouldn't be any better than Eric. He huffed. "I don't know what else to do."

"Do you know his name?"

"Eric Anderson. Dude's got a record but no outstanding warrants."

"Anderson?" Luke's brow puckered as he sauntered into the room. "Is he from Biloxi?"

Bryce's heart rate kicked up. If he couldn't convince

Macey to do something, maybe he could appeal to Luke's protective nature. "Yeah. You know him?"

"I know his old man." Luke exchanged an unreadable look with Macey and strolled into the kitchen.

Macey sighed. "Let it go, Bryce. If she wants to be with Eric, there's nothing you can do about it."

He clenched his fists. "He's an abuser."

"But she won't press charges, and she refused to leave."

"No, I couldn't get her to, but I—"

"She can take care of herself." Her voice turned firm. "You need to let her go." She stood and shuffled to the front door, casting a glance toward the kitchen as he followed her. She whispered, "Seriously, Bryce, don't get involved."

"I already am." He'd been involved since the second he stepped into her hospital room, and he wouldn't give up now when she needed him the most.

Opening the door, she stepped onto the porch and motioned for him to follow. "You're not. Her business doesn't concern you, so please stay out of it."

"The hell it doesn't. Mace, what's going on? You've changed."

She flinched as if he'd slapped her. "What do you mean? Nothing's changed."

"You have. You're missing evidence, blowing off cases, looking for the easy answers rather than digging for the facts."

She crossed her arms. "We're not partners anymore. You don't know how I handle cases."

He stiffened. "That body they pulled out of the river had an internal temperature seven degrees lower than the water they found it in, yet you're calling it animal attack."

She cut her gaze into the house. "Bryce…"

"It's not since I got promoted. Ever since you met Luke, you've been different. You're hanging out with all these people with magical powers. Psychics and witches that I wouldn't have even believed existed if I hadn't seen them work their tricks with my own eyes. Are you in some kind of cult? Is that why Alexis doesn't stick around? Because of what you're involved in?"

She dropped her arms to her sides and tilted her head. "You know me better than that."

"Do I?" He wasn't sure about anything anymore.

"I'm not in a cult." She narrowed her eyes. "I'm married to the man of my dreams who happens to have some friends with abilities similar to mine. I finally belong somewhere, and you're accusing me of nefarious acts?"

He opened his mouth, but the words got stuck in his throat. What the hell was he doing? Arguing with Macey wouldn't help Alexis, and priority number one was getting her out of that abuser's house. "I'm sorry, Mace…"

"Go home, Bryce, and leave Alexis alone. She's not worth it." She marched inside and slammed the door, leaving him alone on the porch.

He'd always held Macey in high regard, but if she didn't give a damn about her own flesh and blood…maybe he didn't know her as well as he'd thought he did.

CHAPTER SIXTEEN

ERIC LEANED AGAINST THE SOUNDPROOF WALL AND crossed his arms. If he could turn this guy into a werewolf, he'd promote him to second as soon as he shifted. Hell, the dude's muscle mass alone was comparable to any alpha he'd ever seen, and man, had he put up a good fight. Tearing him to pieces had been fun.

Sweat beaded on Alexis's forehead as she repaired the damage Eric's teeth had done. She'd screamed at him to stop during the entire attack, her voice cracking with anger or fear…he didn't care which. Seeing her all worked up like that had gotten him all worked up, and now he was so goddamn horny his dick felt like a blocked water pipe about to explode.

He could force her to give him a blowjob, but he didn't trust that bitch's teeth anywhere near his family jewels at the moment. "How much longer you gonna be on your period, babe?"

She wiped her brow with her forearm and glared at him. "A week."

Damn, she was sexy when she was mad. If she'd been

clean, he'd have bent her over the table right then and reminded her why she really came back. She wanted him, whether she was ready to admit it or not.

"How's the patient?" He pushed from the wall and strolled toward his mate-to-be. Peering over her shoulder, he marveled at the final flesh wound stitching itself back together with the help of Alexis's magic.

She turned her face toward him, and her skin had taken on a grayish color. She'd never admit weakness, but healing drained the life right out of her. He gave her shoulder a shove, and she fell onto her side before rolling onto her back and squeezing her eyes shut. *Frail little bitch.*

The man's eyes rolled beneath his closed lids, and Eric knelt, gripping his forearm and waiting for the tingle of werewolf energy to seep into his skin. He felt nothing. "Damn it, Alex, you healed him too fast."

She grimaced as she pushed to a sitting position. "Any slower and he wouldn't have made it. You almost tore his throat out."

He shot to his feet and clenched his fists. "We'll try again then. I'll stay away from his neck this time."

Alexis rubbed her forehead. "No, Eric. He's been attacked and healed three times now. Doing it again isn't going to change anything. Maybe it takes time for the magic to bond with his blood."

"No. It's almost a full moon; it should be immediate." He narrowed his gaze at Alexis. "You're distracted. That's what it is."

She leaned her back against the wall. "Of course I'm distracted. You're insane."

"No. It's that damn cop. You're still thinking about him." He'd seen it in her eyes, even as she'd told the dude to leave her alone. She had feelings for a human. His nostrils flared as a jealous rage boiled in his gut.

"I'm not thinking about him. All I can think about right now is how I wish you'd clean up all this blood. It's making me nauseated."

What could a human cop give her that he couldn't? At the moment, the one thing Samuels had that he didn't was power. That would change soon enough. He had a new strategy in the works. His men were already out finding him someone weaker to practice on. Once he perfected the method, then he'd move on to creating strength in his pack. He'd need weaker wolves to do his grunt work anyway.

"You can clean it up when we're done. We've got a new patient on the way."

"You need to give this one time. Let him at least wake up before you hurt anyone else. The magic might hold."

"No. He's too strong. It's not going to work." A chime sounded in the hall. His minions had arrived with his next experiment. "Stay here with the dead guy."

"He's not dead."

"Not yet." He slipped out the door to meet them at the back.

Alexis took a deep breath and leaned her head against the wall. Her stomach churned at the coppery scent of fresh blood, but she pushed to her feet. She couldn't let Eric see how weak healing made her.

She shook the man's shoulder. "Wake up, dude."

His eyes rolled from side to side, but they didn't open. The third time Eric had attacked him, he'd nearly killed him. It had taken every ounce of energy Alexis had to keep the guy alive, and he was still unconscious.

She put her hands on either side of his head and tried to push more healing energy into him. If she could get him to wake up before the dickhead and his flunkies came back, he might be able to escape out the front door.

"Goddammit, Trevor, I told you no more women." Eric's voice grew louder as they approached the room. "Alexis is going to be my mate."

Her skin crawled at the thought of getting her body anywhere near that meathead. She pressed her back against the wall as Eric slammed the door open and stomped into the room, followed by his two prospective pack members.

"You said you wanted someone weaker," Trevor said as he lowered the unconscious woman to the floor.

"Not that weak. A new pack needs a solid foundation of strong werewolves. I can make males strong, but females aren't going to cut it."

"Sorry." Trevor lowered his gaze, while Justin hovered near the door.

Eric scratched the scruff on his jaw as his gaze danced between the victims, his men, and Alexis. "Here's the plan. Trevor, go get me the kid we talked about."

Trevor rubbed the back of his neck. "The kid? Are you sure you wanna go there, boss?"

Eric puffed out his chest like an overstuffed peacock. "Are you questioning your alpha?"

He lowered his head. "No sir. I'm on my way." He scurried out the door.

"Justin, after I take care of these two, dump them in the river, and then get your ass back here to help Alexis clean up the mess." Eric cracked his knuckles. "I don't want any contamination when the kid gets here."

"Yes, sir." Justin gave him a mock salute.

She stepped toward the woman. "Take care of them? What are you going to do?"

Eric smiled wickedly and shifted into his wolf form.

Alexis screamed.

He lunged for the unconscious man, going straight for the neck, and ripped his throat out before Alexis could move. Then he turned to the woman.

"Eric, no!" She threw herself on top of her. "Don't kill her. Let her go."

He paused, a low growl rumbling in his throat. His gaze flicked to Justin and back to Alexis.

Justin grabbed her arm, trying to haul her up, but she clutched the woman's shoulders, hanging on tight. She couldn't let him kill her or anyone else. This had to end.

"Come on, woman," Justin said. "You heard the alpha. We have to get rid of her."

"No. She hasn't even woken up. Let her go."

Justin pulled his arm back, fisting his hand to deliver a blow, but Eric barreled into him, knocking him into the wall. Alexis clung to the woman, her head spinning from exhaustion, nausea churning in her stomach. Eric would have to go through her if he wanted to kill another innocent human, and in her current condition, she'd be dead before she had the chance to shift.

Eric returned to human form and yanked Justin up by the collar of his shirt. "No one lays a hand on the alpha's mate," he growled.

"I'm sorry." The lackey ducked his head, averting his gaze. "You want me to haul her off and take care of her myself?"

"You'll have to kill me first." Alexis tightened her grip on the victim's shoulders.

Eric arched an eyebrow at her before turning to his minion. "Did she see your wolf form?"

"I knocked her out with the chloroform from behind. She never even saw my face." He smiled smugly.

Eric grabbed Alexis's elbow and dragged her to her feet before wrapping an arm around her. "You heard my future mate. This one lives. Dump her in the woods before she wakes up and leave her." He pressed his putrid lips to Alexis's head, and her stomach turned. "See, babe? I told you this would be a partnership. You saved a life today."

She shook from his embrace. "And you took one, asshole."

He shrugged. "As soon as we figure out the formula, no one else will die."

She clenched her teeth. Someone else would die tonight, and it wouldn't be another human.

CHAPTER SEVENTEEN

EVERY MUSCLE IN BRYCE'S BODY TENSED AS HE DROVE over the Crescent City Connection bridge onto the East Bank. He'd been driving aimlessly for the past two hours, rolling over his conversations with Alexis and Macey in his head, gripping the steering wheel until his knuckles whitened and his joints ached.

Had he been wrong about Alexis? He'd missed every single sign when she'd lied to him about going to the bastard's house. He could hardly see through the thick cloud of love covering his eyes, and his judgment suffered for it. Was he only seeing what he wanted to see?

No, she hadn't used him like she'd said. It was a lie—all of it—but *something* was going on. She may have gone to Eric's willingly, but she wouldn't stay with him unless she had a reason. She was smarter than that.

Whatever it was, she did not need to be anywhere near that abuser. He had to figure out a way to get through to her. Maybe she really couldn't ever love a man like Bryce, but she deserved so much better than an asshole like Eric.

He groaned and exited the highway onto Tchoupitoulas Street and made his way into the Garden District. A few shots of caffeine and a rush of sugar ought to wake his mind up. Help him think straight.

He hadn't slept much last night with Alexis in his bed. The corner of his mouth twitched as images of her sexy body wrapped around him danced behind his eyes. She had feelings for him; of that he was sure.

But he'd come on too strong. What the hell had he been thinking asking her to live with him? He should've been satisfied when she said she'd stay in town, but he'd pushed her too hard and sent her straight into that asshole's house. That's what Macey would have him believe, but the wriggling sensation in the back of his mind told him something else was going on. And in his heart…damn it, in his *soul,* he knew Alexis was the one for him. If he believed in fate and soul mates and all that crap, he'd say she was his. He couldn't deny the strong connection he felt with her. She felt it too. She had to.

He pulled into a parking lot and zipped his jacket as he trekked into the coffee shop. Half a dozen tables sat scattered about the room, four of them occupied, and a row of stools lined the counter in front of the kitchen. The rich aromas of espresso and cinnamon tickled his senses, and a woman laughed, disturbing the quiet hum of conversation filling the air. Grabbing a seat at the counter, he ordered black coffee and an apple fritter, and he played his conversation with Alexis in his mind for the fifteenth time. There had to be something he'd missed. Some clue.

"Hey, Bryce. How's it going?" A tall man with dark hair and blue eyes slid onto the seat next to him.

Bryce sat up straight. "James, right?" He offered his hand to shake. "Good to see you." Macey had so many new friends since she'd married Luke, it was hard to keep up with them all.

James shook his hand and ordered a roast beef po-boy. As the waitress delivered Bryce's food, James chuckled. "Late breakfast?"

"I didn't realize it was already lunch time." He broke off a piece of the fritter and shoved it into his mouth. The combination of apple and cinnamon normally made his taste buds zing, but he could hardly taste it now.

"You okay?" James's eyes held brotherly concern. "You look like you lost your best friend."

He let out a dry laugh. "Close. I might have lost the woman I love."

James palmed his shoulder. "I'm sorry man. That's tough."

"Tell me about it." He scrubbed a hand down his face. He normally kept his mouth shut about his personal life, but at least this guy had some sympathy for his situation. Macey had had none. "She went back to her abusive ex."

He sucked in a breath through his teeth. "There's nothing I hate more than a man who hits a woman. You need any help kicking his ass, you let me know."

"I might take you up on that." He took a gulp of coffee. Lukewarm, like his love life.

James's food arrived and they ate in silence. The waitress refilled Bryce's coffee, and it was a little warmer this time. Still, nothing compared to the fire Alexis had lit inside his soul. He shoved his plate away. If he could clear his head—get his mind off his emotions—then he could look at the facts and figure out how to get her back.

He turned to James. "What's your super power?"

James choked on his iced tea. "Pardon?"

"Seems like all Macey's new friends have some sort of psychic ability. What's yours?"

He bit into his sandwich and took his time chewing before he answered. "I don't have any psychic abilities." He cut his gaze to the side and ran his hand over his mouth.

"Good to know I'm not the only one." Bryce sipped his coffee and eyed the man. "How long have you known Luke?"

"Since we were kids. We grew up together, close as cousins." He rubbed the back of his neck. "Listen, man, I'm serious. If you need help getting your girl out of a bad situation, hit me up."

"Thanks."

"What's her name?"

Bryce straightened his spine and held his gaze. "It's Alexis. Macey's sister."

James's eyes widened briefly, and he pressed his lips into a hard line. He slapped a twenty on the counter before giving Bryce's shoulder a squeeze. "Take care, man." He hustled out the door.

The waitress grinned as she picked up the money James had left. "Is he paying for yours too?"

"No, ma'am. I've got mine."

Her smiled widened as Bryce paid his tab, and he shuffled out of the restaurant. James was hiding something, like Macey and Luke and everyone else she'd gotten herself involved with. From the look on James's face, Alexis was mixed up in it too, and it seemed this Eric guy was at the center of the mess.

He got into his car and started the engine. It looked like he'd be putting his detective skills to the test on this one.

His frazzled nerves should have smoothed as he made

his way toward his home. Being alone inside his apartment always brought him a sense of calm, but the tension wound tighter as he pulled into the driveway and cut the engine. He kept adding pieces to the puzzle, but he couldn't get any of them to fit together.

He climbed out of the car and cut around the side of the house to the staircase, and his heart dropped into his shoes. A mass of white fur lay at the bottom of the steps, and icy dread clawed through his veins as he approached. *Please don't be Sam.*

His throat thickened. It was Sam.

Bryce dropped to his knees and put a hand on his dog's side. Sam's ribcage rose and fell with his shallow breaths, and he whimpered, lifting his head to look at his master.

"Aw, buddy. What happened to you?" Bryce ran his hands along the dog's fur, and Sam yelped as he touched his back leg. "Can you get up? Come here, boy." He scooted a few feet away and patted his legs to call his dog.

Sam wiggled and tried to push to his feet, but he let out an ear-piercing howl and crumpled to the ground.

"All right, goofball, let's get you to the doctor." He scooped the eighty-pound canine into his arms and carried him to the car. Shifting the dog's weight to one arm, he fumbled with the handle, cursing at the damn thing until he got it open.

Sam whined as Bryce positioned him on the back seat and unhooked the leash from his collar. "I'll be right back."

He shut the door and marched to the house. Michael was probably inside, crying on the couch. No telling how Sam had hurt his leg, but the kid would blame himself since it happened on his watch.

He banged on the door. "Hey, Michael? What happened to Sam?"

Silence answered.

He knocked again. Nothing.

Fishing his keys from his pocket, he unlocked the door and poked his head inside. "Michael?"

A lamp burned in the corner of the living room, but all the overhead lights were off. Pausing, he listened for sounds of movement, for any indication someone was home, but the apartment sat silent. Empty. He wiped his feet on the rug and crept inside the eerily quiet living room. His heart sprinted as thoughts of Michael's delicate mental state flashed through his mind. If the kid had done something to himself because Sam was hurt…

He shook the idea from his head and searched the place, finding every room empty. No sign of Michael anywhere. "What the hell?"

He locked the front door and dialed Michael's number as he paced to his car. Sam whimpered as he climbed into the driver's seat and started the engine. Michael didn't answer.

"Hey, Mike, it's Bryce. I found Sam hurt at the bottom of the steps and wanted to check in with you. Call me as soon as you can."

He shifted into drive and headed to the emergency vet as he dialed Karen. The call went straight to voicemail, so he left her a message too. Hopefully they were together, but Karen would have called if she'd known Sam was hurt.

Maybe Michael left the door open, and Sam escaped that way, tumbling down the stairs on his way to freedom. But why would the leash have been attached?

If Michael had left in a hurry, he might have forgotten to unhook the leash and left the door ajar. It was the only logical explanation…but Bryce had glanced up at his apartment from the bottom of the stairs. The door was closed.

He tried both their numbers again, hanging up before the voicemail greeting ended, and then carried Sam into the clinic. The technicians took the dog to the back to sedate him and run tests and X-rays, and Bryce dropped into a chair in the waiting room.

He called Alexis first, but the call went straight to voicemail, so he tried Michael and Karen's cells again. Nothing. He sent all three of them a text before calling the landline at Karen's house. The machine picked up, so he left another message there before shoving his phone in his pocket and wringing his hands.

He took a deep breath, and the scents of lavender and antiseptic greeted his senses. A fake plant stood in the corner of the room next to a short table littered with magazines. A woman and her young daughter occupied two chairs on the opposite wall, the mother reading quietly from a thick-paged book.

He could call Macey, but what good would that do? He'd already pissed her off with his cult comment, and James's strange responses during their conversation had him all the more suspicious.

Bryce had never felt more alone in his life.

Alexis showered and shoved her bloodied clothes into the washer before ducking back into the bathroom and tossing another tampon wrapper into the trash to keep up the charade. With Bryce's gun hidden at the bottom of her backpack, she shoved the bag under Eric's bed and cringed. She'd have to crawl under these blankets with the dickhead tonight if her plan was going to work. She might even have to make out with him. Her stomach lurched, and she covered her mouth with her hand as she shuffled toward the sound-proof room.

She and Justin had cleaned up the bloody mess while Eric jerked off in the bathroom. *Sick bastard.* And now Trevor was probably back with whatever kid Eric planned to turn. Alexis gritted her teeth. She would *not* let him hurt a child.

Glancing toward the bed, she eyed the edge of the backpack beneath it. She could grab the gun and end this now, but she'd only get one shot. If she fired and missed, she'd be dead. Since she'd never shot a gun before, it was better to wait until he slept tonight. She swallowed the sour taste from her mouth and turned away from the bedroom.

Twisting the knob, she pushed open the door, and her heart shot into her throat. Michael sat alone on the floor, gagged, his back against the wall, his hands tied to his ankles.

"Oh, no." Alexis ran to him, dropping to her knees at his side and pulling the gag from his mouth. "Are you okay?" She put up a finger to keep him from answering and rushed to slam the door, blocking the sound from escaping. "Did he hurt you?"

Tears collected on his lower lids. "I'm okay. He knocked me out with something on a rag, but Sam…" His lip trembled and the tears spilled down his cheeks. "He hurt Sergeant Samuels' dog." He sucked in a shaky breath. "Sam was trying to protect me, and he kicked him. I heard something snap, and he yelped, and I tried to help him but…" He bit his lip.

She clenched her teeth. "He won't get away with this." The urge to grab the gun and end this now grew palpable in her core. Her legs tensed, her body willing her to follow through, but she fought the impulse. She had to wait for the right moment.

Squaring her gaze on Michael, she put a hand on his shoulder. "I'm going to help you, but I need you to play along, okay? And when I tell you to run, you need to *run*. No questions asked. Got it?"

He nodded.

The knob turned, and Eric sauntered into the room. "Damn. He's awake." He closed the door. "I wanted to make this fast, so you don't get all teary and soft on me."

Alexis shot to her feet, clenching her hands at her sides. "Leave him out of this, Eric."

"Oh, he's in this, babe. He was in it the moment you ran to that cop for help. Now everyone he knows is in this."

She swallowed her bitter anger and softened her gaze. Eric liked it when she seemed weak. "Please don't hurt him. I'm here. You got what you wanted, and I promise I won't leave you again." She unclenched her fists and clasped them together over her heart, batting her lashes to add to the effect.

He hesitated, his mouth opening a few times as he attempted to speak, and her pulse thrummed.

"I'm sorry, Eric. I'm here." She held out her hands to him. *Please let this act work.*

His brows slammed together in a scowl. "Your body may be here, but your mind ain't." He cracked his neck, and shimmering vibration engulfed him as he shifted into wolf form.

Michael screamed.

"Damn it, Eric." Alexis widened her stance, blocking the kid from his attack.

Eric rocked back, ready to spring, and Alexis had two choices: she could shift and fight him, or she could get torn apart on his way to his target.

"I promise I won't hurt you," she said over her shoulder to Michael before calling on her own wolf and shifting form. Crouching low, she growled a warning but didn't advance. Even with all her strength intact, she didn't stand a chance against a powerful wolf like Eric.

He lunged, feigning right then left. Alexis snapped her jaws, purposely missing on each advance. He was toying with her, and she refused to give him a reason to attack.

Ears back, Eric lowered his head and let out a menacing growl. Michael whimpered behind her, but she didn't dare turn her back on the wolf to check on him. She growled in return, and Eric blew out a hard breath through his nostrils before backing up and sitting on his haunches. He tilted his head, and his body shimmered as he shifted back to human form and laughed. "Come on, babe. Let's not fight."

This was her chance. If she leapt for him now and went straight for the throat, she could take him out before he knew what hit him. But the uncontrollable sobs from the terrified teenager behind her glued her to the spot.

She'd wait. Bide her time like she originally planned. Another warning rumbled from her chest before she shifted to human form. "Let him go." With her wolf hovering near the surface, her voice sounded more like a growl.

"He's seen our wolf forms now. You'll be in deep shit too, if we do that."

She knelt beside Michael, and he recoiled from her touch. "It's okay. I promise no one will hurt you."

He stared at her with wide eyes. "Are you a…are you a werewolf?"

She pressed her lips together and gave a tight nod.

"You'll be one too, by the time I'm done with you." Eric rose to his feet as a speaker in the corner of the room buzzed. He grumbled and pulled his phone from his pocket. "Goddammit. It's my old man."

He slammed his phone onto a table and grabbed two guitars from the wall, shoving them at Alexis. "Hold these."

He yanked the ties from Michael's wrists and ankles and dragged him to his feet. "Give him the bass. Sit there and pretend like you're practicing." He raked his hands through his hair and mumbled as he stomped out the door. "Piece of shit's got the worst timing."

As soon as the door shut, Alexis swiped Eric's phone from the table. It took her less than a minute to download a rideshare app, connect it to his credit card stored in his virtual wallet, and request a car.

She crept toward the door and peeked down the hall. No sign of the men. Eric must have wrangled his dad into the living room.

Motioning for Michael, she whispered, "Hang a right and go out the back door. Keep running straight through the neighbor's yard and you'll come to a road. Go left and head for the convenience store on the corner. A rideshare car will be there to pick you up, and it's taking you to O'Malley's Pub."

He furrowed his brow as his frightened gaze danced about the room. "A bar? I don't understand."

"Ask for Macey Mason when you get there. You know who she is, right?"

"Sergeant Samuels' old partner."

"Right. Now, listen to me, Michael, this is important. You need to tell her *everything* you saw here."

His eyes widened. "Even about how you…?"

"She's my sister. She knows what I am."

He nodded.

"Don't tell Sergeant Samuels anything, okay? He doesn't know, and it's important no one else ever finds out. For my safety and yours. Don't talk about this to *anyone* but Macey. Do you understand?"

"Yes, ma'am. I'll tell Detective Mason everything, and I won't say a word to Sergeant Samuels."

She leaned into the hallway. "Run, Michael. Don't stop until you get in the car. Go!"

Stepping away from the door, she shoved Michael through. He stumbled in the hall, catching himself on the wall before regaining his footing and barreling toward the exit. Alexis held her breath as he fumbled with the knob, and when he finally threw the door open, a chime sounded from the hall speaker.

Alexis's heart pounded against her ribs as she closed the door and settled onto a chair with the guitar in her lap.

Eric stormed into the room with a look of fury in his eyes so hot he could have shot flames. "Where's the kid?"

David stepped in behind him and narrowed his eyes at Alexis.

She plastered a huge smile on her face. "His mom called, and he had to go home." She turned to Eric's dad. "It's good to see you again, David. What brings you out to our neck of the woods?"

"I'm checking up on my son."

Eric's hands clenched into fists, and a vein in his forehead throbbed. "And everything is fine, so you can go now."

Alexis stood and hung the guitar on the wall. "Don't be rude, Eric. He drove all this way." Eric couldn't do a damn thing while his dad was around, so the longer she could keep David in the house, the more time Michael would have to get away. "Why don't you stay and visit a while? Can I get you a beer or some coffee?" She padded toward the door.

David cut a suspicious gaze between Eric and her. "I'll take a beer."

"How about you, babe?" She slapped Eric's ass on her way to the hall. "Want a cold one?"

"Sure." The word was barely audible over the sound of his grinding teeth.

The men shuffled into the living room as she popped the tops on two cans of Bud Light and handed them the beers. David settled into a recliner, and Eric glared at her as he dropped onto the sofa. She flashed him a smirk and perched on the arm of the couch.

David's gaze bore into her as he set his beer on the coffee table and crossed his arms. "After that story you told me about my son, I wonder why you're here."

She swallowed, lowering her gaze and trying to look ashamed. "I'm sorry about that. We had a little tiff, and I was mad at him. I thought getting him into trouble would make up for him hitting my friend, but…" She glanced at Eric. "It was a stupid thing for me to do. I apologized, and he forgave me. Didn't you, babe?"

Eric grunted in response.

David eyed her skeptically. "So you two are together now?"

Forcing a smile, she rested a hand on Eric's shoulder. "'Til death do us part."

She managed to keep Eric's dad in the house for another half hour, and by the time he left, two more veins had popped out on Eric's forehead. He watched from the window as David drove away, and as he turned to face her, his face flushed red.

Her blood turned to ice in her veins, but she held her ground, planting her feet firmly on the floor and lifting her chin defiantly. Eric backhanded her, and searing pain exploded in her cheek, the momentum of his swing knocking her to carpet.

"You'll pay for this." He patted his pockets. "Where the hell is my phone?" He stomped down the hall and returned with the device. "You ordered a car with my phone?"

"You hid mine."

His eyes narrowed. "You sent him to O'Malley's? Isn't that the pack's headquarters?"

"He's being protected now."

"Like hell he is." Growling, he punched some buttons on the screen. "The kid got away. Go find him." He paused as the other person spoke. "I don't give a damn what you're doing; go get that kid."

CHAPTER EIGHTEEN

BRYCE LIFTED HIS HEAD FROM HIS HANDS AS A VET tech shuffled into the waiting room. She had a warm smile, and she looked him in the eyes, putting his fears at ease. "Mr. Samuels?"

"How's my boy?"

"His leg is broken and a few ribs are bruised, but he's otherwise healthy. He's sedated, and we'd like to keep him overnight for observation." She offered him a tablet to sign.

He scribbled his name on the screen. "Can you tell how it broke? Did he fall down the stairs?"

Her eyes tightened. "From the X-ray, it looks like some sort of blunt force trauma caused the break. A boot or something else hard."

He sucked in a sharp breath. Whoever hurt his dog would pay.

"We'll call you when he wakes up and let you know when you can get him."

"Thank you, ma'am." Bryce nodded and turned for the

door. As he exited the building, his phone buzzed, and he fished it from his pocket. Karen's name lit up the screen.

He pressed the device to his ear. "Where are you? Where's Michael?"

She paused. "I'm at work. I was in a meeting when you called, and Michael's at home. Is everything okay?"

Dread sank in his stomach like a brick. "He's not there, and I found Sam at the foot of the stairs with his leg broken and the leash attached to his collar."

She didn't respond.

"Karen? Have you heard from him today?"

"No." Her voice was a whisper.

He scrubbed a hand down his face and climbed into his car. "Meet me at the station. We'll file a missing person's report."

Silence.

He slammed the door and buckled his seatbelt. "Karen? Did you hear me?"

"Yeah. I'll meet you there."

He tossed his phone in the cupholder and sped to the station. When he arrived, Karen was already talking with an officer. Tears dripped from her eyes, and she threw her arms around Bryce when he approached.

"He hasn't been missing for twenty-four hours." She sobbed into his shirt.

Bryce narrowed his gaze at the officer. "He's a suicide risk. File the report."

Karen sobbed harder.

The officer nodded. "Yes, sir. Ma'am, can you give me a description."

Releasing her hold on Bryce's shirt, she wiped her eyes. "He's tall. A little chunky."

"He's one of mine," Bryce said. "Michael Benson. The

report should have everything you need. And put in a call to the area hospitals; he might be injured."

Karen stared blankly at the wall as she sank into a chair. Lacing her fingers together, she clenched them tightly until the tips turned purple. "We're moving."

Bryce sat next to her. "Where are you going?"

She inhaled a shaky breath. "To stay with my mom in Texas. I thought it would be good for Michael to get a clean start. I put in my two-week notice today." She covered her mouth and sobbed.

"Hey." Bryce rubbed a hand across her back. "We're going to find him."

Her phone rang, and she yanked it from her purse. "It's our landline." She held it to her ear. "Michael?"

She let out an enormous sigh and leaned back into the seat, her shoulders slumping in relief. "Are you there alone?"

Her brow furrowed as she listened. "Okay. Stay put. I'm on my way." She shoved the phone into her purse and shot to her feet. "He's okay. He's at home. There's an officer with him."

Bryce glanced at the dispatcher, who lifted his hands and shook his head. "Which officer?"

"I don't know." She strode to the front door.

Bryce followed her home and stood in the doorway as she hugged her son. She showered him in questions and affections, and Bryce cut his gaze to James, who stood in the living room. *Officer, my ass.*

"Good to see you, Sergeant Samuels." James held out his hand to shake. Bryce accepted. "Detective Mason wants to speak with you ASAP. She's at home, waiting."

Bryce lowered his voice. "What the hell is going on?"

James glanced at Karen and gave him a pointed look.

"I'm not at liberty to discuss the case, but Detective Mason will fill you in on the details."

"I'm so sorry, Sergeant Samuels." Michael hung his head and shuffled toward him. "Sam fell down the stairs, and when I couldn't get him to stand up, I freaked out and ran away. Detective Mason found me by the riverbank, and she brought me home." He rubbed at his nose as he spoke, looking anywhere *but* at Bryce. "Is Sam…" He glanced into Bryce's eyes and looked away. "Is he okay?"

"He will be." Bryce glared at James, who clamped his mouth shut. The kid was lying. James was lying. The whole story smelled like a wharf in the summertime.

Karen wrapped her arm around Michael's shoulders. "We'll pay Sam's vet bill."

"I'm sorry." Michael stared at the floor.

"That won't be necessary. I'm glad you're okay." He reached for the doorknob. "If you've got this under control…"

"We're fine. Thank you for your help, Bryce. Officer." Karen nodded at James.

"A word, *officer?*" He jerked his head, silently telling James to follow him outside. Stepping off the porch, he shuffled around to the stairs.

"We've got a man watching each side of the house. They're safe." James handed him a slip of paper. "My number. I meant what I said about getting your girl back, but Luke can't know."

He squinted at the paper. "Luke?"

"Say the word, and I'll be there." James climbed into a pickup truck and slammed the door, revving the engine before Bryce's mind caught up with the conversation. Why did it matter if Luke knew? And what *men* were watching the house?

He got into his car and dialed Macey's number. "What the hell's going on, Mace? Since when is James an officer of the law?"

She paused. "Not over the phone. Come to my house."

He let out a slow breath. "Is Michael safe?"

"We've got...people...watching him. Get over here. Now." She hung up.

Bryce reversed out of the driveway and hightailed it to the French Quarter. His emotions flipflopped between satisfaction that his suspicions about Macey and her new friends were well-founded and sickening dread for the same reason.

He parked two blocks from her house and hoofed it up the sidewalk to her front porch. As he lifted his hand to pound on the door, it swung open and Macey ushered him inside. Luke lounged on the sofa in the living room, and Macey sank down next to him, gesturing to the chair for Bryce to sit.

He paced in front of the coffee table instead. "I want answers, Mace. You've got a man impersonating an officer. Michael's lying about where he's been. James is lying. You. Alexis. Shit, everyone's lying." He threw his arms in the air. "What the hell is going on?"

Macey tugged on her bottom lip and glanced at Luke. "You're going to want to sit down for this."

"I don't want to sit down." He didn't mean to yell, but goddammit, he needed the truth.

Luke leaned forward, resting a protective hand on Macey's knee.

Bryce took a slow, deep breath, trying to calm his sprinting heart. Unclenching his fists, he lowered himself onto the chair and rested his palms on the arms. He pried his teeth apart and tried to keep his voice calm. "I'm sorry. Will you please tell me what's going on?"

Macey sat up straight. "You were right about everything."

"I…" Her confession took the breath from his chest. "What do you mean everything?"

Luke grasped her hand and nodded. "Tell him. It's time he found out."

"You accused me of being different since I met Luke, and you're right. I am. Or…I haven't changed, but I finally understand *what* I am."

"*What* you are? Mace…" He squeezed his eyes shut and pinched the bridge of his nose. "Will you please try to make some sense? I need facts. What happened to Michael? Why is James posing as a police officer? Why are you ignoring the autopsy reports for the bodies we pulled out of the river?" He scrubbed a hand down his face. "And what's going on with Alexis?"

She locked eyes with him. "Werewolves."

"What?"

"We're werewolves."

He held her gaze, waiting for her to crack a smile or roll her eyes and tell him he'd been overreacting. But she returned his stare, her eyes tightening as if she were willing him to accept the absurd remark.

Blowing out a hard breath, he leaned back into the chair and crossed his arms. "C'mon. Be serious." Did she take him for some kind of idiot? "Whatever you're involved in, it's affecting the people I care about. You can either tell me the truth, or I'll figure it out for myself." *Werewolves, my ass.*

She scooted to the edge of the couch and gave him a

sympathetic look. "This is going to require some open-mindedness, so please hear me out."

"My mind is open to facts. Tell me the truth."

"We're werewolves." Her face held the most serious expression he'd ever seen, but there was no way.

He threw his arms into the air. "This was a waste of time. I'm going to get a *real* officer to look out for Michael, and I'm going to get Alexis back." He shoved to his feet.

"Sit down, Bryce." Luke's voice boomed with so much authority Bryce planted his ass in the seat without thinking twice. "My mate is trying to give you the facts, and you're going to listen to her."

His *mate?* What the…? And who the hell did this guy think he was giving an order like that? Bryce opened his mouth for a comeback, but Macey beat him to it.

"It's okay, hon. I've got this." She patted Luke's knee and scooted closer to Bryce, turning to him again. "Are you ready to listen?"

"Yeah, sure. Why not?" She'd probably spin some crazy story about magical creatures lurking in the shadows all around that no one had ever seen, but maybe he'd be able to glean a few bits of actual information from the tale.

"You believe in my ability to read spirit energy, right?"

"I've seen you do it. Of course I do."

"And you remember Chase's wife, Rain? She's a witch; she can cast spells."

He nodded. "She told me spells are like prayers, but they're something else, aren't they?"

"They're a way of manipulating energy. Magic is, at its core, energy manipulation."

Crossing his arms, he arched an eyebrow. "What are you trying to say?"

"Magic is real."

Had she told him that a week ago, he'd never have believed it. Hell, he didn't believe in ghosts until he'd seen how she could read spirit energy. But after the way Alexis healed his burns with a simple touch, he couldn't deny it anymore. "I know. Alexis said you were related to witches."

"We are, way back in the family tree." She furrowed her brow. "What else did she tell you about us?"

He shrugged. "Nothing I didn't already know about your parents dying when you were young. And she showed me her healing powers."

Her eyes widened. "Healing powers? When she was hurt?"

"Yeah. Then she healed me when I was hurt."

Macey gave Luke a quizzical look, and he shrugged. "It's not unheard of," he said. "The witch genes could be active in her system."

She shook her head. "Anyway, you *do* believe in magic, whether you want to admit it or not."

He had no problem admitting to things that could be proven. "Go on."

"Do you remember last year, when those women claimed some kind of animal saved them from the attackers?"

He closed his eyes for a long blink. "I remember."

"And then I saw a wolf in the woods behind the crime scene?"

A lump formed in his throat. This story was starting to make too much sense. She couldn't be serious.

"That wolf was Luke. I didn't know that he…that *we*…were werewolves at the time. Once I figured it out, everything fell into place."

"Hold on, now. You had me going for a minute there, Mace, but how could you be a werewolf and not know it? Do you black out every time you sprout fur and forget?"

"Only the first-born child of a werewolf couple can shift," Luke explained. "Macey was raised by humans, and Alexis went rogue as soon the change came, so she never knew until they reunited."

"Wha—?" He clamped his mouth shut. Questions ricocheted around in his head, but he couldn't grab on to one long enough to speak it coherently. Luckily, Macey knew him well enough to give him the answers he couldn't ask for.

"A rogue is a werewolf who doesn't belong to a pack. Alexis didn't know what she was until the first time she shifted when she was thirteen. She freaked and ran away and has been living on her own ever since."

His mind didn't want to believe it, but somewhere deep in his soul it made sense. Why the hell would something so ridiculous make sense? He'd been working too hard. Too many distractions had his thoughts wound up in a jumbled mess. He needed sleep. Or an appointment with a psychiatrist. "You're telling me that Alexis...is a werewolf?"

"She is."

He shook his head. Nonsense. It was all nonsense. "Werewolves aren't real."

"We are."

He crossed his arms. It wasn't possible. "I'll believe it when I see it."

Macey looked at Luke. "That's your cue."

"I'm on it." Luke stood and strode down the hall.

Leaning toward him, Macey took Bryce's hand as he uncrossed his arms. He hadn't realized how cold his own had turned until the warmth from her palm seeped into his skin. "It took a lot of convincing for me too," she said, "but I think this will do it."

A shuffling noise sounded from the hallway, and in padded the biggest wolf he'd ever seen. Light-brown fur covered its massive body, and as it opened its mouth to pant, fangs the size of daggers filled its enormous maw.

Bryce's heart rate kicked up, and his muscles tensed, ready for fight or flight…he wasn't sure which. "What the hell?"

The wolf approached Macey and sat at her feet as she rested a hand on its neck. "This is Luke."

"No, it's not. It's a pet. A mutated Siberian huskey or something." There was no way. That beast couldn't be… Luke wasn't a…

The animal licked Macey's cheek from jaw to ear. She laughed and pushed it away. "What have I told you about that? Show him."

The wolf paced to the center of the room. A shimmering mist gathered around its fur, almost as if it were glowing, but not quite. Bryce rubbed his eyes and looked again. As the mist grew denser and the image wavered, the wolf rose onto its back legs and transformed into…

"Luke?" Bryce's mouth fell open. How could he—? "But you—"

Luke laughed. "Convinced?"

It wasn't possible. Supernatural creatures didn't exist in this world, yet he'd watched a wolf turn into a man right before his eyes. He stood and paced toward Luke. Reaching out his arms, he hesitated before clapping his hands onto his shoulders.

All the blood in his body seemed to settle at his feet,

making his head spin. "It's really you." He dropped his arms to his sides.

"Yep." Luke patted him on the back and plopped onto the couch next to Macey.

"Do you believe it now?" she asked.

He sank into the chair. "I suppose I have no choice." He'd always been a *seeing is believing* guy, but what he just saw he couldn't explain. Focusing on *how* a giant wolf had waltzed into Macey's living room and transformed into her husband made his head spin. The important thing was that it *had* happened. He'd deal with the how later. "Can Alexis…?"

Macey nodded. "She's first-born, so she can shift."

How could his sweet, soft woman turn into a massive beast? "I never would've guessed it." He shook his head, trying to get the spinning thoughts to form into some sort of coherence. The woman he loved was a werewolf. His partner of the last seven years was a supernatural being. Her husband too. "James?"

"He's a werewolf," Macey said. "So is Chase. Michael is safe with them watching him, but Alexis is in trouble." Her expression softened. The mask of supernatural secrets she'd been keeping dissolved, allowing her true concern for her sister to finally show through, and his doubts about Macey dissolved right along with it.

Her words focused his thoughts into pinpoint precision. His world may have been turned upside down, but having the woman he loved safe and back in his arms was all that mattered. "I assume you're telling me all this because Eric is a werewolf too?"

Macey's expression turned grim. "I haven't been ignoring the autopsy reports on those bodies. I've been trying to cover them up. Those people were killed by werewolves."

"One werewolf in particular," Luke said.

"Eric." He fisted his hands on the arms of the chair. "Why would Alexis go back to him?"

Macey straightened. "We think she wants to stop him. He's trying to turn humans into werewolves, and those bodies we found in the river were his failed experiments."

Bryce rubbed his forehead in an attempt to slow the merry-go-round of thoughts whirling though his mind. "How do you know all this?"

"Michael didn't run away." She cringed. "One of Eric's men kidnapped him."

He slammed his fist on the arm of the chair. "The bastard hurt my dog too."

"Alexis helped Michael escape, and she sent him to me. I think she's safe for now, but we don't know how long he'll keep using her."

His stomach soured. "What's he using her for?"

"If she can heal other people like you say." She took a deep breath and looked at Luke. "He must be attacking the humans and having Alexis heal them in hopes that they'll turn into werewolves."

"Is that possible?" He cut his gaze between Luke and Macey. "Can someone be turned into a werewolf?"

"It's possible," Luke said. "But extremely unlikely to happen. The human would have to lose a considerable amount of blood and put up enough of a fight to cause some damage to the wolf attacking him. Get enough werewolf blood into your system, and it's going to wreak havoc on your DNA."

Bryce scrubbed a hand down his face. "Why attack people then? If he's kidnapping people and knocking them out, why not give them a blood transfusion and avoid the hassle?"

"He probably doesn't realize it's blood his victims need." Thor, Macey's brown tabby cat, jumped into Luke's lap, and he stroked its back. "Werewolves are taught two basic laws from the time we're old enough to understand them. One: never attack a human while in wolf form, unless it's a fight to the death. Two: our blood is sacred and can never be shared." He passed the cat to Macey. "Breaking those laws is punishable by death."

Macey set the cat on the floor. "He probably thinks the first law exists because people will turn into werewolves if they're attacked. Most people think that."

"The chance of survival after losing the amount of blood required for the change is slim," Luke said. "I know of four cases in our history of it actually happening, and they were hundreds of years ago, before the laws were in place."

Bryce's mind spun. It was all too much to process. More than his brain was ready or willing to comprehend. He focused on the one thing he did understand…his own heart. "I have to get Alexis out of there."

Macey swallowed. "Yes, you do."

"That guy is inhumanly strong. Tell me he's not bulletproof."

"You have to hit him in the head or the heart," Luke said. "Anywhere else, and he'll heal easily."

He rubbed the back of his neck. Murder wasn't on his radar, but it sounded like having a civilized conversation with this guy was off the table. He might have to shoot him in self-defense, but the ramifications of what he was about to do could end his career and land his ass in jail.

"Don't worry about the police." Macey seemed to have

read his mind. "Werewolves have been covering up our less-than-humanly-legal activity for hundreds of years. Get Alexis out. We'll take care of you."

He looked from Macey to Luke, and they both met his gaze with sincerity in their eyes. Bryce trusted them to his core, and it didn't matter what happened to him. Eric was a murderer who needed to be stopped, and Alexis needed saving.

"Got it." Bryce shot to his feet. "We'll stop by my place first to get my personal firearm. You've got your own, right, Mace?"

Macey glanced at Luke. "We…can't help you."

He cocked his head. "Why not? She's your sister."

"I know, but…" She sighed. "Eric belongs to the Biloxi pack. If New Orleans werewolves attack, it will start a war between the packs. He's not on our territory."

"War? We're talking about stopping a murderer, not assassinating a political figure."

"It is political. His father is second in command of Biloxi." Luke rose to his feet and paced in front of the couch. "We've contacted the Biloxi alpha and put a call in to the national congress. Our hands are tied until one of them acts."

"But he's killing people."

Macey stood next to Luke. "We don't have any proof."

"We have bodies."

Luke ran a hand through his hair. "And the connection to Eric is based on the word of a human who shouldn't know we exist."

"What about Alexis? She knows what's happening."

"She's…a rogue." Macey lowered her gaze to the floor.

Luke put his arm around her. "The word of a rogue is

as useful as wet toilet paper, no matter who she's related to."

"I don't believe this." Because Alexis wasn't a card-carrying member of their group, they refused to help her? Were they insane? Didn't they even care? He crossed his arms. "You called the Biloxi alpha. I want to talk to the man in charge of New Orleans."

"You are talking to him," Macey said. "Luke is the alpha."

"Damn it, Mace. Why didn't you tell me any of this before?"

"You were on a need-to-know basis."

"And I didn't need to know until now. I get it." It sucked that she'd kept so many secrets from him...but he got it. He reached for the doorknob. "James gave me his number."

Macey drew in a breath. "That's great. You should call him and go have a beer sometime."

"He said—"

She opened the door and pushed him through it. "I'm sure *whatever* reason he had for giving it to you is between you and him." Widening her eyes, she gave Bryce a pointed look before glancing at Luke and closing the door.

"Right." Luke couldn't know because he was the alpha and sending in pack members would start a war. James was offering his help outside the pack.

"I know it seems like I don't care about her, but this is a complicated situation. When a werewolf decides to go rogue, they understand that they're giving up all support from the pack. Alexis has had an open invitation to join us since the moment she came back into my life, but she's chosen to remain rogue."

He shook his head. "Doesn't matter. She's your blood."

"I know. That's why you *have* to help her. For seven years, I've trusted you with my own life. Now, I'm trusting you with my sister's."

"I'll get her out of there." Or he'd die trying.

Macey pulled him into a tight hug. "Be careful. You're living outside the law now."

"She's worth it." He patted her shoulder and stepped away. "I won't let her down."

CHAPTER NINETEEN

BRYCE CLIMBED INTO THE PASSENGER SEAT OF JAMES'S truck and slammed the door. He'd torn his bedroom apart looking for his Smith and Wesson when it wasn't in its drawer. His personal firearm was gone, and he hadn't misplaced it. He chewed the inside of his cheek. "If Alexis can turn into a wolf, why would she need a gun?"

James arched an eyebrow. "Good question. A werewolf using a gun is like cheating. Our teeth and claws are our weapons. My guess is that she knows she can't beat him in a fair fight."

His mind flashed back to the scuffle in the parking lot, and he cringed. One punch had landed Bryce on his ass. "How does werewolf justice work? Since this guy's part of another pack, if they don't want to stop him, he can keep on killing people?"

James started the engine and backed out of the driveway. "Unless another pack can prove he's breaking our laws, attacking him would be equivalent to attacking his pack. That's why I'm going rogue tonight." He shifted into drive and headed for Pearl River.

"What will happen to you if Luke finds out you're helping me?"

Resting his left elbow on the window frame, James rubbed at the scruff on his face. "Depending on how far south this all goes, I could serve time in the pit."

"The pit?"

"Werewolf prison. A human cell won't hold a supernatural being." He cast a sideways glance toward him before focusing on the road.

Bryce stared out the window as they exited the residential area of the city and entered the highway. "You're risking jail time to help me. Why?"

His brow furrowed as if the question confused him. "It's what friends do."

Friends. "Thanks, man." He'd have to buy him a beer when this was through.

The corner of James's mouth twitched. "Jail time is better than execution. That's a possibility too."

He balked. Firm laws and harsh punishments served their purpose, but execution for trying to save someone from a murderer? What kind of man was Macey married to? "Luke would kill you for this?"

"Our laws are strict to keep our existence a secret. They've worked for hundreds of years." He chuckled. "Our alpha is bound by the national congress to enforce them, but he knows when to look the other way. Sometimes laws have to be broken."

"Yeah, I guess they do." He'd spent his entire life playing by the rules, doing what everyone expected of him. Human laws had served him well, but the world as he knew it ceased to exist a few hours ago. Where did he fit in now?

He was in love with a werewolf. How could he

compete with a supernatural being? What could he offer a woman who came from a magical world he'd had no idea existed? A sinking sensation formed in the pit of his stomach. "What if she doesn't want to be saved?" He looked at James. "What if she went back to Eric because she really does want to be with him?"

"She doesn't want to be with that asshole. Believe me."

He wanted to believe him. To believe he hadn't imagined the connection he'd felt with Alexis. But the rug of life had been yanked out from under him, and he didn't have a clue what was real and what wasn't anymore. "How do you know?"

"I know Alexis. She's got a good thing with you."

He rested his arm on the edge of the window and watched the trees zooming by in a blur. "Is it even allowed? If she were in a pack and followed the rules, would she be allowed to date me?"

"We can date anyone we want. We can't reveal our true selves unless we plan to take the person as a mate, but since you're already in on the secret, you're good to go."

A weight lifted from his shoulders, but his stomach tensed as they exited the highway and turned onto Eric's street. James tightened his grip on the steering wheel, and Bryce glanced at his four-fingered hand. "Mind if I ask what happened to you?"

James loosened his grip and flexed his fingers. "Construction accident."

"I thought werewolves were fast healers."

"We are, but we can't regrow limbs." He cut the wheel to the right and stopped in a grocery store parking lot. "We'll walk from here."

Bryce tucked his service weapon into the waistband of his jeans, and they trekked into the field behind the store.

He'd left his badge and holster at home. His cuffs too. He'd lose his job if he got caught in an act of vigilante justice. Hell, he might even lose his life.

The nearly-full moon hung high in the night sky, casting a silver glow on the damp grass. Shadows danced around his peripheral vision, and his pulse thrummed in his ears. If werewolves existed, what other kinds of monsters lurked in the darkness? A shudder ran down his spine. He didn't want to know.

A rustle sounded in the grass, and he jerked his head toward the noise, his hand instinctively reaching for his firearm. Adrenaline coursed through his veins, setting him on edge.

"It's a fox." James stopped walking and pointed. "Look closely and you'll see the light reflect in its eyes."

Bryce repositioned his gun in his pants and squinted into the darkness. A little flash of something glinted in the moonlight, and a shadow darted through the grass. "I suppose you have some kind of enhanced werewolf vision?"

"It's better in wolf form, but yeah. You'll never see a shifter needing glasses."

He huffed and continued his trek toward the house. The eye surgery he'd had a few years back had turned his own night vision to shit. Add that to the list of reasons he couldn't compete with a werewolf, and he began to wonder exactly what Alexis saw in him.

As the house came into view, James let out a whistle. "Looks like our friend has company."

Alexis's car sat behind the Mustang, and an F-150 had parked in the grass by the road. They crept into the yard and scanned the outside of the house. The massive pine trees appeared black against the moonlit sky, and light burned in the living room window. No security cameras hung from the eaves, and no motion-sensor lights turned on as they approached.

"Do you know if he has a security system?" James asked.

"He's got a video doorbell, the kind you can easily install yourself, but I haven't noticed anything else."

James nodded. "Can you pick a lock?"

"If I had the tools."

He pulled a black bag from his pocket and handed it to Bryce. "I'll knock on the door and keep them occupied. You go in through the back and get Alexis out. Got your phone on you?"

Bryce patted his pocket.

"Get pictures. Any kind of evidence you can find. Paperwork, blood, bodies, whatever. If we can prove what he's doing, the pack can move in and end it."

Bryce took a deep breath, centering himself, and the nervous jitters he'd experienced on the way over dissolved, leaving behind nothing but the calm before the storm. "And if there's a confrontation…"

"We end him."

"I'm glad we're on the same page."

James darted around to the front door, and Bryce slipped into the backyard. He pulled the tools out of the bag and jimmied them into the lock. The faint sound of voices emanated from the front, and the tool slipped from his sweaty fingers. He cursed under his breath and wiped his palms on his jeans before retrieving the instrument and shoving it back into the lock.

After a few minutes of fumbling, the bolt disengaged and he pushed the door open. An alert chimed in the darkened hallway, and he held his breath as the voices stopped.

"What the hell's going on?" Eric's voice boomed.

"Stop!" Alexis screamed, and the sound of scuffling ensued. Then a growl. Then a snarl, and the scuffle turned into a full-blown brawl.

Holy shit, he was about to witness a werewolf fight.

Instinct to break it up drew him toward the fray, but he stopped as the sound of footsteps thudded toward him. They needed evidence. He leaned into a door on the left and twisted the knob. Locked.

"Bryce!" Alexis whispered as she ran toward him. "What are you doing here? You have to leave. It's not safe." She tried to push him down the hall, but he caught her in his arms and held her to his chest.

Relief unfurled in his gut, and he pressed his lips against her hair. "I'm here to bring you home." The sounds of snarling and jaws snapping echoed from the living room, and he tightened his arms around her.

"I can't go home. Not until I stop Eric." She pushed him toward the back door. "Please go."

He gripped her shoulders. "I know what you are. I know you're a werewolf."

She glanced behind her toward the living room. Someone yelped as glass crashed on the floor. "Then you should know how dangerous it is for you to be here. I promise I'll come home, okay? Let me finish this."

"What do you need to finish, babe?" Eric stood at the end of the hall and crossed his arms over his barrel of a chest.

Bryce shoved her behind his back and leveled his gun at the bastard's heart.

Eric smirked and raised his hands. "Aren't you going to

read me my rights first, officer? Your case will never stand in a court of law if you don't."

His finger hovered over the trigger. "What you're doing is so far beyond the law that I've appointed myself judge and jury."

He laughed. "If that's how you want to play..." Eric's body shimmered, and in an instant, he transformed into a wolf. Dark-gray fur rolled over his massive body, standing in a ridge along his back. Baring his razor-sharp fangs, he prowled toward them.

Bryce's heart slammed into his throat, and he squeezed the trigger, firing a shot into the wolf's shoulder.

Eric paused and shook his coat as if the bullet had merely stung his skin. Then he rocked back on his haunches and sprang.

"No!" Alexis screamed as she shoved Bryce against the wall and turned into a wolf in mid-air. She lunged at Eric, and Bryce stood motionless as they tumbled over each other snapping and biting at their necks. Alexis yelped, and blood matted in her sandy-colored fur above her shoulder.

Gripping his gun in both hands, Bryce pointed it at the bigger wolf, but he couldn't get a clear shot. A gray wolf appeared behind them, but a black one latched onto its neck and dragged it into the living room. Bryce couldn't tell which one was James, so he'd have to let them fight it out. But Alexis, he would save...if she'd get out of his way.

"Alexis, move," he shouted.

She faltered, whipping her head around to look at him, and Eric latched on to her neck. Lifting her from the ground, he hurled her massive body toward Bryce, and she slammed into him, the momentum busting open the door.

He landed on his back, with Alexis the wolf on top of him, and the air left his lungs in a gush as the gun skidded across the floor. Alexis scrambled to her feet, and Bryce blinked until his vision focused on his surroundings. Musical instruments hung from the padded walls, and the sounds of the other werewolf fight ceased. This must have been the sound-proof room she'd told him about.

Eric's massive body filled the doorway, blood matting his dark fur on his neck and shoulder. Alexis barreled toward him, but he tossed her aside as if she weighed nothing, slamming her into the wall.

"Alexis!" *That's it. This guy is dead.* He scrambled for his gun, but Eric leapt at him, clamping his jaws onto his shoulder. Bryce let out a garbled yelp as dagger-like teeth sliced through skin and muscle, shooting searing pain through his core. With a jerk of his head, Eric dragged him away from the gun and swiped his claws across his stomach.

The flesh on Bryce's abdomen ripped open, the wolf's claws penetrating to the organs beneath. Pain exploded through his gut, first as the pressure of a Mack truck rolling over him, and then the burning, stinging sensation and fear that his guts would spill onto the floor. He groaned as the massive wolf loomed over him, his body growing cold beneath the animal's heated breath. Paralyzed in agony, Bryce gasped for air and turned his head toward where Alexis had lain, his only thought that she should be the last thing he saw before he left the world.

She was gone.

His vision tunneled, and he straightened his head to look into his killer's eyes. Eric reared back, opening his maw for another strike, and time slowed to a crawl. Numbness spread through Bryce's body as he stared into the werewolf's open mouth. Hot saliva dripped from Eric's canines and splashed onto Bryce's cheek. His heart should have been pounding as the teeth neared his throat, but the sluggish muscle barely beat in his chest. He couldn't move. Couldn't fight back, so he prayed for a quick ending.

The explosion of a gunshot pierced the room, and the wolf's head jerked to the side. Another shot, and it went limp, collapsing on top of him, the pressure shooting another burst of agonizing pain through Bryce's body. Stars danced in his wavering vision as the weight of the wolf was lifted, and Alexis's emerald eyes came into view.

Worry knit her brow as she knelt beside him, and he tried to focus on the beauty of her human face. Her flawless skin. Her cropped, blonde hair sticking out in every direction. Darkness closed in around him as he opened his mouth, and no words would pass from his lips. Alexis was alive—uninjured—and he'd go to his grave with the satisfaction of knowing that she'd survived.

She rested her hands on his stomach. "He got you pretty good." Her lip trembled, and a tear slid down her cheek. "You've lost a lot of blood, but I'm going to fix you, and then we'll get you to the hospital. Hold on for me, okay, Bryce?"

He wanted to nod. To tell her yes, he would hold on. That he'd never leave her. But his head spun and his lids fluttered shut, betraying his intentions. His abdomen tingled where she touched him. He forced his eyes open to meet her gaze, and streams of tears ran in rivulets down her face.

"James!" she screamed, her voice hoarse and trembling. "If you're done with Trevor, I could use some help." Her skin paled, and she swayed as she moved toward his shoulder. She closed her eyes and tipped to the side, catching herself with her hand before her head smacked the tile floor.

"Alexis." Bryce's voice came out as a croak.

"I'm here." She sat up and clutched her head. "I healed your stomach. Your shoulder's in pretty bad shape too."

"Stop." He forced the words through his thickening throat. "You're draining yourself."

"I'll be fine." Though her voice sounded calm, it didn't mask the anguish in her eyes. "Let me heal you so we can go home."

He touched his stomach. Cooling blood congealed on his torn shirt, but he couldn't find a trace of injury. Lifting a hand to her face, he brushed the hair from her forehead, leaving a swipe of red across her skin, and she closed her eyes, nuzzling her cheek into his palm. "Where is home?" he asked.

She smiled weakly. "It's anywhere you are, dummy."

A werewolf snarled behind her, and as she turned toward it, the wolf lunged, clamping onto her throat. It shook her violently, dropping her on top of Bryce, and her body fell limp. Lifeless.

The growl of a second wolf and sounds of another fight retreating through the open door barely registered in his mind, and the pain shooting through his shoulder paled in comparison to the agony of his heart wrenching in his chest.

"Alexis?" His throat thickened, and tears stung his eyes as he tried to move her with his good arm. Her head lolled like her neck had been snapped, and his breath hitched. *No.*

She couldn't be dead. She was his soul mate. The

woman he was meant to spend the rest of his life with. "Darlin', you have to heal yourself." He stroked her matted hair and then rested his hand on her back, searching for the gentle rise and fall to prove she was breathing. That she was healing.

She lay utterly still.

This couldn't be happening. She had to live. This amazing woman who could heal with a touch had accepted him for who he was, and she'd taught him to accept himself. She meant the world to him; she couldn't be gone. "Come on, sweetheart. Don't leave me now." Damn it, he needed her. Tears rolled down his cheeks, choking his words. "I love you."

When she didn't respond, a sob bubbled up from somewhere deep in his soul—the sound of his heart breaking beyond repair.

He nudged her, and blood gushed from her wound, flowing into the gash on his shoulder.

It seared the exposed muscle, and the fiery sensation shot down his arm and into his chest, spreading through his body as if he were being burned from the inside out. He tried to scream, but he couldn't get any air into his scorched lungs. An inferno raged inside his body, and agony consumed him as a burst of blinding white light flashed in his vision.

Then the world went dark.

CHAPTER TWENTY

ALEXIS GASPED AND SHOT TO A SITTING POSITION. "Bryce!" Her heart sprinted as she clutched a soft fabric in her hands and blinked her eyes into focus. "Where?"

"He's here." Macey sat next to the bed and gestured to the spot beside Alexis.

A knot formed in her throat as she shifted her gaze to Bryce. He lay on his back, his arms by his sides, a peaceful expression softening his handsome features. Too peaceful. "Is he…?"

"He's alive."

"Oh, thank God." She reached for him, running her fingers down the side of his face, and a tingling sensation seeped into her skin. She cupped his cheek in her hand, and the faint prickling shimmied up her arm. "Why do I feel magic in him?"

"We were hoping you could answer that." Luke stood beside Macey and rested a hand on her shoulder. "James found you both unconscious on the floor. He thought you were dead."

She looked from Luke to Macey and finally took in

her surroundings. Sheer drapes covered a bay window, and morning sunlight filtered through the glass, softly illuminating the bedroom. She sat in their bed, the alabaster duvet covering her legs. The white cotton T-shirt and flannel pajamas pants she wore didn't belong to her, and as she ran her fingers through her hair, flakes of dried blood drifted onto her lap.

Blood. Her breath caught. *Bryce's shoulder.*

She put her hand on his chest and gazed at his unmarred skin. No trace of the bite marks remained. Tugging on the neck of his shirt, she moved it aside to see what should have been a massive gash. He was uninjured. She hadn't healed him, had she?

"Can you tell us what happened?" Macey put her hand on Alexis's leg.

Alexis blinked, her mind reeling to understand. "I was healing him. Eric had torn him up, and I healed his stomach. I shouted for James, and I was about to heal his shoulder when…" She cupped her neck in her hands. "Trevor tried to rip my throat out. He broke my neck." Her body trembled as the memory ran through her mind. "What happened to James?"

"I'm fine." He stood in the doorway, leaning against the jamb. "Sorry, Trevor got away from me. I took care of him, but I really thought you were dead. There was blood all over you. All over him. I thought it was Bryce's blood, but when I rolled you off him, he didn't have a scratch. Your neck healed pretty quick after that, but neither of you would wake up."

"How did we get here? What's going to happen?" She took Bryce's hand, lacing her fingers through his. The same faint tingle of magic seeped from his warm palm. "Is Bryce…did Eric turn him?"

"Rain is on her way over to read his aura." Macey squeezed her leg and stood.

Luke put his arm around her. "I don't think Eric turned him. The shot to the head killed him, but he didn't lose much blood before that. Only werewolf blood—a lot of it—has the power to turn a human into a shifter."

Blood. That was why Eric's plan didn't work. It never would have worked, no matter how violently he attacked his victims, but… "Then why does Bryce have a magical signature?" She rubbed her temple, trying to put the pieces together, but it didn't make sense. Bryce had lost too much blood. Even with her healing powers, she couldn't have saved him without a transfusion. He'd needed a hospital.

"We think you turned him." Macey gave her a sympathetic look.

She gazed at Bryce. "But it's not possible."

"It's possible," Luke said. "If he lost enough blood, and then yours mixed with his…with your healing ability…he could have magic in his veins now."

Magic in his veins? *Her* magic. What had she done?

Bryce drew in a deep breath and mumbled, "Alexis."

"I'm here." She put her hand on his cheek and hovered her face above his.

His lids fluttered open, and his brow pinched in confusion. "How? I watched you die."

"I'm not that easy to kill." She smiled and stroked the hair away from his face. She may have forced him into a supernatural life, but he was alive. That mattered most. "How do you feel?"

He rubbed his shoulder where the bite had been and glanced down at his body. "Not hurt." He pushed to a sitting position and leaned his back against the headboard. "But not quite…right."

He looked at Luke and Macey, and his eyes widened as if he'd just realized they were there. "Where?" His gaze danced around the room, and he clutched his shirt.

"You're in our house," Macey said.

"Whose clothes are these?"

"They're mine." Luke shuffled closer to him and bent down to look into his eyes. "You're not in any pain?"

"Surprisingly, no." He tossed back the blanket and swung his legs over the side of the bed. "I feel weird though. What happened?"

James pushed from the wall and sauntered toward him. "We got your girl."

Bryce looked over his shoulder at Alexis and took her hand, pulling her toward him. "We sure did."

She moved to sit next to him, holding his hand in both of hers. "Eric is dead." Her chest tightened, and she looked at Luke. "I don't want to cause any trouble with the pack. Should I…leave?"

Bryce's grip on her hand tightened. She didn't want to go anywhere without this man, but if killing Eric would bring war to the pack, she'd have no choice.

Luke shook his head. "You stopped a madman who was breaking the law. You don't have to go anywhere."

She let out a slow breath and leaned into Bryce's side.

"We found a body in Trevor's fridge," James said. "Found his roommate casing Michael's house, and he was in on it too. Confessed to the whole plan."

"I've contacted the national congress and Biloxi." Luke crossed his arms. "We're in agreement that Eric was to blame and he was killed in self-defense."

Alexis nodded. The ordeal had been messier than she'd planned, but it was over. Eric couldn't hurt anyone else.

The doorbell rang, and she glanced at Bryce. "That'll be Rain."

"I'll let her in." James strode out of the bedroom.

"More company?" Bryce gestured to the sweatpants he wore. "I'm not dressed for guests."

"We need her to read your aura," Macey said. "If you're both feeling okay, let's move to the living room."

Bryce stood. "My aura? That's really a thing?" He shook his head. "Of course it's a thing. I keep having to remind myself this is all real."

Alexis held tight to his hand as Luke and Macey shuffled into the living room. The guilt of not revealing her secret to Bryce herself gnawed in her gut. She was done keeping things from this man. Moving to face him, she rested her hands on his shoulders. "I need you to know something."

He grasped her hips and gazed into her eyes. "Tell me you didn't mean what you said before about wanting to be with Eric."

The lies ended now too. From this moment on, she planned to tell him everything. She swallowed the thickness from her throat. "I didn't mean a word of it. I was trying to stop him."

His lips tugged into a smile. "That's all I need to know." He flicked his gaze to the door and leaned in, taking her mouth with his. Vibrating energy danced across her lips, shooting straight to her heart.

She'd been an idiot to think she could handle Eric on her own, defaulting to her old ways when her future stood right in front of her. When she'd held her fate-bound in her arms. She didn't have to be alone anymore. She had her sister, a pack who would accept her, and a man who loved her.

She brushed his lips once more and pulled away to look into his eyes. "There's something else you need to know, and it's something I should have told you a long time ago." Brushing his hair from his forehead, she cupped his face in her hand. "I love you."

He smiled. "I love you too."

She threw her arms around his shoulders and hugged him tight, the wolf and the woman rejoicing in her acceptance of what she'd known deep down all along. She belonged with him, and now, she could spend forever with him. "There's one more thing I need to tell you before we go out there. It might come as a shock."

"In the past twenty-four hours, I found out that werewolves are real and I'm in love with one. I don't think anything you can say will shock me."

She pulled from his embrace and furrowed her brow. "You might *be* a werewolf now."

He blinked.

Macey popped her head in the doorway. "Rain's ready."

"How?" Bryce cocked his head and narrowed his gaze at Alexis before following Macey into the living room.

Alexis held her breath as she sank onto the couch by Bryce. Rain sat on a chair next to the sofa, and Chase stood behind her. Macey perched on the arm of the couch, and Luke stood in front of them.

"What do you see, *cher?*" Chase asked.

Rain's eyebrows pinched as she studied Bryce, and she opened her mouth a few times as if to speak, but then she clamped her lips together.

Alexis's stomach sank. Why did she get the feeling the witch didn't have good news?

"He's…" Rain tilted her head. "He has two auras. I see

a pale-blue hovering around an orange one like a halo. It's…I've never seen anything like it."

Bryce swallowed. "What does that mean?"

Alexis took his hand. "It means you have werewolf magic in your blood now."

He looked at Luke. "You said it wasn't possible. You said no one would survive the kind of attack it would take…"

"You shouldn't have survived." She drew in a shaky breath. "Your stomach was…" A shudder ran up her spine at the memory. "You'd lost so much blood." She bit her lip to hold back the tears threatening to spill down her cheeks.

His eyes widened. "It was your blood…from where the wolf bit you. It burned."

"Burned?" James gave Luke a wary look. "That doesn't sound good."

"Can you describe the burn?" Luke asked.

"It felt like my whole body was on fire. I thought I was dying." He rubbed his forehead. "What does this mean? Am I going to be like you?"

"You might." Alexis put her hand on his leg and gave him a squeeze. "Or the magic might not hold, and the moon will draw it out of you. Either way, we'll find out soon. The next full moon is tonight."

"I wouldn't mind having super strength like you guys. That's not so bad." He laughed, but it sounded forced. "And the night vision would come in handy at work."

Luke's expression turned grim. "The magic could also be too much for your body to handle. You might not make it."

Macey gasped and covered her mouth. Rain lowered her gaze to her lap as Alexis tightened her grip on Bryce's hand. He had to make it. Her blood coursed through his veins. Her power. Her healing ability. The magic—the wolf—in her blood was bound to Bryce as much as her heart was. Her wolf would never hurt the man she loved.

"Super strength," he said through clenched teeth.

"Sorry." She relaxed her grip and swallowed the bile from the back of her throat. "You're going to make it. If the magic is too much, I'll heal you. Whatever it does to your body, I'll fix it."

Bryce nodded absently and looked at Luke. "So, I might not make it through the night?"

Luke pursed his lips, his brow raising apologetically. "It's a possibility."

He pulled from her grasp and cracked his knuckles. "Hey, Mace? Can you take me home?"

"Bryce." Alexis reached for his hand, but he shot to his feet.

"I need to go home."

"I can, but, Alexis, we brought your car back," Macey said. "It's parked down the street."

Alexis stood. "I'll take you home." She couldn't begin to imagine what he must've been feeling, but she planned to be there for him through the full moon and every second that led up to it. All of this was her fault. She'd run to Eric to ensure Bryce's safety, and now he might die because of her.

Clenching her fists, she strode toward the door. She wouldn't let it happen. She couldn't live without him.

Macey padded into the hallway and returned with Alexis's backpack. "The guys found it in the bedroom." She handed it to her. "I washed your clothes, and Bryce, your keys and wallet and both your guns are in there too."

He looked at the backpack and nodded before shuffling toward Alexis. "Thank you, everyone, for your help. Really, I can't thank you enough, but I need some time alone to..." He inhaled deeply. "This is a lot to take in."

"We'll need to take you to the swamp tonight for the full moon." Luke shook his hand. "Whatever happens, you won't be alone."

"Thanks." He glanced at Alexis and walked out the door.

Bryce's mind reeled as he stepped onto Macey's front porch and jogged down the steps. He'd learned werewolves existed less than twenty-four hours ago, and now he might be one?

Or he might be dead before dawn.

The brisk morning air raised goose bumps on his skin, and he rubbed his arms to chase away the chill. Alexis followed behind, but he didn't dare turn around. With the amount of pressure building in the back of his eyes, looking at her would probably make the tears fall, and he refused to look weak in front of her.

Spotting her car on the curb, he slid into the passenger seat, closing the door before she caught up. He managed two deep breaths before she got in the driver's side. She shoved the key into the ignition and started the car, but she didn't drive.

Dropping her hands into her lap, she looked at him with sadness in her eyes. "Please talk to me. Tell me what you're thinking."

What *was* he thinking? Between the strange electrical sensation tingling through his body and the news that he might have less than twelve hours to live, not a single coherent thought had formed in his mind in the last twenty minutes. "Take me home. Please."

Her breath caught, and she nodded before pulling away from the curb. They meandered through the French Quarter, and Bryce stared out the window at the architecture. The festive displays in the windows of the historic buildings reminded him of the upcoming holidays.

He glanced at Alexis, who clutched the steering wheel in a death grip and stared straight ahead. He might not see Christmas this year—or tomorrow for that matter—but if he did survive, and she stuck around, he wouldn't have to spend another holiday alone.

He needed to say something. To let her know he planned to spend the rest of his life with her, whether that meant the rest of today or the next fifty years. But he couldn't make his mouth form the words. Instead, he shifted his gaze to the scenery.

They reached Canal Street and stopped at a light, waiting for a streetcar to pass before heading onto St. Charles and leaving the French Quarter behind. Highrise hotels and more modern architecture replaced the nineteenth-century buildings, and the roads widened as the traffic increased.

They entered the Central Business District, and he glanced up at the twelve-story building where Michael's life had almost come to an end. A heaviness settled on his shoulders. Would the kid and his mom be safe living below him now that he was part of this supernatural world? At least they were moving in two weeks, but what would happen with the new neighbors?

As they left the CBD and approached the Garden District, he admired the Colonial and Greek Revival houses. How many times had he driven by these homes, not even noticing the grand columns and pristine gardens surrounding the structures? Today, he took it all in. The ornate fences, the detailed trim, the elaborate wreaths hanging from the doors, and the Christmas trees illuminating the windows. He'd overlooked the beauty of this city for far too long.

The beauty of life.

Alexis turned onto his street and stopped on the curb in front of his house. "Here we are."

"Home sweet home." He reached for the handle.

She put her hand on his thigh. "Can I come inside?"

He glanced at her, and the pressure in his eyes built again so he looked away. "I expected you to."

As he climbed out of the car, Karen's front door opened, and she struggled to drag a giant suitcase down the porch steps. He jogged toward her and lifted it from the ground. "Where you headed?"

She hit a button on her key fob, and her car chirped, unlocking the doors. "To my mom's."

"I thought you were staying another two weeks." He followed her to the driveway, lugging the suitcase.

"After what happened yesterday, I…" She opened the trunk, and Bryce put the bag inside. "I want to get Michael away. It's time."

"I understand." They'd be safer there, and if he didn't make it tonight, at least they'd be far away. "Take care of yourself." He gave her a hug.

"Oh, I have something for you." She rummaged in her purse and pulled out a white envelope. Handing it to him, she glanced toward Alexis's car and gave him a half-smile. "It's a gift certificate for couple's cooking classes. I thought it might be something you'd have fun doing together."

She turned to Alexis as she approached. "I'm sorry we

got off on the wrong foot. I judged you when I should have gotten to know you."

Alexis smiled. "Thank you."

"Take care of him. He likes to pretend he can handle himself, but he needs a good woman around."

"I will."

Michael brought out another suitcase and paused, his gaze cutting from Bryce to Alexis. The corners of his mouth twitched like he wasn't sure if he should smile or not. "Is…everything okay?"

Bryce forced a smile. "Never better. I'll see you around, kid."

"Bye, Sergeant Samuels."

Alexis slung her backpack over her shoulder and followed him up the stairs. As they reached the landing, she handed him his keys, and he unlocked the door. Silence greeted him as he stepped into the living room, and a sense of calm settled in his core.

"Where's Sam?" Alexis asked.

"He's at the emergency vet. Someone beat him up when they kidnapped Michael. Do you have my phone?"

She dug in her backpack and handed it to him. He had several missed calls and a voicemail from the vet. As he listened to the message, he let out a slow breath. "He's okay. I'm going to take a shower and go pick him up."

"I can get him. He'll be good as new by the time I get him home." She smiled weakly. "It's my fault he got hurt to begin with."

"It's not your fault." None of this was her fault. He'd gotten involved of his own free will, and he'd tell her so if he could compose himself enough to speak. If she'd give him five minutes to breathe, he might be able to pull all the broken pieces of his thoughts together and talk to the woman. He took a credit card from his wallet. "But if you could get him, I'd appreciate it. I'm not sure I should be driving with the way I feel."

She put a hand on his arm. "How do you feel?"

"Like I've got electricity running through my veins, battling with my blood."

"What do you feel when I touch you?"

He put his hand over hers. "Soft skin. Warmth. Concern, though I think that's because I see it in your eyes."

"Nothing else?"

"No. Should I feel something else?"

She dropped her arm to her side and lowered her gaze as her voice softened. "I guess not. I'll go get Sam."

CHAPTER TWENTY-ONE

A WEIGHT THE SIZE OF A BOWLING BALL SETTLED IN Alexis's stomach as she drove to the emergency vet clinic. Getting more than two words out of Bryce had felt like wringing grape juice from a raisin. The moment he learned about the magic in his blood, he'd become distant, acting as if she were nothing more than an acquaintance.

He had every reason to hate her. She'd endangered his job…his life and Michael's…all because she was a rogue. She never should have tried to collect the money from Eric in the first place, much less gone back to him a second time to try and stop him on her own.

What the hell was her problem? She parked in the back of the clinic parking lot and smoothed the wrinkles out of her sister's shirt as she strode to the door.

The receptionist stopped talking mid-sentence and stared as Alexis made her way to the desk. "Can I help you?" Her gaze lingered on Alexis's hair.

She ran a hand through her locks, cringing as little flakes of dried blood rained down on her shoulders. She should have showered and changed clothes before she came, but Bryce had needed some alone time. "I'm here to pick up Sam, the Siberian husky."

"Right, his owner called and said to expect you." She rose to her feet, but hesitated. "Are you okay?"

Alexis smiled. "I was painting an accent wall. Forgot I got it in my hair."

The receptionist let out a nervous giggle. "A technician will be bringing him out. He'll need to lie on his side. Do you have room in your back seat?"

"Sure do." She gave the woman Bryce's credit card and cringed when she saw the eight-hundred-dollar charge. She'd pay him back, even if it took her five years to save up the money.

A door swung open, and a burly man cradling the dog in his arms stepped through. Sam whimpered, and she sucked in a sharp breath as guilt stabbed her in the heart. *Poor boy.* She stroked his head, and his tail swished.

"Thank you." She held out her arms to take the dog.

"He's heavy. I'll carry him to your car."

"I can handle it." She took Sam into her arms and shuffled toward the door. Taking a deep breath, she began healing his bruised ribs on the way to the car. As she situated him in the back seat, she focused her energy on his leg.

Her head spun as the bone mended, and she stumbled around to the driver's seat when she finished. Sam sat up and licked her cheek, leaving a trail of warm saliva on her skin.

She laughed. "Thanks, boy. We'll get the bandages off of you after we get home, okay?"

Sam let out a quiet woof and sat in the back seat. The dog had forgiven her. Now, she'd have to work on the man.

Thankfully, Karen and Michael were gone by the time she brought Sam home. She killed the engine and let out a sigh. At least she wouldn't have to explain how the dog had magically recovered. She opened the back door, and Sam jumped out and hobbled on his cast to the staircase. It took him a while to climb all the steps, which gave her time to figure out what she would say to Bryce.

A profuse apology would be step one. She'd follow that with another confession of her love…and hope he could find forgiveness somewhere in his heart.

She opened the door, and Bryce's face lit up as Sam limped inside. He dropped to his knees and took the dog in his arms. "Hey, buddy. How you feeling?" He lifted his gaze to hers but quickly looked down. "Can we take the cast off?"

Her throat tightened. Was he so angry he couldn't even look at her? "Yeah. He's all healed."

He rummaged under the sink and took out a small saw. "Can you hold him?"

"Sure." She wrapped her arms around the dog's chest as Bryce cut into the cast. Sam wiggled, desperate to be free, and Bryce grunted, making tiny back and forth motions with the saw.

Sam twisted in her arms again, and Bryce rubbed the dog's head. "Be still, buddy. I don't want to saw your leg off."

"I can probably get it from here."

The corner of his mouth twitched as he set the saw on the counter and took the dog in his arms. "Super strength?"

"Something like that." Grasping the cast in both hands, she pulled it apart at the cut he'd made. Sam shimmied free from Bryce's grasp and danced around the room, wagging his entire body.

She handed Bryce the receipt and his credit card. "I'll pay you back for this."

His eyes widened at the amount before he dropped the paper on the table. "There's no need. You saved him from a week or two of pain."

With her hand on the back of a chair, she traced her finger along the smooth wood, unable to meet his gaze. "He wouldn't have been in pain at all if it weren't for me."

Bryce rested his hands on her shoulders and finally looked her in the eyes. "None of this was your fault, so stop blaming yourself. I don't blame you."

Her breath hitched. "You don't?"

"No." He dropped his arms to his sides, and the sadness in his eyes caused his brow to pinch. "But considering what could happen tonight…I'm going to see my mom."

Sam nudged his leg, so he leaned down to pet him.

Alexis swallowed the lump from her throat. "I understand." Of course he would want to see his mom and anyone else he cared about. Spending the day with the person who doomed him to possible death wouldn't rank high on his last-day-of-life to-do list. "I'll wait here for you."

He straightened. "I was hoping you'd come with me."

She missed a beat. "Really?"

"It could be the last time I see her, and I'd like her to meet the woman I love."

A swarm of butterflies unfurled in her stomach, flitting its way up to her chest. "I thought you were mad at me."

He sighed and took her face in his hand. "I'm sorry if

it seemed that way. I needed a moment to gather my thoughts, but I'm okay now. If anything, I love you more after everything that's happened." He chuckled. "I didn't think that was possible, and maybe it's because I've got your blood…your magic…running through my veins, but I feel connected to you."

He had no idea the connection she had to him. Now that he had werewolf magic inside him, could he possibly feel the bond between their hearts like she did? She rested a hand on his chest. "We're bound by fate."

"More like by blood, but you can call it fate if you want to." He shrugged. "Whatever it is…blood, magic, something supernatural…I could never be mad at you."

He didn't believe in fate, but after tonight, he would. Once the magic took hold, he'd understand. They were meant to be together. To be mates.

"I'm either going to end the night as a werewolf, a human, or dead, so I'm going to make the most of the day. Will you come meet my mom?"

She smiled and pressed a kiss to his lips. "I would love to meet your mom. Let's go."

He stepped back and gazed at her, the corner of his mouth tugging into an adorable grin. "I think you look beautiful like you are, but the nurses might not appreciate the blood in your hair."

She cringed. "Maybe I should shower?"

"Probably a good idea." He dropped onto the couch and held out his arms to Sam. The dog bounded toward him and licked his face.

Alexis shuffled toward the bathroom and paused in the doorway, turning to look at him. Her fate-bound. "I love you, Bryce. I mean that."

He smiled. "I love you too."

"Don't expect much." Bryce pressed the elevator button and took Alexis's hand. His heart felt like it was beating in his throat as the doors slid open and they stepped inside. "She might not recognize me. Sometimes she thinks I'm my brother."

"That's got to be hard." She squeezed his hand. "Don't worry about me. I'll follow your lead."

He kissed her on the cheek, and they exited the elevator, heading to his mom's room. Pausing outside the door, he took a deep breath to calm the hummingbird trying to escape his chest. He lowered his head, saying a silent prayer to whatever gods—supernatural or not—that might be listening for his mom to be coherent. If this turned out to be the last time he saw her, he'd like to go out knowing she remembered him.

Alexis rested her hand on his back, calming him. "Are you okay?"

He forced a smile. "I'm good."

Cold metal greeted his clammy palm as he twisted the knob and opened the door a crack. He leaned his face in the space between the door and the jamb. "Hey, Mom? You decent?"

"Bryce? Is that you?"

He closed his eyes and tipped his head back as he whispered, "Thank you," to whomever answered his prayer. He opened the door wider and smiled at his mom. She sat propped against a mound of pillows in her bed, her legs covered with the blue afghan she'd knitted a few years back, before the arthritis in her hands forced her to give up the hobby. Someone had curled her hair and applied bright-pink rouge to her cheeks.

Grasping Alexis's hand, he tugged her through the door. "You look like you're having a good day."

She beamed a smile, and her eyes were bright and coherent. "I am. And who is this lovely young lady?"

"I'd like you to meet my girlfriend, Alexis." His smile widened as Alexis gave his hand a squeeze.

She waved. "Hi, Mrs. Samuels. It's nice to meet you."

"Come here, hon." His mom held out her arms. "I'm a hugger. You too, Bryce, honey, I haven't seen you in ages."

He'd visited his mom last week, but she hadn't recognized him at the time. Alexis shuffled forward and leaned over the bed to give his mom a hug, and he sucked in a shaky breath. He'd never believed in fate or getting signs from above or any of that nonsense. But after everything he'd learned about the supernatural, he couldn't shake the feeling that his mom being coherent was a sign he wouldn't make it through the night. Maybe fate was granting him one last visit with his loved ones before his life ended.

"That's a beautiful ring." Alexis gestured to his mom's wedding ring.

She held it up and admired the stone. "It's been in the family for ages. It belonged to Bryce's grandma, and I think his great-great-grandma before that. Keeps getting passed down."

"What a lovely tradition." Alexis moved aside for him to hug his mom, and pressure built in the back of his eyes.

She held him tight and whispered in his ear, "She's a keeper. I like her."

"So do I." He swallowed the thickness from his throat and blinked back the moisture threatening to drip from his eyes as he settled into a chair next to Alexis.

They chatted for another twenty minutes, Bryce filling

her in on how he'd come to date his ex-partner's sister after all these years working with Macey. When her lids started to flutter shut, he gave her a kiss on the cheek and led Alexis to the door.

His mom sucked in a sharp breath as she woke. "Wait, Bryce. I need to talk to you."

Alexis patted his shoulder. "I'll be in the hall."

He shuffled to his mom's bed and sat on the edge. "You should get some rest."

"I will. I will." She tugged the ring off her finger and put it in his hand. "You love this girl?"

"With all my heart."

"Then you better put that ring on her before she gets away."

He gazed at the stone, a one-carat diamond nestled in a scalloped circle of tiny diamond flecks. "Are you sure you're ready to give it up?"

She closed his fingers around the ring. "I'm ready for you to make good use of it."

He kissed her forehead. "Thanks, Mom. I will."

Bryce dropped the ring into his pocket and shuffled toward the door. Pausing with his hand on the knob, he glanced back at his mom, sleeping peacefully, and a sense of calmness settled over him. Had he come to terms with the fact that this might be his last night on Earth? Not really. But if he did go, at least the people he loved knew he cared about them.

His throat thickened as he toyed with the ring in his pocket. He'd like to drop to one knee and put it on Alexis's finger as soon as he stepped through the door, but he'd wait. If he asked her to marry him now, she might say yes out of guilt or pity, and that was no way to spend the rest of his life with the woman of his dreams.

If he survived whatever the full moon had in store for him, then he'd propose. She could say yes…or no…with a clear conscience.

A tiny smile tugged at the corners of Bryce's mouth as he stepped through the door, and Alexis couldn't help but smile in return. His nervousness had rolled off him in waves on the way to visit his mom, but now he seemed calm. Maybe even at peace with everything that had and would happen.

She took his hand. "Everything okay?"

"I never thought my fate would lie with a lunar cycle, but yeah. Let's go home." He guided her to the elevator, and they stepped inside.

She waited until the doors closed before turning to him. "I thought you didn't believe in fate?"

The elevator stopped and opened into the parking garage. "That's the first time my mom has been coherent when I've visited her in a month. It could be a coincidence, or it could be God or the *gods* or fate or…whatever…granting me one last moment with her before I die."

Pain gripped her heart, and she stopped walking. "Don't talk like that."

He took a few more steps before turning to her. "Whatever's gonna happen is gonna happen. Nothing I can do about it, right?"

"I'm not going to let you die." She marched past him and got in her car, slamming the door. This nonsense had to stop. There was no way in hell she'd let anything happen to him, and he needed to stop talking like this was the end. She started the engine and checked the clock on the radio. They had four hours until they had to meet the pack in the forest, and she intended to use those hours to show Bryce she was worth living for.

He sidled into the seat next to her and buckled his seatbelt. "I'm sorry."

"Don't." She ground her teeth as she pulled out of the parking lot and headed to his home…*their* home.

He didn't say anything else on the drive, but he reached across the console to hold her hand, and tears almost spilled from her eyes.

They greeted Sam as they entered the house, but even his signature full-body wag couldn't lift the weight pressing down on her shoulders. When he was satisfied with their affection, the husky returned to his favorite spot on the couch and curled into a fluffy ball.

Alexis looked at Bryce. "You are not going to die, so don't even mention it again today, okay?"

He knit his brow and cupped her cheek in his hand. "It's a possibility, darlin', so we have to consider it. And by the look on Luke's face, it seems highly likely."

She slapped his hand away. "No. Luke doesn't know what I can do. He's never seen me heal." She'd survived a hundred-foot fall from an electrical tower that broke every bone in her body. The same magic that saved her now ran through Bryce's veins. Fate didn't lead her to this man—give her the ability to heal him—to take him away from her when she needed him most. He *would* survive this. He had to.

"You said yourself you can only heal physical injuries. This one might be in my blood."

Her entire core tightened, twisting her insides until she couldn't breathe. She grabbed his shoulders and shook him. "I can't lose you. Do you understand? For the first time in my life, I've found something worth staying for. That something is you, Bryce. You've made this place my home. *You* are my home."

A thousand emotions danced with the brown and green flecks in his eyes as she held his gaze, and the corner of his mouth tugged into a grin. "That's the nicest thing anyone's ever said to me. I still might die, though."

"Stop talking." She took his mouth with hers, and the tingle of werewolf magic on his skin mingled with the electricity shooting through her body. He responded with a masculine growl emanating from somewhere deep in his core as he slid his arms around her waist and pulled her close.

A spark of hope ignited in her chest. She'd never heard such a wolf-like growl from Bryce before. Taking his face in her hands, she pressed her forehead to his. "What do you feel when I touch you?"

He kissed her jaw, trailing his lips down the curve of her neck before whispering in her ear, "Passion. Adoration. Love."

Sweet, but not the answer she wanted to hear. "Do you feel my magic?"

"Everything about you is magical." He gripped the hem of her shirt and tugged it over her head before stepping back to admire her. "Wondrous." Grabbing the back of his shirt, he yanked it over his head.

She ran her hands up his chest, resting them on his shoulders. "You don't feel a tingling sensation when I touch you?"

"Should I?"

She lowered her gaze. "If you were a werewolf, you would."

"Hey." He hooked his finger under her chin, lifting her

head toward his. "That's not to say I won't be after the moon comes out. We have no idea what's going to happen tonight, so let's enjoy right now while we can."

She inhaled deeply and gazed at him. Whatever fate had planned, she couldn't do anything about it now. All they could control was this moment. "That's the best idea I've heard all day."

With his hand on the small of her back, he pulled her to his body, taking her mouth in a kiss. She parted her lips, and as her tongue brushed his, fire shot through her veins. This was *her* man. Whether he became a werewolf or stayed human, she didn't give a damn. At this moment, he had magic in his veins, and that magic called to her, awakening a primal instinct in her soul. The overwhelming need to possess him had her burning with desire. Throwing her arms around his neck, she pushed him against the wall and crushed her body to his.

He grunted and broke the kiss. "Watch out with that super strength. I know you can heal me, but I'd rather not get broken."

She nipped at his collarbone, gliding her tongue up his neck to take his earlobe between her teeth. "I'm sorry. You have no idea what it's like to finally be able to be my true self with someone. For you to know everything about me and want me anyway."

"I know *exactly* how you feel." The heat of his breathy whisper warmed her ear, sending shivers down to her toes.

She fumbled with his belt, trailing kisses across his chest, as she finally unbuckled it and yanked it from his jeans. She couldn't undress him fast enough. Jerking at the buttons on his fly, she shoved the rest of his clothes to floor and took his dick in her hand. She needed to be closer. To be part of him. To make him understand how much he meant to her and that dying was not an option for him tonight or any night in the next fifty years.

Gripping her hips, he leaned his head against the wall, his lids fluttering shut as she stroked him. He was thick and hard, and as a bead of moisture collected on his tip, she had to taste him. Lowering her head, she circled her tongue around him before taking him into her mouth and reveling in the salty-sweet taste of him.

Sliding his fingers into her hair, he rested his hand on her head—not to move her or force her into a rhythm—but to gently caress her scalp as she sucked him.

Another growl rumbled from his chest, and he stilled her head, moving his hand to her shoulder to guide her back up to his mouth. He undid her pants as he kissed her, working them over her hips and pushing her clothes to the floor.

He toed off his shoes and stumbled out of his jeans before grabbing her by the ass and lifting her onto the table. Pushing her onto her back, he dragged a hand down her body and stroked her clit with his thumb.

Electricity shot through her core, and she bit her bottom lip as he pulled her pants from her ankles and spread her legs with his broad shoulders. He caressed her inner thighs, and she rose onto her elbows to find him gazing at her with so much passion in his eyes that it took her breath away.

"You're so beautiful, Alexis."

"I need you inside me. Please."

He pressed his lips to one thigh, and then the other. "If this is my last night on Earth, I want to savor you first."

"Stop saying—"

The warmth of his tongue bathed her sensitive nub,

taking the words from her lips. She lay back and closed her eyes as he lifted her legs onto his shoulders and stroked her folds before slipping a finger inside her. She sucked in a breath between her teeth when his tongue circled her clit again. An *mmm* vibrated across his lips, the sensation intensifying the climax coiling in her core.

He continued pleasuring her, adding a second finger inside, working her in circles until she lost control. Her orgasm slammed into her center, ricocheting through her soul and shattering her senses. She tangled her fingers in his hair, panting his name until he brought her down. But she was far from satisfied.

She needed this man inside her like she'd never needed anything in her life. Sitting up, she pushed him into a chair and straddled him. He inhaled deeply, gazing at her with passion-drunk eyes as she guided his cock to her center.

He moaned as she sheathed him, and she stilled, pressing her naked body to his, memorizing the way he filled her, relishing the magic emanating from his skin. Taking his face in her hands, she pressed her forehead to his. "I love you, Bryce."

"I love you more than you can imagine."

"I can imagine." She rocked her hips, and he gripped her thighs as he sucked in a sharp breath.

Clutching his shoulders, she held him close as she moved up and down his thick shaft, delicious friction making every nerve in her body hum. He held her hips, moving his own in unison, creating a choreography that felt as if it were ingrained in her soul. She belonged to this man. Every part of her.

His rhythm increased, each thrust of his hips sending a thrilling jolt through her core. Her climax built slowly, steadily, and when her name crossed his lips in his growl of release, she lost control. Her orgasm consumed her, burning her in its flames, and Bryce raised her from the ashes.

A sleepy, satisfied smile curved his lips as he ran his fingers through her hair. "Talk about going out with a bang."

This would not be the last time she made love to him. They had many, many years ahead of them, and tonight was only the beginning.

So, why did her throat thicken at the thought? Tears she'd refused to shed collected on her lower lids, and she wrapped her arms around his shoulders, burying her face in his neck to hide them.

He held her and stroked the back of her head. "Are you crying?"

"No."

"Then your eyes are leaking on my neck. Hey." He gently pushed her back to look at her. "I'm sorry. I shouldn't have said that."

"No, you shouldn't have. You're not going to die."

"You're right." He touched his own chest and then hers. "This connection I feel with you is going to hold me here. I haven't spent nearly enough time with you, and if fate decides it's my time to go, well…fate can kiss my ass."

CHAPTER TWENTY-TWO

BRYCE HELD ALEXIS'S HAND AS THEY CREPT TOWARD A clearing in the trees. The sinking sun cast long, jagged shadows across the forest floor, and the sound of dry leaves crunching beneath his boots filled the silence. The sense of calm he'd achieved with Alexis earlier was slowly draining away, and a ball of nervousness twisted in his gut.

A week ago, no amount of money would have been enough to convince him to venture into the swamp at night unarmed. Snakes, gators, and who-knew-what other kinds of creatures lurked in the shadows, waiting to make an unsuspecting human their next meal.

Well, now he did know what other kind of creatures hunted these woods, and all he could do was hope they didn't have the taste for human flesh.

Alexis squeezed his hand. "Almost there. Luke and some other weres will be there to help you if you shift, and I won't leave your side no matter what happens. You won't be alone through any of this."

If he shifted. But if he didn't? "What do werewolves eat?"

"Boar, gator, whatever. You can start with a prey animal—a deer or even a nutria for your first hunt."

"Swamp rat?" He curled his lip. The idea of killing any animal with his mouth and then eating it raw made his stomach churn.

She shrugged. "It's what I went for my first time. Of course, I was hunting alone and had no clue if I'd even turn human again."

"That must have been scary."

"It was terrifying." She stopped walking and looked at him. "But it won't be like that for you. You've got a pack and a woman who loves you to guide you through it."

Her words loosened the knot in his chest. For once in his life, being alone didn't sound the slightest bit appealing. "Do werewolves ever eat humans?"

Now it was her turn to curl her lip in disgust. "We aren't cannibals."

"You aren't exactly human."

"We are half-human, and that's the side that's in control. Even in wolf form, our human minds are fully functioning." She cupped his cheek in her hand. "Don't be scared. No one is going to hurt you tonight."

He stiffened. "I'm not scared."

She kissed him on the cheek. "I would be."

Who was he kidding? He was scared shitless. Not that he thought his friends would actually eat him, but the list of things that could go wrong tonight was too long to count.

They reached the clearing and found Luke standing with his thick arms crossed over his chest. Was the alpha always the biggest man in the pack? Once the shock of this situation wore off, he'd have to wrangle the mess of questions running through his mind into a manageable list.

Chase leaned casually against a tree trunk, and James stood with his hands in his pockets as if a bunch of French Quarter men hanging out in the swamp was the most natural thing in the world. For these men, he supposed it was.

Alexis nodded at the alpha, and he stepped forward to shake Bryce's hand. "Welcome to our hunting grounds. This goes without saying, but no one can know about us or where we hunt."

"Your secret's safe with me." He stared into the trees. "I'm still having a hard time believing it myself."

Alexis held his bicep. "Even after everything you've seen?"

"When you've been a skeptic your entire life, and you're suddenly thrust into a world you never knew—refused to believe—existed, it takes a while for your brain to catch up."

Chase pushed from the tree and strode toward them. "We're running out of daylight. You ready?"

His pulse thrummed. Could he ever be prepared for what could possibly happen to him in the next few minutes? "As I'll ever be. Hey, can you really talk to ghosts?"

Chase laughed. "Nah. I'm just a werewolf."

"So those weird cases you helped on…"

"I was determining if they were supernatural or not and what evidence we'd need to hide. We're like the paranormal police force of New Orleans."

The pieces of the puzzle finally clicked into place. All the evidence that went missing over the years wasn't from poor management of the lab and the morgue. The werewolves had been stealing it. And if Bryce became a werewolf, he'd have to find a balance between enforcing the law like he'd been doing his entire adult life and breaking it to keep supernatural secrets.

Could he do that? If the safety of humanity was at stake, he damn well could. Super strength. The task of protecting humans from real-life monsters. This werewolf gig didn't sound half-bad.

James grinned. "Breaking laws has its advantages." Luke cut him a sideways glance, and he stiffened. "Only human laws. I never break pack laws." He clapped Luke on the shoulder and winked. "I swear."

The last rays of sun disappeared behind the horizon, and everyone looked at Bryce.

Alexis wrapped her arms around his waist. "How do you feel?"

He took a deep breath and focused on his body. The hormones he'd released by making love to Alexis continued to course through his veins, giving him a natural high. But adrenaline and—if he were honest with himself—a trickle of dread created a nauseating, hyper sensation that made him feel like he needed to jump out of his own skin.

Otherwise…nothing unusual. "Honestly, I feel completely human. I don't even feel that battle in my blood anymore."

She furrowed her brow and took his face in her hands. "I feel the magic on your skin." Every time she mentioned the magic she felt in him, she got a hopeful look in her eyes. While he'd be thrilled if he simply survived the night, he couldn't shake the feeling Alexis wanted him to be a werewolf. With all the things he *couldn't* do as a human, he didn't blame her.

He took her hands and held them against his chest. "You want there to be magic in me, don't you?"

"I couldn't care less. I want you to be you, whether the magic binds with your soul or leaves you completely. As long as you're my sexy, sci-fi loving, introverted, tough guy, I'll be the happiest woman in the world." She held his gaze with conviction in her eyes. She meant every word.

Maybe he wasn't a fake after all. If she could be both a wolf and a woman, why couldn't he be the scrawny, bullied kid from his past and the cop of today? Hell, he could even be a wolf too. They were all parts that made up the whole, and he was done hiding behind a mask.

"Feeling anything yet?" James asked.

He shook his head. "If I shift, is it going to hurt?"

"It shouldn't." Alexis kissed his cheek.

"Well…" Luke rubbed at the scruff on his face. "It might. Werewolves are born with the magic already ingrained in their souls. Yours needs to bond with your blood, so it might be painful at first." His eyes tightened. "It probably will be."

"Fantastic." He tipped his head back and looked at the moon. A light mist of clouds stretched across the silver sphere, and stars glistened around it. How could a hunk of rock orbiting the Earth have so much control over his future? He sighed and shook his head. If it could control the tides, why not his fate?

"Still nothing?" Alexis asked.

"Do I need to say some kind of magic chant or pray to the moon god or something?"

They all chuckled, but he'd been serious.

He let out his breath in a huff. "Maybe nothing's going to happen. Maybe—" He clutched his stomach as a burning sensation expanded in his gut.

Alexis grabbed his shoulders. "Are you okay?"

"Unless this is really bad heartburn, no." He doubled

over, supporting himself with his hands on his knees. "God, it feels like it did when you bled on me." His jaw involuntarily clenched, his teeth cutting into his tongue. The coppery taste of blood filled his mouth, and he dry-heaved as the burning intensified.

Alexis held on to him, pressing her lips to his ear. "I'm here. Whatever happens, I'm here."

He spit blood onto the ground, and she gasped. "Oh, God. What's hurt? Let me heal you. Is it your stomach?" She tried to make him stand upright, but he pushed her away.

"I bit my tongue. I'm fine." He dropped to his knees. His blood burned like acid, each beat of his heart forcing another pulse of caustic sludge through his veins. He wanted to scream, but he couldn't get enough air into his lungs.

Alexis knelt beside him and wrapped her arms around him. "Why is it hurting him so bad?" she screamed at Luke. "Why is it taking so long?"

"I don't know. Nothing like this has happened in hundreds of years. This is new territory for all of us."

Bryce squeezed his eyes shut and prayed for a quick ending. He would either spontaneously combust or he'd black out from the pain. At this point, he'd take either.

"I don't know what to heal." Alexis rubbed his back. "I can't find anything broken."

"It's okay." He forced the words out in a breathy whisper as he turned his gaze to meet hers. "If this ends the way it feels like it's going to end, please know that I loved you with every fiber of my being."

Tears streamed down her cheeks. "You're not going to die. Do something, Luke!"

Luke straightened his spine and nodded. “Everyone shift. Maybe seeing our wolves will bring his out.”

Bryce squinted through his wavering vision as Luke, Chase, and James became wolves. They circled him, their intelligent eyes boring into him as if they were willing him to shift too. “That’s not helping.”

Alexis stroked his hair. “I’m going to shift too. It’s my magic doing this to you, so maybe *my* wolf needs to bring yours out.”

He nodded and dropped his hands to the ground to stop himself from collapsing.

“I won’t be able to talk once I shift, but I’ll still be me, okay? Just…whatever is happening inside you…don’t fight it. Give in and let the magic take over.” She rose to her feet. “I love you, Bryce.”

Her body shimmered, and in seconds, she transformed into a beautiful, sandy-colored wolf. She lay on her stomach, resting her head between her paws, and gazed at him with emerald-green eyes.

His chest squeezed, and a swarm of wasps seemed to come to life in his stomach. The stinging, fluttering sensation spread through his body, electrifying his veins and making his head spin. He closed his eyes to stave off the dizzying effect and tensed his muscles against the pain.

Don’t fight it. Alexis’s words rang in his ears. *Let the magic take over.*

He inhaled the deepest breath his starving lungs would allow, and then he let go. Collapsing onto his side, he let the world slip away and focused on Alexis’s eyes. Her gaze grounded him, her wolf silently calling to something deep in his core, and a cooling sensation spread from his chest out to his fingers and toes.

His body vibrated, and Alexis rose to her feet. She

whimpered as she took a tentative step toward him and nudged his shoulder with her nose. Something inside him responded, and the vibration intensified until it consumed every cell in his body.

Then, it stopped. The pain ceased. He inhaled a deep breath and was met with an array of scents from the swampy forest. Dirt, cypress, decaying foliage, and the distinct aroma of dog fur danced in his senses.

He lifted his head and gazed at the wolves surrounding him. The forest seemed almost as bright as day. Raising his gaze to the full moon above, a shudder ran through his body, and he shot to his feet.

No…to his paws. And did he have a…? He swished his tail, and Alexis trotted toward him, bathing his face with her tongue. He was an honest-to-God werewolf.

He tried to laugh, but the sound came out as a grunt. Alexis nudged him toward the bayou, and he gazed at his reflection in the water. Dappled, reddish-brown fur covered his entire body, but his hazel eyes somehow looked like his own.

His stomach growled, and the urge to hunt overwhelmed him. He looked at Alexis, and she met his gaze, seeming to understand what he needed. Somehow, the thought *follow my lead* entered his mind, and he knew it came from her. Could he read her mind?

He stared at her intently, trying to figure out her thoughts, but what he received was more of a feeling. She was urging him to hunt with the pack, though no words were exchanged telepathically.

He turned around to find the other wolves watching him, and Luke's command to follow him registered in his mind. Bryce hesitated. Hunting had never appealed to him before, and he expected to be repulsed at the idea. But his wolf's needs outweighed his own.

He ran with the pack, reveling in the exhilaration of the hunt and the sensation of using his senses for what felt like the first time. Every sound, from leaves crunching underfoot to rodents scurrying to hide, registered in ears, and the scents of the forest delighted his senses.

Alexis stayed by his side, silently guiding him, being a calming force like she had been since he awakened with magic in his blood. Magic that it seemed would be with him forever now.

As the expedition concluded, the rest of the wolves shifted back into human form, laughing and congratulating each other on their successful hunt. Bryce's heart thrummed as Alexis sashayed toward him, her hips swaying and a smile lighting on her lips. He had no clue how to turn human again and no way to tell her his problem.

She took his face in her hands and stroked his fur. "You are the sexiest wolf I've ever seen, but you're even sexier as a man. Come back to me, Bryce."

He whimpered.

"Focus your intent and imagine yourself human again. Let the magic running through your veins change you."

He blew out a hard breath through his nostrils and did as she said. As the image of himself as a human formed in his mind, his body vibrated, the sensation running up and down his form in a wave as he transformed into himself.

As soon as he was upright, Alexis hugged him and showered his face in kisses. His skin tingled each time her lips brushed his cheeks, and as she took his mouth with hers, magical energy shot straight to his heart. "Is this what you were wanting me to feel before? This electricity dancing on your skin?"

Her smile brightened her eyes. "Yes, it is."

He felt it, and his love for her had grown exponentially in a matter of minutes. The wolf inside him loved her as much as he did, and it was time to make her his. He sucked in a sharp breath and pressed his hands to his pockets. "Oh, shit." Where was the ring?

Alexis laughed. "Everything you had on you is there. It gets absorbed by the magic and returns to its proper place when you shift back."

He ran his finger around the circle of metal in his pocket and let out a breath.

The men approached, and Luke clapped him on the shoulder. "Glad to have you back, my friend. Macey insists y'all come by the bar to celebrate."

Alexis took his hand. "Is that okay with you? We can stop by tomorrow if you're too overwhelmed."

A few days ago, his first instinct would have been to say no. To retreat to the quiet and comfort of his home. But he was a pack animal now, and he couldn't ignore the new duality of his nature. His wolf craved the company of his friends. "I'm the first human-turned-werewolf in hundreds of years. I'd say that's something to celebrate."

"I'd also like you to join the pack," Luke said. "You can be rogue if you want." He glanced at Alexis. "But there are benefits to joining the pack…if you don't mind following a few more rules."

Bryce laughed. "More rules? Where do I sign up?"

Luke smiled. "Let's not waste the full moon then. We can perform the induction ceremony when we get back."

"I want to join too." Alexis wrapped an arm around

Bryce's bicep. "I'm ready to stay in one place, if you'll have me."

"How can I say no to my mate's sister? Macey will be thrilled." Luke shook both their hands. "I'll see you two at the bar."

Alexis started to follow Luke and the others, but Bryce didn't move. Slipping his hand into his pocket, he moved his lips as if silently practicing lines for a play. He must have been overwhelmed, his mind reeling.

The first time Alexis had shifted, she'd felt the call of the moon and run deep into the woods. But what happened once she'd gotten there had turned her entire world upside down. She could imagine what Bryce must have been feeling, but he'd have the pack and her for the rest of his life. He'd be fine if she could get him out of the woods and back to humanity.

She laced her fingers through his and gave his arm a gentle tug. "We don't want to keep the alpha waiting."

He blinked, focusing on her. "No, I guess we don't."

She led him to her car, and they rode in silence to the bar, Bryce letting everything sink in, and Alexis basking in the joy that her fate-bound had survived. They parked a block away, and as soon as they reached the sidewalk in front of the bar, Macey ran out and threw her arms around Bryce's waist.

"I'm so glad you're okay." She hugged him tightly and grinned at Alexis. "I bet you're glad too." She let Bryce go and hugged her sister.

Alexis wrapped her arms around her, and those pesky

tears collected on her lower lids again. "I'm going to take care of him."

Macey pulled back and wiped a tear from her cheek. "I know. Luke said you're joining the pack."

"I am." She reached for Bryce's hand. "*We* are."

"Come here." Macey wrapped her arms around both of them and kissed their cheeks. "I am *so* happy."

Rain and Chase stepped onto the sidewalk, and the witch smiled. "His aura is all werewolf now." She moved closer and squinted at him. "The orange has completely taken over."

Macey let them go and stepped into Luke's arms as he and his sister, Amber, joined them on the sidewalk.

A giddy sensation bubbled up from Alexis's chest as her wolf rejoiced in the company of the pack. She'd be with her sister and the man she loved for the rest of her life. As she slid her arms around Bryce's waist, the woman in her celebrated too.

James leaned out the door. "Would all you happy couples care to come inside and have a drink?" He scanned their faces and sighed. "I'm going to have to find some more friends. All you lovebirds are cramping my style."

Amber laughed. "Enjoy your style while you can, my friend. I'm sensing change in your future."

He narrowed his eyes. "I'll pass."

Alexis laughed. "You won't have a choice."

"You can't fight fate." Bryce kissed her on the cheek. "What's meant to be will always be."

She squeezed his hand. "Oh, you believe in it now?"

"How could I not?"

Luke motioned toward the door. "Let's go in and get this induction ceremony started, so we can celebrate."

They all filed in, but Bryce held her back. “Hold on. I need to talk you about something.” He reached into his pocket and pulled out a ring. Holding it in both hands, he gazed at the stone.

Her breath caught in her throat, and a shiver ran through her body. “Is that your mom’s ring?”

He let out a nervous chuckle. “It is. She gave it to me when you left the room this afternoon.” He held it up to the light, and the diamond glinted. “It can never replace your own mom’s ring, but I would be honored if you’d wear this one. Alexis, will—”

“Wait.” She held up a hand. “Before you say anything else, you need to know something about werewolves. In order to get married, we would have to become mates.”

His brow furrowed. “Mates?”

“It’s kind of like marriage, but it’s an oath you take under a full moon to be together forever. Werewolves mate for life, so once you’re in there’s no way out. There’s no such thing as werewolf divorce.”

“I like the sound of that.” He closed the distance between them. “I’ve never been a quitter. Anyway, you said yourself we’re bound by fate. I didn’t understand what you meant at first, but after what happened tonight in the woods, I finally do. We’re connected somehow, and I couldn’t imagine myself with anyone but you. I’m in this for the long-haul. Forever.”

Forever was exactly what she wanted. For him to be a permanent fixture in her life. She was done with temporary. “You are my fate-bound.”

“We’re each other’s fate-bounds.” He took her left hand in his. “So…can I put this ring on you now?”

“I would be honored to wear it.”

He slipped the ring on her finger and pressed his lips

to her hand. "It looks good on you. Now, call me old-fashioned if you want…I did spend most of my life as a human…but, werewolf or not, I want to marry you. How do we become mates so I can make you my wife?"

She slid her arms up his shoulders to hold the back of his neck. "The alpha performs the mating ceremony on the night of a full moon."

He arched an eyebrow. "Really?"

"Mm-hmm." She licked her lips in anticipation of what she hoped he'd suggest.

"There happens to be a full moon tonight, ma'am, and the alpha is already performing one ceremony. Do you think he'd mind adding one more to the agenda?"

"I doubt he'd mind."

He smiled and ran his fingers through her hair. "Well, what do you think about becoming mates tonight?"

She gazed up at the full moon glowing brightly in the midnight sky and offered a silent thank you to fate for finally forcing her to get her life together and for bringing this amazing man to her. Looking into Bryce's eyes, she ran a finger down his chest and hooked it into the waistband of his jeans. "I think we should stop burning moonlight. Let's get hitched."

ALSO BY CARRIE PULKINEN

Crescent City Wolf Pack Series

Werewolves Only

Beneath a Blue Moon

Bound by Blood

A Deal with Death

A Song to Remember

Crescent City Ghost Tours Series

Love & Ghosts

Spirit Chasers Series

To Catch a Spirit

To Stop a Shadow

To Free a Phantom

Stand Alone Books

The Rest of Forever

Reawakened

Bewitching the Vampire

Young Adult

Soul Catchers

ABOUT THE AUTHOR

Carrie Pulkinen is a paranormal romance author who has always been fascinated with things that go bump in the night. Of course, when you grow up next door to a cemetery, the dead (and the undead) are hard to ignore. Pair that with her passion for writing and her love of a good happily-ever-after, and becoming a paranormal romance author seems like the only logical career choice.

Before she decided to turn her love of the written word into a career, Carrie spent the first part of her professional life as a high school journalism and yearbook teacher. She loves good chocolate and bad puns, and in her free time, she likes to read, drink wine, and travel with her family.

Connect with Carrie online:
www.CarriePulkinen.com

Made in the USA
Columbia, SC
12 November 2021